WINNING THE BULL RIDER'S HEART

MELINDA CURTIS

HEARTWARMING

ISBN-13: 978-1-335-46038-7

Winning the Bull Rider's Heart

For questions and comments about the quality of this book, please contact us at CustomerService@Harlequin.com.

Harlequin Enterprises ULC
22 Adelaide St. West, 41st Floor
Toronto, Ontario M5H 4E3, Canada
www.Harlequin.com

HarperCollins Publishers
Macken House, 39/40 Mayor Street Upper,
Dublin 1, D01 C9W8, Ireland
www.HarperCollins.com

Printed in U.S.A.

"Just like old times," Noel said.

Too late, Sophie Jean realized her error. "I don't want to get back together."

Noel must think she'd chosen Betty's Bakery for nostalgic purposes. One severe case of heartbreak was enough for her.

Oh, that felt like a lie. Every time Noel got too close, a distortion of the truth seemed to be required to protect her from being hurt again.

"Huh." Noel sipped his coffee, smiling softly. "I guess I should learn how to rephrase things. I remember coming here fondly. Just like I remember our time together. Fondly. And you. Fondly."

Sophie Jean took a big piece of apple fritter and stuffed it in her face.

Noel grinned.

"What's...so...funny?" she managed to ask without choking on a mouthful of sugary pastry.

"Whenever I asked you something too personal, you'd eat. It's nice to know some things never change.

This is one major stroll down memory lane I shouldn't have taken.

Dear Reader,

I've always loved the song "Desperado" by the Eagles. It's the tale of a range-riding cowboy who is being encouraged to hang up his spurs and come home. I always wanted to use that idea as inspiration for a story. And so, *Winning the Bull Rider's Heart* was born.

Noel Emerson had it hard as a kid. And that hardened him into a top bull rider. Now he's thirty-eight. And most of his friends on the circuit have retired. After an unexpected injury, Noel decides to return home to Clementine for his seventy-year-old foster mother's birthday party. Little does he know, that in his long absence, the woman he gave up for bull riding has somehow found a place, or taken his, in the hearts of his foster family. Worse, there are still sparks between them. And now, he's back to square one, torn between a busy life traveling and competing, and a contented life with the cowgirl who still owns his heart.

I hope you enjoy Noel and Sophie Jean's second chance at happiness, and come to love the cowboys and cowgirls of The Cowboy Academy as much as I do.

Happy reading!

Melinda

Award-winning *USA TODAY* bestselling author **Melinda Curtis**, when not writing romance, can be found working on a fixer-upper she and her husband purchased in Oregon's Willamette Valley. Although this is the third home they've lived in and renovated, it's not a job for the faint of heart. But it's been a good metaphor for book writing, as sometimes you have to tear things down to find the core beauty and potential. Melinda has written over forty books for Harlequin, including *Dandelion Wishes*, which is now a TV movie, *Love in Harmony Valley*, starring Amber Marshall.

Brenda Novak says *Season of Change* "found a place on my keeper shelf."

Books by Melinda Curtis

Harlequin Heartwarming

The Cowboy Academy

A Cowboy's Fourth of July
A Cowboy Christmas Carol
A Cowboy for the Twins
The Rodeo Star's Reunion
Cowboy Santa
The Cowboy's Wedding Proposal
Country Fair Cowboy
The Christmas Cowboy

Visit the Author Profile page at Harlequin.com for more titles.

To all those who struggle to decide if they should take a chance on a second act in life

I say go for it!

CHAPTER ONE

WHOEVER SAID YOU can't come home again, because things won't be the same, was annoyingly correct.

Noel Emerson walked across the graveled ranch yard toward the arena at the Done Roamin' Ranch, unnoticed by his foster family, who were working livestock on this sunny Saturday spring afternoon in Clementine, Oklahoma.

He'd expected a hero's welcome at the ranch. Last week, Noel had ridden several bucking bulls to a big purse in a rodeo in Austin, Texas. Given the Done Roamin' Ranch supplied roughstock to rodeos, Noel had assumed they'd heard about his win. He'd also assumed they'd be on the lookout for him since there was a big shindig happening this week—his foster mother's birthday—and most of his foster brothers would probably attend.

But… No one greeted Noel.

Just proves what assuming does to a man.

That was his biological father's voice, grating and authoritative in his head. His father didn't tolerate excuses or failure.

Dad doesn't respect what's mine, either.

Just the thought of what awaited Noel at his own ranch—his next stop—made his head hurt. Not that it hadn't been hurting all day. Noel gingerly rubbed the lump on the back of his skull, silently grumbling about the head-hunting bull that had given him a kick in Austin.

Cheers rose from within the arena, bringing Noel back to the present. But the enthusiasm wasn't for him. No one looked his way as he approached.

Noel was close enough now to work out what was going on.

The arena was filled with a small herd of cattle, maybe twenty head. Cowboys on horseback were roping them by their horns, laughing and shouting gleefully as they caught and released each one. Their activity wasn't for sport. Roughstock needed to be handled frequently to make rodeo travel more manageable.

Noel smiled as he reached the arena railing, recognizing a few of his foster brothers on horseback—Chandler, with gray sprinkled through his hair; Wade, a newly retired bucking bronc champion; Ryan, a team roping champion; and…

Noel tipped his cowboy hat back, squinting at an unfamiliar silhouette in the arena. Is that…?

No. It can't be.

The cowboy in question expertly wheeled their horse around, revealing they weren't a cowboy at all, but a cowgirl.

My cowgirl.

Noel shook his head.

She's not mine anymore.

He drew his cowboy hat brim lower over his eyes, not wanting to be caught staring at his former girlfriend. What was Sophie Jean Shearer doing here?

On my home turf.

Sophie Jean had her dark brown hair pulled into a bun beneath the rim of her compact straw cowboy hat. She sat in the saddle of a black-and-white paint gelding competently, as if she earned a living as a ranch hand. Sophie Jean was, in fact, a beautician. And yet, she was laughing and joking and tossing a lasso as if she'd grown up as a Done Roamin' Ranch foster, not a townie.

Just watching Sophie Jean made Noel feel melancholy because his heart didn't belong to her anymore.

No. He gave his head a little shake, refusing to acknowledge he missed her. Noel felt sad because *he* didn't belong here anymore. It looked like Sophie Jean did.

And he resented her for it.

He knew that wasn't fair. But feelings seldom were.

Noel rubbed a hand over his chest, reliving that fateful day four years back when Sophie Jean had asked him what his intentions toward her were.

"We've been together for years, Noel." Sophie Jean's warm brown eyes had captured Noel's gaze while her slender arms encircled his neck. "I love you. I want to be by your side through thick and thin. I want to be happy. Make you happy. And grow old with you. But in order to do that, you need to settle down and ask me to marry you."

"No more rodeo, you mean." The thought had sliced through Noel like a sharp knife through a ripe tomato, dividing him into two equal parts—the man who wanted to stay in Clementine and make a life with Sophie Jean, and the man who needed to prove to the world he was a winner. "But… I still haven't amounted to something."

"Hey!" Chandler called from astride a fine-looking bay, pointing toward Noel, bringing him back to the present once more. "Let's give this long-lost cowboy a Done Roamin' Ranch welcome." He swung his rope, riding toward the arena rail. "First one to rope him wins a steak dinner. On me."

As one, the four riders in the arena turned their horses toward Noel, spinning their ropes in the air, parting the steers between them. Cattle was no longer the practice target. Noel was.

This was the way of the Done Roamin' Ranch. Good, clean cowboy fun. Reject it or run away and you didn't belong.

Noel held his ground.

The pounding of hooves. The echo of laughter. Both drowned out the rush of blood in his ears.

Four lariats landed on Noel, stinging his shoulders before being drawn snugly about his torso.

"Caught like a wanted man." That was Sophie Jean's voice. "My rope hit him first."

"Fair enough," Chandler said with a chuckle. "I owe you a steak."

The ropes about Noel loosened. He shrugged them off and stepped free.

Someone gasped.

Noel glanced up, his gaze colliding with Sophie Jean's.

My Sophie Jean.

Except she wasn't his anymore. He'd chosen himself over a future with her.

Regret sidled up Noel's throat like an old almost-friend, crowding too close and testing his defenses.

"You're home," Sophie Jean said as if in awe. Then she seemed to collect herself and said in a firmer voice, "Noel's home."

Noel nodded, clearing his throat. "Wouldn't miss my mom's birthday celebration." Foster mom, he meant. Although in the scheme of things, Mary was the only mother who loved him enough to be present in his life and he looked forward to seeing her.

But he would have liked to have missed seeing Sophie Jean again.

If only to protect his pride and his heart.

Not necessarily in that order.

I DIDN'T EXPECT to see Noel today.

Or any day for that matter. Around Clementine,

her former boyfriend was considered a former resident. A man seldom mentioned or thought of.

Except by Sophie Jean on cold winter nights.

Or on lazy Sunday afternoons.

Or after a dreamy, romantic novel with a hard-won happy ending.

That's enough of that, Sophie Jean Shearer.

But it wasn't. Sophie Jean's heart pounded as if Noel had smiled at her with welcome, rather than averted his gaze after a second or two.

A bit of pride resurfaced, tattered and worn, stuffing love and sentimentality for Noel in a far corner of her mind, out of reach of foolish impulses.

Sophie Jean gathered her lariat, looping the stiff length and then hanging it on her saddle horn. She glanced at the ranch foreman. "Are we done, Chandler?"

Chandler nodded, then turned to direct another cowboy to open one of the arena's side gates for the cattle's exit. The atmosphere in the arena had sobered, as if every cowboy knew this was a reunion no one wanted.

A reunion I don't want.

As the cattle trotted out a side gate leading to a nearby pasture, Sophie Jean hopped off Teddy and led the paint gelding toward the main gate nearest the barn. When it came to Noel, she was in the rip-the-bandage-off-the-wound camp. No sense delaying the awkward reunion. She'd waited years for this and rehearsed what she'd say—*Hi, nice to see you. So long.* Or some variation thereof.

Sophie Jean tied her reins to the arena rail and then approached the man who'd tossed her heart aside like an old, unwanted bed pillow.

And while she walked, she took inventory of her appearance—something she took care with. At the moment, she didn't live up to her standards. She had steer snot on one pant leg. The back of her checkered button-down was damp with sweat. Loose strands of hair fluttered free around her face, lifted by the breeze, while other strands were sweaty and plastered to the back of her neck. Her face felt gritty with arena dust.

Sophie Jean held her head high anyway, meeting Noel's gaze squarely.

Four years ago, she'd told Noel plainly how she felt about him after nearly a decade of dating—through her establishing herself as a trusted beautician, through his broken bones and concussions from paying his dues on the bull riding circuit. And in the end, she hadn't been what he wanted.

How could a man claim to love me yet not want to marry me?

That was a question she'd been unable to answer. And there was no way she was asking it of Noel now, especially since protocol for greeting an ex-boyfriend required her to give him a polite hug and pretend she'd never pressed her lips to his.

"Good to see you, Noel," Sophie Jean fibbed,

opening her arms to give him the barest of hugs. "I know Mary will be happy you've come home."

There was going to be a big celebration for Mary Harrison's seventieth birthday next weekend. Mary and her husband, Frank, had fostered more than fifty teenage boys, all while building a rodeo stock business and being actively involved in Clementine's community. That left quite the imprint. It was going to be quite a party.

"Good to see you, Soph."

She stiffened at Noel's use of her nickname and pulled away, only to lose herself for a moment, taking in the whole of him—muscular, compact body, shaggy black hair in need of a trim, stubborn chin and sharp blue eyes. His clothes, black cowboy boots and hat were new but he looked worn out. Defeated and distant.

There was no mischievous smile. No hearty laughter. No warmth to him at all.

Earning another bull riding championship hasn't done him good.

"When did you start working here?" Noel asked, as polite as a stranger.

Oh, that hurt.

"I'm just part of the family." Sophie Jean attempted a carefree smile. "I'm still at the Cozy Clip."

"But..." Something akin to confusion flashed through his blue eyes. "You haven't opened your own beauty shop? That was always your dream. Did you give up?"

Sophie Jean thrust her nose in the air.

Noel hasn't been back five minutes and he's already plucked a nerve.

"It's still my dream. The right place is turning out to be hard to find." A unicorn, in fact. She had viewings of potential locations scheduled for Monday. But his assumption that she'd quit stung. "Some dreams take a long time to achieve, as you well know."

"And require a good bit of sacrifice." Noel nodded. He ran a hand around the back of his neck. Not to rub his neck. *No.* It was more like he was checking something in his hairline at the base of his skull. He had a habit of touching his wounds. Bruises, gouges and the like.

Concern cinched around her chest, squeezing out her tattered pride. "Are you all ri—"

"Noel Emerson? Is that you?" Mary Harrison, Noel's foster mother, came down the front porch steps of the main ranch house, one of three homes and a bunkhouse on the large property. Mary had never regained weight after her last battle with cancer two years back. Her blue jeans drooped at the waist and her pink-checked button-down billowed loosely in the spring prairie breeze. But she still had game. She trotted over to join them—all of them, since several cowboys from the ranch had gathered round Noel and Sophie Jean, waiting for their turn to greet him. "Why didn't you tell me you were coming back, Noel?"

"Do I need to tell you?" Noel's voice was infused with a warmth that had been missing when he'd greeted Sophie Jean. His smile was bigger. His open arms seemed more welcoming. "I wouldn't miss your birthday, Mom."

"You missed it last year," Mary gently chided, swallowed in Noel's effusive hug.

"That means I'll stay twice as long this year," Noel promised.

Other cowboys tossed in their greetings, including Mary's husband, Frank, who was wearing his trademark wide-brimmed white cowboy hat. Hugs were passed around.

Sophie Jean eased her way to the perimeter of that hug-zone.

Or she tried to.

"I can't believe Noel is back." Mary somehow managed to loop her arm through Sophie Jean's, holding her mere feet away from Noel. "Come inside and wash up, Sophie Jean. We'll make cookies for him. Chocolate chip." Noel's favorite.

"With nuts," Sophie Jean murmured. And then she said a bit louder, "You go on, Mary. I need to unsaddle Teddy and get going." Anywhere but where Noel was.

"Nonsense." Mary poked another foster son's shoulder with a slender finger. "Chandler, do me a favor and put Sophie Jean's horse away. We've got some baking to do."

"Yes, ma'am." Chandler put up no fight. He may

have been the foreman and Frank the ranch founder, but everyone obeyed Mary's commands. She was the heart and soul of the Done Roamin' Ranch.

"I'll walk with you back to the house to wash up, Mary," Sophie Jean said, allowing herself to be led along by the older woman. "But then I really have to go."

And she meant it. She really did.

Especially when she caught the intent way Noel was looking at her…as if he wanted to take her hand and draw her close to whisper an apology for what happened between them.

Wishful thinking.

Sophie Jean scoffed, dismissing the impression as a figment of her imagination. After they broke up, he'd left town without looking back, proving her belief that love didn't last forever.

"What's wrong?" Mary asked, drawing Sophie Jean farther away from the cowboys wanting to catch up with Noel.

"Nothing." Sophie Jean had thought she'd built immunity where Noel was concerned.

Turned out, she was nearly as susceptible to his presence as she'd been four years ago.

If he was staying the week, she needed to rectify that. Fast.

CHAPTER TWO

"WHAT ARE WE doing for your birthday, Mom?" Noel entered the kitchen of the main house at the Done Roamin' Ranch, seeking a less bright environment since his concussion made him sensitive to light. The spring sunshine was strong today. Even a hat and dark glasses couldn't protect his sensitive eyes completely.

Noel stopped when he saw Sophie Jean at the oven, held in place by a deep-seated yearning. For the longest time, she'd been home to him.

Sophie Jean caught him staring and looked away.

No more of that, cowboy.

Noel tried to ignore Sophie Jean and the resurgence of guilt over putting himself first four years ago. Instead, he smiled at his foster mother. "Can't have a milestone birthday without something big planned, Mom."

"Says who?" Sophie Jean muttered, poking at his ego. She was filling a cookie sheet with spoonfuls of chocolate chip cookie dough with walnuts.

My favorite.

But his ex-girlfriend had laid down a challenge

against the idea that Mary deserved a big shindig and he had to clap back.

Challenge accepted.

And this was a challenge he wasn't going to lose.

"Who says my mom needs a big to-do? That'd be me, Sophie Jean," Noel shot back, coming to stand next to Mary's chair at the kitchen table. His foster mother had always been open to his style of fun in the past, claiming it lifted her spirits. "When you have a great family, you celebrate it." Wouldn't find him doing the same for his biological parents.

"Everybody's got a different birthday preference, son." His foster father, Frank, sat across from Mary, making an outline of a heart on the kitchen table with chocolate chips, eating as many as he put down. "As I recall, you like to celebrate your birthday with a large crowd. That hasn't changed, has it, Noel?"

"Nope. The more, the merrier." Trying not to squint, Noel turned his back to the bright sunlight coming in through the sole kitchen window and glanced around his second home.

Other than Sophie Jean's presence, the kitchen hadn't changed. There was still the extra-large wooden table in the center surrounded by a dozen or so chairs. The oversize bulletin board still hung on a wall with pictures of various fosters as teens and then as young men. Photographs of babies and children had been added since he'd been home last.

Sometimes, Noel was envious of the families

his foster brothers were building, especially when his winning bull riding trajectory experienced setbacks. Like this week.

His head pounded at the reminder of his forced career pause. He reached to the back of his skull and touched that troublesome lump, feeling again the sting of contact from the bull's hoof. It had been nasty even through his helmet.

"Is there a reason you've got your sunglasses on?" Sophie Jean asked, dulcet tones ringing with faux innocence.

Oh, she suspected he was hiding something. And oh, he intended to keep his secret.

"I forgot is all." Noel slid his dark glasses to the top of his head and tried not to squint. But his eyes felt as if they'd had a dose of dilation drops and the only thing he could do to keep from narrowing his eyes was to keep his back to that window over the sink. And the only way to do that gracefully was to move closer to Sophie Jean.

"Now, Noel. I don't want a fuss for my birthday," Mary insisted, stirring a bowl of dense cookie dough. She'd aged visibly since Noel had seen her last. Her short hair was more bright white than soft gray. The laugh lines around her eyes more prominent. "Truthfully? It's enough to have family around."

"It's not enough," Noel insisted, frowning. His foster mother deserved the moon. And Noel was determined to give it to her, wrapped in love and laughter. "The Chairman of Fun has returned to make sure you have family around *and* more than a smidge of fuss." Noel moved to the kitchen sink, where he washed his hands, sneaking sidelong glances at Sophie Jean.

Unlike Mary, Sophie Jean hadn't changed, other than to become more beautiful. But her presence here was a distraction.

He turned his back on that window and leaned against the sink, within touching distance of Sophie Jean, but it was Mary he spoke to. "What do you think, Mom? Want to go to a rodeo? Have a rodeo here? Invite the whole town over for cake?"

"I've already planned a party, son," Frank said in that even-keeled way of his. "We're having an open house at Brown's Brewery next Saturday during happy hour."

"I'm assuming that's for the extended community, friends and such," Noel surmised. "I think we need to have a little shindig with the family. And by little… Well, you know, I mean *big*." Noel grinned. "Besides, Mom deserves it." Because unlike his biological mother, Mary Harrison stuck by her foster sons through all their highs and lows.

"Why is everything a production for you, Noel?" Beside him, Sophie Jean scooped another spoonful of cookie dough meant for the baking sheet. When Noel moved closer and tried to stick a finger in the bowl for a taste, she hip-checked him aside, making him smile. "Mary just wants to blow out her candles and enjoy her loved ones. You should respect her wishes."

"I think I know my mom better than you," Noel said, earning a sharp glance from Sophie Jean.

"In this case, Sophie Jean is right." Mary turned in her chair to face Noel. "I don't want a fuss. I don't need presents or speeches."

Several bodies entered the mudroom, out of sight from the kitchen. High-pitched, excited voices indicated the group's youth. The sound of boots dropping on the floor preceded the pack invading the kitchen—young cowboys and cowgirls, not all of which Noel recognized. Nor was he familiar with the two Labradoodles that galloped in with them—one a reddish-brown, one black as night. The two dogs greeted his foster parents, then Sophie Jean and, finally, Noel.

I'm last even among the dogs.

Tension pinched his shoulder blades. Tension and a feeling that he didn't belong.

"That's Rusty and Biff," Sophie Jean told Noel, working her way around him to wash her hands after petting the dogs. She pointed to a pair of kids who looked to be about eight or nine. "They belong to Sam and Mae, Chandler's kids."

I should know that.

Noel surveyed the youngsters as they went straight to the cooling rack on the counter and helped themselves to cookies.

Sam, one of the young dog owners, came to

stand next to Mary's chair, putting a proprietary hand on her shoulder. He nodded toward Noel. "Who's this, Grandma?"

"Don't you recognize him, Sam?" A slim teenage cowgirl with braces and brown pigtails gave the boy a disparaging look.

Noel put a name to her face: *Ginny.*

"That's Uncle Noel," Ginny said, gracing Noel with a worshipful smile. "Repeat bull riding champion. And in the Professional Bull Riding circuit, too, not in some of those minor circuits." The ones meant for beginners and older cowboys who just didn't know when to retire.

That'll never be me.

Noel smiled at young Sam, waiting for accolades and recognition.

"Never heard of him," Sam deadpanned, giving Noel a disparaging glance.

Really?

"How can you not have heard of me, Sam?" Noel teased, tapping a faded photograph on the bulletin board. "This is me and your dad." A picture taken twenty years ago when he and Chandler were both still in school. They sat on an arena railing after competing in a junior bull riding event, grins nearly splitting their dirt-streaked cheeks.

Sam stared from the picture to Noel, expression unchanged. "Nope. I got nothin'."

Ouch.

While Noel processed his shock, Sophie Jean

slid the cookie tray in the oven and said, "Come on, Sam. You must remember the story about a bull tossing Noel from his back to the back of your father's horse."

"That was you?" Sam brightened. "Dad tells that story all the time."

"He's a legend," one of the teenage boys Noel didn't recognize said, staring at Noel as if he were a myth come to life.

And Noel realized with a sinking heart that to most of this young generation, he was identified by a story. He wanted to be known to his found family—his face, his character, his heart. He wanted to be considered a member to every generation. Because family didn't have to prove themselves over and over again. Family was built with the arms of unconditional love. Family was safe. Noel had never found that outside the Done Roamin' Ranch.

Except with Sophie Jean.

"You need a reintroduction to your nieces and nephews, Noel," Mary said kindly. Then she pointed at each of the kids in turn. "That's Sam and his sister, Mae."

"Mae moved onto the ranch after Izzy and Chandler got married a few weeks back," Sophie Jean explained.

Noel nodded. He'd missed Chandler's second wedding in the pursuit of points on the circuit.

"Our family continues to grow," his foster father added, feeding the leggy Labradoodles dog treats he'd stored in his gray-checked shirt pocket.

Mary continued her introductions. "And you know Ginny and Piper." The two teenage girls with pigtails and braces.

Ginny had on a frilly, flowered blouse while Piper wore a peach-colored T-shirt from last year's county fair.

"They're best friends." Sophie Jean continued to prove that she was more plugged in to the doings of Noel's family than he was. "Freshmen in high school. Barrel racers and ballerinas."

Noel hadn't known any of that. He hadn't felt this adrift among family since his biological mother packed her bags, wrote him a brief note and left, leaving Noel to try and cajole his father out of his dark funk with forced mischief and false cheer. But seemingly in answer to Noel's jokes and high jinks, his father had decided Noel needed to get more serious about the sport of rodeo. Mired in memories of lost tempers and attempts to run away, Noel missed the rest of Mary's introductions.

"And I'm Ford," a sturdy little cowboy piped up, coming to stand in front of Noel. "Your brother Zeke is gonna marry my favorite aunt in the whole wide world, which makes us family even if it seems weird."

"Family is weird," Noel murmured. "Found or otherwise."

"There'll be a test on their names later," Sophie

Jean teased from the vicinity of the stove. "Chandler thinks the family has gotten so large that we need to make a family tree."

We? Sophie Jean considers herself part of my foster family's tree? "Noel?" Ginny fiddled with the hem of her ruffled blouse. "Are you Ike Emerson's older brother?"

"I am." Noel smiled. Ike was Noel's half brother and more than twenty years younger than Noel. "You look to be about Ike's age."

"Ike's in my algebra class." Ginny's cheeks turned a rosy shade Noel associated with teenage crushes. "He's actually a year older than me."

"I'll put in a good word for you when I see him later," Noel promised. Ike lived on Noel's ranch in Clementine with their father, who'd managed to drive his second wife away just as cleanly as he had his first wife.

And me.

"Oh." Ginny's eyes went wide. "You don't have to say anything to Ike."

"Just that you said hi." Noel nodded.

Ginny gasped, cheeks flaming red.

"Noel's forgotten what it's like to be a teenager, Ginny." Sophie Jean handed Noel a warm chocolate chip cookie, coming close enough that he could smell the flowery product she used in her dark brown hair and remember how soft her locks were to touch. "Ginny doesn't want you to mention her to your brother, Noel. That would be embarrassing."

Ginny's head began bobbing and didn't stop until Noel spoke.

"Right." Noel regrouped, banning thoughts of Sophie Jean to a far corner of his brain. "What happens at the Done Roamin' Ranch stays at the Done Roamin' Ranch."

"Exactly." Sophie Jean moved back to the oven. More wisps of dark brown hair had escaped from her low bun, tempting him to curl one lock around his finger and—

"Grandpa Frank, will you play video games with us?" Sam wrapped his arms around Frank's shoulders. "Pretty please."

"Not now," Mary said in a firm, commanding tone that Noel recognized all too well. "I agreed you kids could come over during your break assuming that you'd head out on a ride or practice your rodeo skills. It's too fine a day to be hunched in front of a television killing aliens."

Excuses were tossed about like corn popping in a lidless pan.

"We go riding all the time."

"It's spring break."

"I didn't bring my riding gloves."

"No one would saddle a horse for me."

"Max and I both wanted to ride Shirley."

At that last comment, everyone in the kitchen

whinnied. Everyone but Noel, that is. He had no idea what they were neighing for.

"Everybody wants to ride Shirley," Sophie Jean said, chuckling as the assembled whinnied once more.

"Who's Shirley?" Noel asked, taking a bite of his cookie as another wave of whinnies filled the room. That sweet chocolate taste was small consolation for him feeling so out of the loop with his found family.

"Shirley is my draft horse," Mary said, smiling deeply enough to bring out all her familiar wrinkles when the kids whinnied again. "She's a talker and too big for a saddle."

"Which is why the kids ride her bareback," Sophie Jean pointed out.

"And me," Mary added. "I ride her bareback, too."

"Is that wise?" Noel wondered aloud.

Mary shot him with a piercing look. "If you're implying I should stick to a porch rocking chair instead of living…"

"Nope." But, of course, he was. He wanted Mary to be safe and live to be one hundred. Noel held up his hands in surrender anyway. "Never." Always.

Mary had slowed down over the years, sure. But the day he'd met her, she'd been in the Done Roamin' Ranch arena riding a young bull. Mary could cowboy with the best of them. She was every bit Frank's partner, in love, life and the rodeo livestock supply business. Nonetheless, now that she was older, she should think twice about riding any more bulls or bareback horses.

"She's careful," Sophie Jean said in a voice meant just for Noel.

He suspected Sophie Jean was trying to be helpful and keep him in the loop but every time she did, it just proved how out of touch he was.

"Noel," Frank began. "I gave Shirley—"

Whinny!

"—and her surrey to your mother two Christmases ago," his foster father finished proudly, watching kids gobble the chocolate chips he'd laid out on the table. "One of my best gifts ever, I think."

Mary nodded, glowing at her spouse. "The best gifts are the ones that keep on giving."

Gifts. Giving. Noel was reminded of his intention to make Mary's birthday special this year. "Hey, kids, I was just saying to your grandmother that we should have a blowout celebration for her birthday."

That generated heartfelt support from the assembled minors.

"Can we get a bouncy house?" Sam asked, watching Sophie Jean take more cookies out of the oven.

"No." Noel was adamant on that score. Couldn't have his foster mother breaking a limb on her birthday. She wasn't one to let fun pass her by when presented with something new.

"What about a clown?" Sam asked.

"No," Noel repeated, reminded that Sophie Jean didn't like clowns.

"How about a petting zoo?" Sam kept trying.

"No." Noel shook his head. "You live on a ranch. You can pet animals anytime. We want something fun for all."

"I don't think you know anything about fun," Sam grumped, crossing his arms over his little chest.

"Go easy on him, Sam." Sophie Jean moved next to Noel at the sink to rinse the now-empty cookie dough mixing bowl. "As I recall, those are fighting words from Noel's perspective." She lowered her voice as if imitating a man, "*No fun? No way!*"

Is that supposed to be me? She's making me sound arrogant.

Noel's shoulders pinched once more. "I've got thicker skin nowadays." He liked to think so anyway.

"I hope you have a thicker skull." Sophie Jean was close enough to kiss but couldn't seem to bring herself to look at Noel. Not directly, at least. "I saw online that a bull tried to dropkick your head recently."

She follows my career?

Noel shouldn't have smiled. He didn't want anyone to know his head was wonky. They'd fuss. And this week, the fuss should be for Mary. "I'm fine. Bull strikes are par for the course."

Some of the kids nodded.

Respect!

"I think we should give Noel's proposal a chance," Mary said slowly, gaze drifting from Noel to Sophie Jean and then back again. "He plans good parties. And the gathering at Brown's Brewery isn't exactly kid-friendly."

"Great point." Noel put his hands on his hips and his foggy brain into gear, sifting through ideas for excitement. But the right idea seemed elusive, especially given the skeptical scrutiny he was under.

The kids stared at Noel dubiously. Sophie Jean stared at Noel dubiously. Even his foster parents stared at Noel dubiously.

I've been gone so long, I've lost my party cred.

Of course, he'd been a teenager when he'd first earned that reputation, a teen with the need to be the life of the party to earn his place. It hadn't been hard to entertain a pack of foster teens. There were plenty of opportunities for mischief on a ranch that supplied stock for rodeos, including organizing Fun Days, which were competitions involving livestock.

That's it!

"What if we have a Fun Day on Friday?" Noel grinned, feeling more like the Done Roamin' Ranch cowboy who belonged here. He pointed at the next generation of Done Roamin' Ranch kids.

"That's a competition just for you *young-uns.* We'll hold unusual games, plus a few rodeo events. It'll be fun."

"We rodeo all the time," Sam said, heavy on the sarcasm. He had another chocolate chip cookie in hand. "Rodeo isn't supposed to be fun. It's work. My dad says so."

Almost everyone laughed. Everyone except Sophie Jean, who stared at Noel with a thoughtful expression.

When the laughter died down, Noel said, "You can't excel at something you don't enjoy, Sam. You kids can compete in all kinds of events at a Fun Day competition and really show Grandma Mary your talents. In fact, she'll be our Fun Day Queen."

"Like a rodeo queen?" Mary preened in her seat, fluffing her short white hair. "I've never worn a crown."

"We'll get you a sparkly one." Noel felt the tide turning. He smiled.

"We should have teams." Sam wiped chocolate from his mouth with the back of his hand, then submitted to Sophie Jean taking a wet paper towel to his hand and face. "The big kids are on the rodeo team at school. They have a coach and everything."

Compliments were passed around by the teens in the room for how awesome Coach Griff, another former foster teen, and Coach Bess were.

"Teams are perfect." Actually, Noel didn't like teams. It meant he had to rely on others to win. People had often let him down when he was younger. He avoided being vulnerable now.

He'd been invited to coach a professional bull riding team a few weeks ago and had declined. He still had plenty of bull rides in his future. And yet, the team's ownership wouldn't let it go. Noel's phone was full of text messages and emails from them asking for a meeting. It had made his head hurt long before that bull had bushwhacked him.

And despite all that, Noel kept smiling as if he loved teams. "I'll coach one side and Griff can coach the other." Griff was a kindred spirit when it came to defeating the ho-hum.

Again, that dubious silence. Those dubious stares.

How did I lose the room so quickly?

"There should be two coaches per team." Ginny glanced at Sophie Jean, tracing the weave of a brown pigtail with her fingers. "A boy and a girl coach. I want Sophie Jean as mine."

"*Why?*" Noel blurted, although his response seemed to go unnoticed because several kids echoed their agreement with Ginny.

Sophie Jean turned away, running water in the sink over the dirty mixing bowls.

"If Griff is coaching, he'll want to coach with his wife, Bess." Mary smiled at Noel, pointing out the obvious. "That puts you and Sophie Jean together."

Dishes clattered in the sink. Everyone looked toward Sophie Jean. Even Noel.

"Say you'll do it, Sophie Jean," Ginny urged, coming to stand next to her, forcing Noel farther away. "I'd ask my mom but she's always busy, especially now that we've got the new baby."

Sophie Jean half glanced over her shoulder. She didn't look amenable to working with Noel.

Just like I don't want to work with her.

She challenged him on too many levels, like still being incredibly tempting—*those lips!*—and her having displaced him in his foster family's hearts—*so upsetting!* If they hung around too much this week, he'd either kiss her or say something he'd regret.

Like I didn't already do that four years ago.

"I don't know why you'd want me to coach," Sophie Jean said in a small voice.

"Because you're so good," Ginny said staunchly. "I remember when you first started hanging out here and could barely throw a lasso, much less ride without bouncing in the saddle." Ginny glanced around at her cousins. "But now..."

"She roped me." Noel frowned. Now that he thought more about it, it was odd. "How much time do you spend here, Sophie Jean?"

"She's always at the ranch." Sam wriggled between Ginny and Sophie Jean, bumping Noel to a small space in the corner as he did so. He wrapped his arms around Sophie Jean's waist, earning her smile. "We love her." Sam released her and turned toward Noel. "And we don't know you."

"That's a bit harsh, Sam." Mary defended Noel.

"You'll know me soon enough," Noel promised Sam, determined to follow through on that statement. "I'm here all week. We'll be good buds by the time the birthday celebrations are over."

Sam considered Noel with an upturned nose. "We'll see."

Noel gave a brisk nod. "Challenge accepted."

But he noticed Sophie Jean hadn't agreed to be his coaching partner.

BAKING DONE. KITCHEN CLEAN. Farewells spoken. Sophie Jean walked toward her truck, eager to get home and away from Noel.

Granted, the Fun Day was a good way to get the plethora of kids with emotional ties to Mary involved in her birthday. And crowning Mary the Fun Day Queen seemed to make the older woman smile. But as for Sophie Jean's involvement…

I will never agree to coach with Noel.

It would be too hard on her heart, which had already gone out to him in the kitchen where he'd seemed out of place and behind the times at every turn. For all he'd been on the road when they were dating, he'd always easily slipped back into his place at the Done Roamin' Ranch. But a four-year absence had created a noticeable rift. The poor man didn't fit in.

As if summoned by her thoughts. Noel called to her. "Hey, Sophie Jean. Wait up."

Escape was so close. Sophie Jean had her truck key fob in hand. Her small, bright red truck was just a few feet away. But she turned to face the man her heart still desired with a small, civil smile in place. "Hey, Noel. What's up?"

"I wanted to talk more about the Fun Day." Noel caught up to her, a similar polite smile on his fine-looking face. His expressive eyes were hidden behind those dark glasses.

Not that his cool composure diminished his appeal in any way. For years, she'd considered him her person, which was odd since she'd sworn to go through life alone, having been subjected to more than her fair share of stepfathers over the years. Witnessing her mother's repeated heartbreak, Sophie Jean had come to the conclusion that love didn't last. And Noel had proved that belief to be true.

Now, four years since their breakup, it seemed she hadn't been able to wipe her heart's memory banks. With him near, something inside Sophie Jean seemed to gather and lean toward him, like a compass always pointing toward true north.

She took a step back, reaching for her pride and her heart's defenses. "Maybe we should talk about your injury instead, Noel." That topic always threw Noel off. He liked to pretend he was as invincible as a superhero, something that she'd considered endearing. He probably didn't realize how often he'd touched the back of his head since he'd arrived, giving away his injury. "The video I saw showed you getting knocked out cold."

Noel's smile broadened. "You've been following my career."

"Nope." She lied. "I follow rodeo. I get a daily update in my email inbox. And one day last week, there happened to be a link to a video clip of your last bull ride." That was true. Watching that bucking bull's hoof strike the back of Noel's helmeted head had stolen her breath away. "So, I'll ask you again. How bad is it?"

"I'm not banged up any more than usual." His denial didn't quite ring true. The cowboy with big plans for a big Western party gave Sophie Jean a big smile, one that made her heart skip a beat but did nothing to change her opinion that he wasn't physically fine. "Since we're going to be coaching together, Sophie Jean, we should schedule time to plan the Fun Day schedule."

"I haven't said I'll coach. And I won't until you get Griff and Bess to agree to do it." Sophie Jean's smile felt strained. And why wouldn't it? Noel was her heart's kryptonite…even though he'd always focused more on the next win than the woman he claimed to love. "Call me when Griff and Bess say yes and we'll all meet up. The four of us."

Griff and Bess were busy running their ranch and coaching the high school rodeo team. Plus, Griff still picked up shifts at the Done Roamin'

Ranch. The chances they'd agree to help Noel were slim to none.

Thank goodness.

"You're afraid." Noel studied her face. His gaze might have lingered on her lips. "Afraid of spending time with me."

Oh, yeah!

But Sophie Jean put her hands on her hips and a frown on her lips, trying hard to sell her denial. "That's so like you to attribute my hesitation to being involved in your Fun Day as being rooted in *you*. News flash—*I'm too busy to coach*."

"How can you say that?" Noel frowned, tugging down the brim of his straw cowboy hat, and repositioned himself so that the late afternoon sun was at his back. "You haven't opened your salon. Have you gotten sidetracked? Marched down the aisle?" His gaze strayed to her bare left hand. "Had kids?" This last question drifted between them on a whisper.

Another sore point. They'd talked about having a family together. They'd talked about filling a home with warmth and love.

It was just that. All talk.

Sophie Jean held her head high. "No salon. No husband. No kids. But Mary's roped me into volunteering around town." That filled up most of her spare time. "I'm on the Easter egg hunt committee." The event happening this weekend. "The library fundraising committee. The Twelve Parties of Christmas and the Santapalooza parade committees. In July, I'm helping Mary with the big Done Roamin' Ranch shindig on the fourth. And various other community needs that come up, like chaperoning high school dances or coordinating donations to the local food bank."

Noel studied her in silence, smile in place. Only his smile… It felt pitying.

He still thinks I'm a coward.

Four years ago, Noel had told Sophie Jean she needed to go for her dream of owning her own salon, even if the situation wasn't perfect, even if she had to give things up, like him. He'd told her she should do that or let her dream go.

"I'm not running from my dream," Sophie Jean said now, defensively.

"Uh-huh. But you heard those kids." Noel deftly changed tactics, although his smile didn't change at all. "They want you to coach them. You should be flattered. To them, I'm chopped liver."

More like prime rib. To me, that is.

She'd given up those indulgences. But that was beside the point. "Chopped liver? Come on, Noel. Those kids don't even know what chopped liver is." Sophie Jean allowed herself a small smile. "A better analogy might be beets or broccoli."

"I'd rather be cake, Soph." How easily he used the nickname he'd given her. "And you can help me be cake, by coaching with me."

And risk my heart? No way!

Realizing she'd been boxed in, Sophie Jean held up a hand. "Let's not pretend this Fun Day is about the kids. Or that you want to coach with me." She suspected it had to do with his drive to win at all things.

"Soph, you're one of my favorite people in the world. Of course I want to coach with you." That smile changed, took on a more devil-may-care slant.

Sophie Jean's breath hitched.

The past pressed into the present, taking over Sophie Jean's thoughts. The firm feel of Noel's lips against hers. The warmth of his breath wafting across her neck. The tender way his arms encircled her.

The clinical way he'd said he couldn't marry me.

Sophie Jean sucked in air as if she hadn't filled her lungs in far too long. "I'm not one of your favorite people, Noel. Not anymore." She pressed the unlock button on her truck's key fob. "And don't call me *Soph* or…or anything!"

Sophie Jean hopped in her truck and drove away but not without glancing at Noel in her rearview mirror.

He stood and watched her go as if rooted in one spot, the same way he'd watched her leave four years ago.

CHAPTER THREE

BY THE TIME Noel pulled up to his small ranchette outside Clementine later that afternoon, his spirits were low and his head heavy.

He'd had too much sunshine in his eyes, too many miles under his belt and too many disappointing moments at the Done Roamin' Ranch. Not to mention, his conflicting feelings about the former love of his life and her snub that felt a lot like déjà vu.

She's making a habit of driving out of my life.

It didn't make Noel feel better to see a new wrought iron gate guarding the drive to his home, a new truck in the ranch yard and a flashy-looking black horse in the pasture with his piebald gelding. His biological father, a retired bull rider himself, managed Noel's small ranch in Noel's absence and had done so since his second divorce four years back. But dear old dad put more stock in material possessions than Noel did. He was always upgrading things, like the air-conditioning unit and the refrigerator, sprucing up the ranch without asking, like that fancy gate. But he'd never sunk high five figures into a horse before.

That explains why my bank balance was surprisingly lower last week.

Frustration made a thick knot in Noel's gut.

Is nothing mine anymore?

Noel's place at the Done Roamin' Ranch had been usurped by Sophie Jean. His control over his own ranch was...out of his control. And a little niggly voice in his fuzzy head whispered, *"It's all your fault."*

Noel hated making mistakes. In his experience, errors created an unpleasant ripple effect in his life—parents gave up on him, angry bulls got their revenge, girlfriends left him but not his found family.

Thankfully, everything else looked the same at the Emerson Ranch—the white, rambling ranch house, the large red barn, the golden pastures beyond. But there was no telling what he'd find inside either building.

Noel got out of his truck, squinting against the glaring sun low on the horizon. His vision grew hazier. He pulled his hat brim low over his sunglasses and waited to feel better. And waited...

How demoralizing.

The clock on his career was winding down. Noel had already defied skeptics by staying in the elite professional arena for over a decade and rising to the top ten in his thirties. Was his recovery time growing longer based on his age and injuries?

I'm not ready to retire.

Despite the fact that most guys his age had already done so. Champion contenders were younger every year. And when he talked to any of his retired friends, each one raved about how full his life was, how fabulous life off the road was, how wonderful his kids were.

My life is full, fabulous and wonderful. I don't want for anything.

And yet, when Noel looked around his ranch, it felt…empty. The flower beds to either side of the front porch were choked with weeds. The windows dull with a layer of dirt and dust. His father and brother didn't come out to greet him. Not even Pie, his strawberry roan with the piebald face, ambled over to the fence to say hello. What was the point of coming home when no one missed you?

The ground beneath his feet didn't feel solid.

What am I killing myself for?

Memories of Sophie Jean crowded into his head. She hadn't just filled his arms when they were a couple. She'd filled his heart. She'd always raced to greet him when he came home, showering him with kisses before inspecting his body for damage, not believing him when he said he was fine. She'd always known he wasn't 100 percent. No rough rider ever was after a rodeo.

Maybe we should talk about your injury.

That's what she'd told him today.

Sophie Jean still cares for me.

But not the way she did before.

Noel didn't know how to process that. Or anything that had happened to him lately—the injury, the feeling of being an outsider at the Done Roamin' Ranch, the lack of emotional connection to the ranch he owned, the request to coach before he was formally retired.

I'm like an old tractor and my engine timing is off.

A garbled shout came from the barn, drawing Noel out of his funk and spurring him forward.

In no time, Noel was in the barn and out of the sunshine, eyes and brain feeling near-immediate relief.

The rest of him, though…

The rest of him tensed as he took in the scene before him.

It wasn't his barn that stopped him cold, the front interior of which served as his workout facility—weights, a treadmill, a bull riding machine. And it wasn't what lay beyond his exercise equipment that bothered him—tack room and eight stalls. It was *who* was in his barn, or more precisely, *what* they were doing that made Noel's gut clench.

"That'll get you no points!" His biological father shouted at the teen on the bull riding machine, showering the air with spittle. Dad's broad, muscular back was to Noel as he gestured wildly and criticized harshly. “Your arm needs to be held higher! *Higher!*” And then Dad spat. “Ike, you’re not trying!”

If the high-pitched whine of the mechanical bull was any indication, Noel’s younger half brother rode the machine at a high setting. Trying was a necessity or he’d have been tossed off already. But the teen clung to the bull with more determination than skill. His long legs and his free arm flailed about as the bull spun. His bare head snapped back alarmingly with each intense pitch.

Noel’s temples throbbed.

Ike should be wearing a helmet.

“*Come on, Ike!*” Dad cried, although his words sounded more like a putdown than encouragement.

How many times had Noel heard those same words? That same tone? Directed at him?

Too many.

How many times had Noel felt inadequate and unloved after those berating training sessions?

Too many.

Instinctively, Noel wanted to close in on himself and retreat.

That voice… Those words… They were why he’d run away from home as a teen. Again. And again. And again. Until Dad decided he’d be better off living at the Done Roamin’ Ranch during the week and traveling to rodeos with him on weekends for the duration of high school. Noel hadn’t imagined his father would repeat his mistakes with his half brother, Ike.

My ranch is supposed to be a safe place.

For the second time that day, Noel had assumed the wrong thing. The Emerson Ranch wasn't safe for Ike.

Something inside Noel hardened with purpose. He planted his cowboy boots, crossed his arms and said in a loud voice, "I'm home."

"Woo-hoo!" Ike flew off the bull without any grace in his lanky teenage limbs. He landed in a clumsy heap on the crash pad. Unfazed by his ungainly landing, Ike rolled over and grinned at Noel. "Hey, brother."

Oh, to be young again and bounce...

Noel's father turned, frowning. Both of his sons had inherited Steve Emerson's thick black hair, intense blue eyes and stubborn jaw. But there, the similarities ended. Dad was shorter and more solid than either of his boys. And unlike Noel and Ike, their father never seemed to be happy.

Dad frowned at Noel. "Shouldn't you be competing at a rodeo in Tucson right now?"

"Nope." Noel held tight to his smile. "I'm home for Mary Harrison's birthday week."

"And I, for one, am glad to see you, bro." Ike scrambled to his feet, grabbed his cell phone and cowboy hat and then barreled into Noel for a hug. "What's it been? Three years without more than an occasional phone call?"

"Four," Noel admitted gruffly. "And texts count, you know." But limiting contact to texts hadn't prepared Noel for the physical changes in his kid brother.

Ike was a head taller than Noel and had yet to grow into his gangly frame or his size-thirteen cowboy boots…if he still wore size thirteens. Could be larger by now. Although Dad hadn't asked Noel for free boots from one of his sponsors in months.

Noel held on to Ike a little too tight and a lot too long before releasing him. "You should be playing basketball or volleyball with that wingspan of yours." Not trying to ride dangerous beasts. His long build wasn't suited to bull riding. Dad should know that. All that shouting was for naught.

"What are you saying, Noel? That I shouldn't follow in the family footsteps and ride bulls?" Ike chuckled, a humorless sound. The teen's gaze darted toward their father and then away. He stroked two long black whiskers growing on the side of his mouth. Then Ike stuck his cell phone in his back pocket and his fine-looking brown cowboy hat on his thatch of black hair. "That's family treason, bro."

"My boys rodeo. Case closed," Dad said, none too happy with Noel's opinions. "Did you just get into town? You didn't stop at the Done Roamin' Ranch first?" There was a jealous undercurrent in his father's tone. He resented Noel's connection to the Harrisons and the Done Roamin' Ranch.

"I stopped there first," Noel begrudgingly admitted.

Dad's frown deepened to a scowl. "You always give priority to your foster family when it's Ike and me who need you."

All you need is my bank account password.

But now wasn't the time to argue.

Noel brushed a hand over Ike's back, as if to slough off their father's bad vibes. "The Done Roamin' Ranch is on the way here, Dad. Stopped and paid my respects before coming home."

"Smart." Ike grinned. "Saved you gas money."

Dad's expression was stony. "We're your family."

"*Too*," Noel qualified. "I have two families. Now… What's for dinner? I'm starved."

"Have you gotten a workout in today?" Dad's sarcasm cut deep. He assumed Noel was a slacker, his wins based more on luck than hard work and hard-won skill. "These are the last of your top earning years, Noel. You've been lucky to have lasted this long. You can slack off when you're—"

"*Dead*," Noel finished for him, choosing to grin at Ike. "Yes, I know. There are so many things I'll do in my rodeo afterlife. Eat junk food. Spend all day playing video games. Go to honky-tonks every night."

Win the love of a brown-eyed girl whose smile turns my heart upside down.

Ike chuckled, making their father's scowl deepen even further.

"No workout for me today, Dad," Noel said quickly and with a smile, trying to keep the peace for all their sakes. Besides, he was under doctor's orders. No heavy lifting. No quick movements. Definitely no bull riding, real or otherwise. Not until the pounding fog lifted from his hoof-struck brain. Noel tipped his cowboy hat back but didn't remove his dark sunglasses. "No arguments, Dad. I racked up points and prize money for six weeks straight. Sometimes, you need to take a break to recharge."

"Fine." Dad's jaw worked. "Ike, get back on."

"He's had enough for one day, too." Noel turned and guided Ike toward the door. "It's not every day his brother comes home."

Dad grumbled but Noel ignored him.

He walked out into the afternoon sunshine, squinted and drew his hat brim lower. "Dad's been working you hard?"

"Yeah." His gangly brother flanked him. "Things haven't gone so well since I grew six inches." Ike's words sounded as if they'd been carefully chosen. Perhaps carefully considered long before he put them out there for Noel. "Or the three inches before that. He started me riding bulls after you and

Mom left. It's been a ride." And not a good one if Ike's tone was any indication.

Their father hated to lose. Hated for his sons to lose, too.

Things are worse than I thought.

"Whose horse is that?" Noel pointed toward the black gelding in the pasture.

"Ace is mine," Ike said flatly. "Dad suspects I won't make a good bronc or bull rider, although he's not giving up just yet. We added roping to my training. Ace is one of Jo Pierce-Oakley's roping horses."

Pricey, he meant. Jo's horses commanded top dollar and were sold to only the best rodeo contenders. The purchase was unwise. Or a sign of desperation on Dad's part.

"Can you lasso?" Noel was reminded of Sophie Jean roping him earlier and winning a steak dinner from Chandler. It was possible Ike had more talent with a rope than a bull.

Ike stroked those two whiskers. "Dad started teaching me this year but even though my brain hears what he's telling me, my body… My body doesn't always follow along."

Noel scowled. It was just like their father to jump in whole hog without proof that Ike had the skill or passion for roping. Just like Dad to demand Ike work on fine motor skills needed to rope when Ike's young body was in a state of flux, growing too rapidly to adapt easily.

Noel drew a calming breath. "You should be enjoying your time in school."

"Easy for you to say." Ike rolled his eyes. "You barely graduated high school and now you're a champion. While me… It's not like I'm going to be a rocket scientist. Might just as well rodeo."

"Rodeo isn't a sure thing. You should have a fallback plan." Noel wished someone had told him that long ago.

They reached the front door.

Noel blocked his brother's entry. "Ike, don't you have any idea of what you want to be when you grow up? There has to be something that interests you."

"I'm fifteen," Ike said in a deep voice he hadn't had when Noel had last been home. "My dreams involve getting my driver's license and dating Cindy Hidalgo."

If only life were that simple.

"Ike…" Noel wanted to get his point across without raising his voice. Hard wish, that. "What about graduating high school and going to college?"

"I get decent grades but Dad… He has my life planned out. You want me to think about the future? With Dad around… That's like trying to swim upstream in floodwaters. Can't think about the rest of my life when I'm just trying to survive each training session and junior rodeo. Sometimes I just want to…" Ike removed his cowboy hat and slapped it against his thigh, staring at the western horizon. "I don't know."

"Run away?" Noel guessed, going cold inside.

Ike nodded, grimacing. "Don't tell Dad."

"This is my house, Ike. You don't need to be running anywhere. I'm here now. And things are going to change."

But from the expression on Ike's face, his brother didn't believe that was true.

And the reality was Nate couldn't stand behind his word unless he stayed in Clementine.

And retired.

SOPHIE JEAN SLID her key into the lock of her apartment door and turned the key.

The lock bolt didn't slide free…because the door wasn't locked.

Sophie Jean froze, fears of a break-in holding her in place.

Is the burglar still inside? Do I go in to look or stay out here and call the sheriff? Had they let the cat out?

While Sophie Jean debated, she heard a familiar sound—a cell phone company jingle from an overplayed TV ad. Whoever was inside had made themselves at home.

Sophie Jean pushed open the unlocked door, half suspecting Noel of pranking her. He still had a key to her place, after all.

Instead, she found her mother sprawled on the

sofa with Sophie Jean's long-haired calico cat in her lap. Mom gave a little wave. "Surprise!"

"Hello." Sophie Jean set her keys and purse on the narrow table by the door, pulse beginning to calm. "I didn't know you were coming to visit. Is Byron with you?"

"No." That was an unhappy reply. Mom looked away.

Uh-oh. That doesn't bode well.

Kiki leaped to the floor and strutted over to greet Sophie Jean. Or at least, strike a feline pose in front of Sophie Jean with a flick of her long tail, an indication of impatience for affection and food.

Sophie Jean picked up the calico and gave her a cuddle, earning a rumbling purr and head rubs on her chin in return.

Meanwhile, she took in her mother's disheveled appearance. The short brown hair with highlights that was in desperate need of a brushing. The chipped green nail polish that looked as if it had been picked off bit by bit but not completely. The flowery teal dress that was hopelessly wrinkled, as if it had sat too long in the dryer and had never been ironed.

"I'm moving back in with you, sweetheart." Mom sat up, rubbing what might have been tears in her eyes, making her eyeliner raccoon-like. "I hope I can stay until I land on my feet. Byron and I are getting a divorce."

Sophie Jean's insides did a slow, upsetting churn.

Her mother's love life was a roller coaster. She fell hard. She fell fast. And then the bottom dropped out and Mom shut everything down. When Sophie Jean was younger, she'd had her heart broken when each father figure left them. It was why she was so careful with her heart. Why she'd been content to date Noel for nearly a decade without a commitment. Why she hadn't dated anyone seriously since. Love didn't last. A good pair of cowboy boots was a better investment.

Mom blew her nose, then added the crumpled tissue to the pile on the coffee table next to a maroon quilted tote with her name embroidered on it: *Charlene*. "And before you start… Yes, it's my fifth divorce. Don't judge. I'm still a believer in rainbows, fairy tales and happy-ever-afters."

"Maybe you should be a believer in couples therapy," Sophie Jean murmured under her breath. But since she hadn't been able to get Noel to talk to her productively about their relationship four years ago, much less go to couples therapy, she said in a louder voice, "I'm sorry, Mom," and set Kiki on the floor.

"You're my rock." Mom stood and hugged Sophie Jean. She smelled of lemon furniture polish and sounded like regret. "I have no more need of men. But you… You're young and fancy-free. There's plenty more catfish in the creek."

This, too, was predictable. If Mom's relationships fell apart, her recovery process involved projecting a happy-ever-after on Sophie Jean.

Sophie Jean sighed, taking in her gleaming coffee table and TV hutch. Apparently, her mother had been busy stress cleaning since she'd arrived from Oklahoma City. "I'd rather open my own salon than rush to the altar."

"Why do you want the headache of running your own shop?" Mom returned to the couch. "There is nothing wrong with renting a station at someone else's salon."

"And nothing wrong with being the boss. Granny Oswald owned her own salon." Sophie Jean glanced at the black-and-white photograph on her wall of Granny Oswald in front of the Cozy Clip on Main Street. Her maternal grandmother had started the salon fifty years ago. "She was fearless." Leaving her husband in Oklahoma City and starting over in Clementine with three kids. "Grandma Oswald took chances."

Whereas Sophie Jean let fear get in the way of risk-taking, especially when it came to opening her own business.

"You don't have to follow in my mother's footsteps. She walked alone," Mom said, dabbing at tears with a fresh tissue. When Granny Oswald died, Mom had inherited the salon and promptly sold it to pay for her third wedding. She didn't have the sentimental attachment to the Cozy Clip the way Sophie Jean did. "Some of us weren't meant to be the boss. I actually find it freeing to be able to pick up and move on when it suits me." Mom was a nail technician, not that you could tell by the ragged state of her nails today. "Speaking of, does Cozy Clip have an open nail station?"

"Yes. You should call Helga if you're interested." Helga was the current owner of the Cozy Clip, an older woman with a big heart and no plans to retire. Helga was so kind, she wasn't bothered by Sophie Jean's plan to open a salon of her own. There was enough business in town to support two salons and, even if there hadn't been, Helga would still respect Sophie Jean's desire for a place of her own. But Sophie Jean had other things on her mind besides her unfulfilled dreams. "What about Byron? Shouldn't you discuss things with him before you get a job here?"

Her mother's expression crumbled. "He's working a county fair upstate." Byron owned a traveling kiddie carnival.

"Does he know you left?" Because Mom wasn't good about talking through her feelings. She had a habit of calling relationships done and not looking back.

"No." That word came out in a discordant sound. "But he will when he gets back in a week."

Kiki latched onto Sophie Jean's pant leg, claws piercing the dusty denim enough to be felt. Then she released a displeased meow that promised a deeper dig if dinner wasn't forthcoming.

"I know it's time to feed you, Kiki." Sophie Jean gently shook her leg, ridding herself of one spoiled kitty, at least temporarily. "Give me a minute."

"I'm hungry, too." Mom preferred cleaning to spending time in a kitchen. "It's late. And your freezer is empty. Maybe we should order pizza and… Why are you home so late on a Saturday? I stopped by the Cozy Clip first and it was closed."

"It was a light day and my last appointment canceled, so I went to the Done Roamin' Ranch. They were working some new cattle." And Sophie Jean enjoyed riding with the crew, enjoyed being a part of that large, extended, supportive family. It helped fill the hole Noel had left in her heart. "I'm going back tomorrow." She'd promised Mary that she'd bake with her after church. Mary enjoyed having sweets ready for whoever visited. "Noel Emerson showed up while I was there." Sophie Jean pressed her lips together. She hadn't wanted to admit that.

Mom smiled. "I always liked Noel. Are you getting back together?"

"No. That ship has sailed." Too bad it left attraction sitting on the dock.

"Ships can always be turned around, sweetheart." Mom reached for the remote. "I'm living proof. I married your father twice, you know."

And divorced him twice.

But Sophie Jean kept that observation to herself.

CHAPTER FOUR

"ARE YOU TRYING to make Dad blow his top?" Ike asked Noel as they got into Noel's truck and headed out late on Sunday morning. "I don't get days off from rodeo practice. And I *never* go to the Done Roamin' Ranch. Dad considers the Harrisons the enemy."

"Dad will get over it." *Or not.* Noel was prepared to take the heat later, since they'd left the ranch while their father was in town at the feed store.

Noel hadn't told Dad they'd be gone when he returned. For now, Noel was just happy that the sky was overcast and the sun couldn't blind his light-sensitive eyes. He hadn't slept well last night, plagued by memories and regrets about Sophie Jean. He'd awoken with no apparent improvement in his concussion. Frustrating, that.

"This is your spring break, Ike, and I'm organizing a Fun Day with kids connected to the Done Roamin' Ranch. And since you're connected to the Done Roamin' Ranch through me, I'd like to take you there every day this week. There are great ropers at the ranch. Working cowboys. And Frank, my foster father, is no slouch in that department, either. Our dad should be happy you'll be getting good instruction."

Roping wasn't their father's forte. Neither was teaching.

"Dad's going to have a coronary," Ike predicted. He shifted his back to the passenger door, presumably so he could stare incredulously…dramatically at Noel. "If you were going to be home every day from now on, it might be worth it to upset him. But you said you were leaving after Mary Harrison's party next weekend."

"A lot can change in a week, even with Dad," Noel said firmly, pulling out onto the two-lane highway and heading toward town. The Done Roamin' Ranch was on the other side of Clementine. "Let's look on the bright side. You might pick up some useful roping tips." And make that expensive horse purchase pay off. "At the very least, you'll have a bit of time to clear your head and think about the future." They could always sell Ace to fund Ike's college education.

"I'd like to marry Cindy Hidalgo, please," Ike said without missing a beat. "I could dream about her all day."

"And you probably do but let's keep this PG and focus on what you want to do to earn a living."

"Said no fifteen-year-old ever." Ike slumped in his seat. A few more miles of cattle-filled pastures went by before he spoke again. "If this is about being a part of Fun Day, why did you call in a grocery order?"

"Because…" Noel had forgotten how surly teens could be. "After church on Sunday, my foster mother bakes, filling her kitchen with goodies in the hopes that people will visit." Every Sunday. And Noel hadn't been by in four years.

Guilt was a bitter taste at the back of his throat.

"Why don't we make it easier for Mary and just pick up doughnuts?" Ike asked, stroking those two whiskers of his.

"The point isn't to bring her food." Noel turned onto Main Street. "The point is to bake with her. Shared activities help you bond with people." He'd learned that from Mary.

Ike made a noise that sounded like a scoff. "And you want me to bond with the people at the Done Roamin' Ranch because…"

With effort, Noel held on to his temper. "It'll give you a network to rely on when things with Dad get difficult."

"So I won't run away from Clementine, you mean."

"Yes." Noel stopped in front of the grocery store, glad they were finally on the same page. "Running away isn't as cool as it sounds. You're either too hot or too cold, don't have a pillow to lay your head on and most likely have no idea where your next meal is coming from."

Ike was silent while Noel called the store and

waited for someone to bring out his grocery order. Once the bags of baking supplies were in the back seat of the truck, Noel headed toward his foster family's ranch.

"I don't bake," Ike admitted, still in that churlish tone. "I don't cook, either, other than putting frozen food in the microwave."

"Is that what Dad feeds you?" Noel was surprised. Their father was a decent cook. "Frozen food?"

"No. But I'm like a hobbit, Noel." And there was his kid brother's smile, long missing this morning. "I have to have a second dinner before bedtime."

"Or you could eat more at dinner," Noel pointed out.

"If I learn how to bake," Ike countered, smirking now, "I could make myself dessert every night."

Noel grinned. "Then consider this outing worth your while."

"MOM, DID YOU call Helga?" Sophie Jean had changed out of her church clothes and into jeans and a jean jacket to ward off the nip in the air. She grabbed various baking ingredients from her cupboards and the refrigerator, maneuvering around her mother, who was sitting at the small kitchen table finishing decorating her nails with images of small, colorful Easter eggs.

That was heartening. She'd been a lump under a blanket on the couch when Sophie Jean left for church this morning.

"I'm meeting Helga tomorrow morning to discuss renting the nail station." While Mom admired her Easter-themed nails, Kiki jumped up in her lap. Mom flinched and steadied the feline with her elbows, hands in the air. "Kiki, you're lucky I'm to the nail-drying stage. I'm not so forgiving of kitty love ruining my nail art."

The large, fluffy calico kneaded Mom's jean-clad legs, making her squirm.

But Mom didn't dump her off. "This cat is a lover. How old is she?"

"Four." She was Sophie Jean's consolation prize when Noel left. She'd sometimes wondered what, or whom, he'd replaced her with.

Don't go there.

"Your nails look fabulous." Sophie Jean paused to admire her mother's work. "Very cheerful."

"Can't ask Helga to rent a nail station with neglected nails." Mom spread her fingers out for better viewing. "If my nails look good, I can pretend not to be heartbroken." A tear spilled over Mom's cheek. Then another.

Sophie Jean used her thumbs to wipe her mother's tears away. They never talked about deep feelings. Sophie Jean had learned her role was that of moral support. "I feel the same way about hair and clothes." If Sophie Jean dressed to the nines, she could pretend everything was fine. She'd worn one of her favorite dresses to church this morning, straightened her hair, carefully applied makeup.

All in the hopes that Noel would attend and see she was doing all right, even if she hadn't opened a salon yet.

He hadn't shown.

"I can do your nails, Sophie Jean." Mom smiled weakly. "Bunnies and Easter baskets would be so cute."

"No, thanks. Nail polish doesn't last long when I rope." Sophie Jean finished bagging up her supplies.

Her mother gave Sophie Jean a sharp stare. "I thought you were baking with Mary today."

"I am." Sophie Jean took Kiki from Mom's lap, earning a gentle love bite, a nip that didn't break the skin. She placed her on the cat hammock attached to her dining room wall. "But it's not every day I can take a ride or practice roping. So while I'm out there, I'm going to get my cowgirl on if the opportunity presents itself."

Kiki found a place in the hammock where the day's meager sunlight came through the window. She curled into a tight ball with a contented sigh.

"I don't understand." Mom frowned. "You don't own a ranch, honey. Why are you roping? Are you going to start competing in rodeo? Are you going to stop doing hair and be a ranch hand?"

"No." Sophie Jean plopped a straw cowboy hat with a peacock feather hatband on her head. "I just… I like the cowboy lifestyle. It has nothing to do with rodeo or competing."

"How is that possible? You love fancy clothes and city-girl shoes." Her mother came to stand in front of Sophie Jean. Less than twenty-four hours after arriving, she looked a bit more like herself, which was comforting. "Why did you head down this path of being a horsewoman?"

Because at first, I felt closer to Noel.

And yet, that wasn't the reason she continued to hang out at the Done Roamin' Ranch. She felt like her own person there. Independent. Complete all on her own. "I like to ride, okay? But barrel racing is more about the horse and good barrel racing horses are expensive. When I started roping, it made me feel better, stronger. I like the challenge. And for some reason, I'm good at it."

"I see." Mom's gaze was assessing, her smile sly. "There's a special cowboy you've got your eye on."

"No, ma'am." Sophie Jean gathered her things. "It's just… I know I won't fit in at the Done Roamin' Ranch forever but for now, being a part of the doings over there makes me happy."

"I used to feel that way about the knitting circle." Mom nodded slowly. "I do like to knit, and I'm good at it. Maybe I'll call them up and see when they meet. You can never have too many friends or too many hobbies that bring you joy."

Especially when love was fleeting.

Sophie Jean promised to be home by dinner and then left.

"HELLO, LADIES." NOEL set his grocery bags on the kitchen table at the Done Roamin' Ranch and began unpacking ingredients. While he did so, Noel took stock of both his foster mother applying green frosting on a cake on the kitchen table and Sophie Jean assembling what looked like monkey bread dough in a pan by the stove. "I thought Ike and I would crash your baking session."

"No need to crash. You have an open invitation," Mary assured Noel. "Doesn't he, Sophie Jean?"

"If you say so." Sophie Jean's cool gaze collided with Noel's. "I'm not in charge of invitations."

Yet, even with her reticence, Noel felt the stress inside him ease just by having her near.

Ike hesitated at the mudroom opening. The poor kid had removed his boots and cowboy hat only to discover one of his socks had a hole in the toe.

"Come in and sit, Ike." Mary pulled out a chair next to her.

Ike didn't budge. He was still in mulish-teen mode, hiding his exposed toe behind his other foot. "I can hang around outside. I heard there'd be roping and stuff."

"That's later. Come on." Mary patted the seat next to her. She was excellent with ornery teenage boys. "Wc don't bitc."

"I don't bake, ma'am," Ike admitted, although he eyed the cake Mary was frosting and licked his lips.

"You don't bake because no one's taken the time

to teach you, I'd wager." Mary patted the cushion on the chair once more. "I taught every one of my foster boys how to make cookies. In no time, they learned not to be scared in the kitchen."

"I'm not scared in the kitchen," Ike said, slowly coming over to sit next to Mary. His tugged his sock over his right foot, holding the excess material in place by curling his toes. "I like the fridge and the microwave."

"That'll get old quick," Noel predicted.

"He's just like you, Noel." Sophie Jean chuckled, the sound bringing a smile to Noel's lips. She put the monkey bread in the oven and ignored Noel, choosing instead to go to his brother's side. "Do you have a favorite cookie, Ike?"

"Snickerdoodle." Ike eased back in his seat to look up at her. "They're tasty and they don't melt if you take them somewhere."

"That's very logical." Sophie Jean patted his shoulder. She was dressed for the overcast day in blue jeans and a purple blouse. Her brown hair fell thickly, smoothly, temptingly over her shoulders.

Temptingly...

Noel took a step back, frowning. He couldn't let Sophie Jean back into his head like this. She'd already messed with his sleep. When he cleared concussion protocol, he had to focus on bull riding and nothing else. Not Sophie Jean. Not family. Not Clementine.

"What's wrong?" Sophie Jean asked, always in

tune with Noel's moods. She peered into his eyes, making him want to draw her closer and kiss her.

I'm losing focus again.

Noel blamed it on that blasted bull and the slowly diminishing lump on his noggin.

"We'll get you started on a batch of cookies, Ike," Mary was saying. "Being skilled in the kitchen is one way to a woman's heart. And I hear you're a much sought-after catch at school."

Ike blushed the same way Ginny had yesterday. Bright red and sweaty. And then he ran his fingers over those two-inch-long whiskers framing his mouth.

"Are you trying to encourage more whiskers to grow on your face?" Noel teased.

"Yes. I'm gonna grow a beard like Eric Fernet." Presumably, a high school acquaintance of Ike's with more facial hair.

"How many whiskers does Eric have in his beard? Three?" Noel grinned.

"Ike, I heard that shaving encourages whisker growth. Maybe I should get Frank's razor for you." Sophie Jean grinned.

They grinned at each other while Ike sputtered and blushed.

And for a brief moment, happy memories of the past tumbled through Noel's head—of sparkling afternoons spent picnicking in a pasture with Sophie Jean, nights with Sophie Jean in his arms on the dance floor, long rides traveling to a rodeo with Sophie Jean's head on his shoulder.

But in a blink of her pretty brown eyes, the moment ended and she looked away.

Smart gal.

Of the pair of them, she'd gotten the better heartache-survival genes, at least when it came to their broken relationship.

No one seemed to notice their brief connection now. Mary was focused on Ike, who still blushed furiously and mumbled about not touching a razor.

"Oh, by the way, ladies." Noel gave the kid a break, drawing attention to himself. "Although I'm enjoying watching my kid brother squirm, I have an announcement to make." Noel rubbed his hands together and then spread his arms wide. "The carrot cake chef is back in town."

"Carrot cake?" Ike's brow furrowed. "Is that why you bought carrots? You're going to bake them. I thought you were just being nice and restocking Mary's kitchen. But…hang on." His gaze found Noel's, blush fading. "You put *real* carrots in carrot cake?"

"Yep." Noel was amused by his brother's naivete when it came to baking. "You have a lot to learn in the kitchen. You can start by helping me grate carrots."

"What a great idea." His foster mother beamed at Noel. "I *love* your carrot cake." Then Mary nudged

Ike with her elbow. "That's something you should aspire to—a specialty in the kitchen."

"Agree on both counts," Sophie Jean said, sparing Noel a careful smile. "Ike should learn to bake and Noel's carrot cake is good."

"Sophie Jean, I believe the term you used to describe my carrot cake was *divine*," Noel teased, moving to the sink to wash his hands. She'd also said his kisses were divine. He'd like to show her they still were if the chance arose. Despite his better judgment, Noel spared her a glance.

Sophie Jean's pretty brown eyes were wide and she was definitely blushing as he trapped her in his gaze. The spark was still there between them, like a light left on to guide a weary traveler home.

To guide me home.

"*Sophie Jean*," Noel began in a gruff voice.

Her cell phone rang and their connection was lost. Sophie Jean excused herself and headed outside to take the call without a word about who was on the line.

Is she dating someone?

The lump on the back of Noel's head throbbed.

He tried his best to ignore it. But he couldn't ignore his curiosity. "Sophie Jean seems to be hanging out here a lot," Noel said tentatively, grabbing bowls and measuring utensils, while he tried to remember all the single ranch hands that might have caught Sophie Jean's interest.

"Sophie Jean's been a blessing." Mom sprinkled

grated coconut on the green-frosted cake. "Most of you boys have wives and fiancées and are busy. Other than a handful of my friends, Sophie Jean has been a consistent presence around here. Helping me bake. Going with me on surrey treks and horseback rides. Joining all the volunteer committees I'm on. Plus, she doesn't take any guff from the cowboys in the bunkhouse."

It's not just me.

Sophie Jean had filled the void the Harrison foster boys had left behind.

That was noble, Noel supposed. "Where did she learn to rope?"

"I taught her." His foster father entered the room. "Haven't taught anyone how to rope in a long time. She's got skill. I think it's because she used to be a cheerleader. She applies adjustments I suggest to her form quickly." Frank smiled at Ike. "Haven't seen you in an age, young man. How are you?"

"Good. And you might be seeing more of me. I've taken up roping," Ike announced, blush now long gone. "I've never been a cheerleader but I'd be honored to apply any adjustments you have in my technique."

Frank nodded approvingly. "That kind of attitude will get you far."

Sophie Jean returned to the kitchen. "All right, Ike. Time for your first baking lesson." She flipped through Mary's recipe book on the kitchen counter without saying a word about her phone call.

Is she dating someone?

The unanswered question burned in his chest.

"Hang on, Sophie Jean." Ike turned a pleading gaze toward Frank. "Mr. Harrison, maybe we can go outside and you can give me some roping instruction now."

"Let's get your cookies made and in the oven first." Mary laid a hand on Ike's shoulder, presumably to keep him seated. "Both skills are important to learn."

"Um..." Ike shifted in his chair.

"Plenty of time to rope after making a batch of cookies, son," Frank told Ike. "Haven't seen you in roping competitions before. But I heard your father bought a fine roping horse. What made you interested to learn?"

While they talked roping, Noel moved closer to Sophie Jean and asked softly, "Everything all right?"

"Yes." His ex-girlfriend tried to shrug it off but he could tell by the fine lines emanating from her brown eyes that she was worried. Plus, she was hugging the flour tin to her chest like it was a comfort pillow. "If you must know... My mom is back in town and staying with me. She couldn't find a tissue box or a spare roll of toilet paper. She was...flustered."

"Getting divorced again, is she?" Noel guessed. Sophie Jean's mother fell in and out of love more often than Ike got new socks.

Sophie Jean frowned. "Why would you assume Mom's marriage is breaking up?"

Noel held her gaze, raising his brows. He knew her mother's history. He knew it colored Sophie Jean's belief in love. And he also knew he'd done nothing to disprove Sophie Jean's belief.

"Okay. Yes," Sophie Jean relented. "My mom is getting a divorce. *Again.* She's trying to be brave but..."

"That's gotta be hard on both of you," Mary commiserated, turning the green cake around and sprinkling more shaved coconut on the sides. "Divorce is often seen as a failure when it shouldn't be."

"It's like trying on hats," Frank said matter-of-factly, leaving off his roping talk with Ike. "Takes some folks a while to find the right fit."

"No." Noel didn't like that metaphor. "It's like finding the right horse. One that doesn't throw you or bite you—"

"*Too hard,*" Sophie Jean murmured with a private smile.

"—or refuse to come when you call." Noel took a good, long look at Sophie Jean. "Why do I get the feeling my metaphor struck out with you?"

"Because if I go by your relationship rules, I'm in a bad relationship with my cat." The worry on Sophie Jean's face gave way to the beginnings of a smile. "Kiki can get testy and give me love bites." Sophie Jean set the flour canister on the counter.

The smile she gave Noel was unguarded and full of joy.

That joy spread inside him—warm, comforting and yet also exciting.

His pulse ticked faster.

If I thought we had a future I'd...

Noel touched the lump on the back of his head. He didn't know what he'd do if they had a future together. He wasn't even certain what the next few weeks would bring.

Someone entered the mudroom and called out, "The prodigal son has come home." There were sounds of boots being removed.

"Of course you're talking about me, Griff," Noel said, having recognized the voice as one of his best-loved foster brothers. The one he'd texted last night about coaching a Fun Day.

"Noel Emerson is *not* the prodigal son." Griff entered the kitchen, and crossed the room to give Noel a backslapping hug that rattled Noel's brain. And when Griff released him, he said, "*I'm* the prodigal son, Noel. You're the nomadic son. How long are you back for?"

"Just until Mary's birthday bash," Sophie Jean said for Noel, taking Ike by the arm and guiding him over to the counter, presumably to start measuring and mixing snickerdoodle ingredients.

Noel frowned at her. He might not clear concussion protocol by next weekend if his lingering headache was any indication. The last time he'd had one, it had taken three weeks to feel normal enough to ride into the prize money. He had an appointment with Doc Nabidian tomorrow morning to check on his recovery progress. But he wasn't holding his breath on a clean bill of health. "Might stay a bit longer than planned. I haven't decided."

"Really?" Sophie Jean cut Noel with a curious gaze before returning her attention to Ike and the recipe book.

"Seriously, Noel?" Griff looked shocked. "You aren't here today, gone tomorrow?"

"You don't have a departure date?" Frank looked just as stunned. "Rodeo season is in full swing. To qualify for the big money at the end of the year, you need a steady stream of points."

"You're preaching to the choir, fellas," Noel said good-naturedly, trying to hide his own worries. He turned to Griff. "Are you here to talk about the Fun Day?"

"Yep." Griff retrieved a cake knife, plate and fork, then sat down at the kitchen table and eyed the green cake Mary had sprinkled with coconut flakes. "Best take a picture of that beauty, Mom, because it's not going to last long. I call first dibs."

"Prodigal sons go first." Noel confiscated Griff's plate and fork. Mary's coconut cakes were nearly as good as his carrot cake.

"I'll take a piece, too," Ike said from his place at the counter. His toe protruded from his sock but he didn't seem to notice.

Frank chuckled. “Just like old times. I’ll take a piece now or I won’t get one later, my love.”

“No to all of you,” Mary said in a warning tone of voice. She tucked her short white hair behind her ears. “My cake is for dessert tonight. It’s meant to be eaten *after* dinner.”

“I won’t be here for dessert.” Griff pouted. “Bess is expecting me home for supper. That means I’ll miss out on your famous Easter coconut cake, Mom. And it’s so good, I don’t want to go without. Pretty please.”

“Pretty please,” Noel echoed.

“*Oh, please*, guys,” Sophie Jean teased.

“I can see Mary’s going to relent.” Frank came to stand behind his wife, resting his hands on her shoulders. “It’s why she bakes, after all. For our boys to come visit, stay and eat.”

“Like you don’t enjoy the spoils, too.” Mary took hold of his hands and stared up at her husband. The love in her eyes was inspiring to witness. It was proof that there was someone for everyone.

Noel glanced at the back of Sophie Jean’s head.

“I don’t need a slice of cake,” Ike said kindly. “Not if it’s meant for dessert.”

“Oh, you’ll want a slice, little brother,” Noel assured him.

“If I let you eat cake now, what will we have after dinner tonight?” Mary demanded of her grown foster boys.

Griff and Noel exchanged glances. Griff shrugged, as if to say he had no idea how to answer that.

But Noel smiled, because he had an answer. "You'll have my world-famous carrot cupcakes for dessert, Mom."

"Oooh. That's a fair trade," Griff added, reaching across the table to high-five Noel.

Griff and Noel turned to stare at their foster mother with pouts and puppy-dog eyes.

"Oh, all right," she relented. "I never could resist a good round of pleading from my boys. But first, you've got to earn this cake." Mary carried the cake and knife to the counter. Then she got out more plates and forks. "I believe you're here to talk about the Fun Day, Griff."

"Yep." Griff ran a hand through his shaggy brown hair.

"Haven't had one of those here in what feels like forever," Frank mused, taking Mary's seat. "The competition was always fierce among you boys and entertaining to watch."

"I won the last Fun Day I organized," Noel said cheerfully. He was feeling happier than he had in months…years, even. Ike was here and Noel was getting a slice of Mom's cake, after all. And he'd be sure to eat one of his own cupcakes later. Double win. Triple, if you counted Sophie Jean's presence.

Noel paused, realizing the wayward direction of his thoughts. Since his arrival, his thoughts always circled back to Sophie Jean.

"Everything's a competition to Noel, Ike," Sophie Jean continued in a teasing tone, making Noel's kid brother chuckle. "And every competition must be won."

Even though that was true, it stung coming from Sophie Jean. She'd always been his staunchest supporter.

"Noel only won the last Fun Day because he cheated on the boot race." Griff didn't look happy to be reminded of losing the barefoot race to reclaim cowboy boots. In fact, he looked as if he'd enjoy a little payback. "You threw my boots on the far side of the pile." Making it harder for his rival to reach them.

"I don't cheat. I just don't play *nice*." Noel said that last word at the same time that Griff talked over him and said, "*Fair*."

"Not that I bear a grudge," Griff added, smirking when he said it. He clearly still bore a grudge.

"Let's consider this Fun Day a rematch. Winning coach gets absolved of any grudges." And Noel planned on winning. He extended his hand. "Deal?"

"Deal." Griff gave Noel's hand a hearty shake. "Oh, you are going down, Emerson."

Noel laughed. "Not likely."

Sophie Jean and Mary released put-upon sighs.

"This is why we can't have you two coaching the Fun Day teams alone," Frank mused, glancing around to check on Mary's cake-cutting progress.

"Kids need to learn empathy, to play fair and know how to get along. They need to learn to have pride in giving their all, whether they win or lose."

"Your grandkids aren't as cutthroat as we were," Griff assured him. "We don't *need* to give them a life lesson or to baby them."

"In fact, it might do them some good to see what cutthroat competition is really like." Noel floated that idea past Griff and his foster father.

"And it might not," Sophie Jean answered for them, leaning against the counter and crossing her arms over her chest. "I played cards with Ginny and Piper a few weeks back and they let me win. It was a lovely gesture."

"*Softies!*" Noel exclaimed in mock horror. "Winners never give the competition an even break."

"Really, bro?" Ike looked appalled. "Tone it down a notch. You're sounding like Dad."

Ouch.

Griff laughed. "Same old Noel."

"Exactly," Sophie Jean said. And not in a flattering tone. "What do you think, Mary? Should the Fun Day be cutthroat or kind?"

"We're planning a family Fun Day." Mary slid a cake plate toward Griff. "If our big, extended family can't field a friendly competition, I'm calling the whole thing off."

"The next thing you know," Noel said to Griff, "she'll be telling us that every kid needs to be crowned a winner."

"The next thing you know," Griff said in a louder voice to Noel, "she'll be telling us we can't play musical horses at this year's Fun Day."

"There will be no roughhousing events, including musical horses." Mary took the cake slice she'd nearly set in front of Noel and gave it to Frank. "Remember some of these kids are elementary school age."

"Do you approve of mutton busting for the kidlets?" Griff asked. "And letting the older kids ride some young bulls?"

"Of course! That's practically tradition," Noel agreed, even if Mary hadn't yet.

"I will approve rodeo sports on a case-by-case basis," Mary allowed with a small smile. "But there will be no scrums. Boot racing and musical horses are out."

"Sounds like we won't have any prizes for the winners, then." Griff dug into his slice of cake.

"The prize is to make me happy. I'm the Fun Day Queen, remember?" Mary said adamantly, handing Ike a slice of cake. "And what they'll take away from the Fun Day are the joys of being part of the Done Roamin' Ranch family. That includes you, Ike. And you, Sophie Jean. You'll both be a part of Fun Day. I insist. And *fun* will be the word of the day." Mary pointed at Noel. "Not competition. Or winning."

"Where's the fun in that?" Noel wondered aloud.

But he had to apologize and promise to play by the rules or Mary wouldn't give him a slice of cake.

"WE AGREE TO start with Bareback Ride-a-Buck." Griff had a sheet of paper full of scribbles. He and Noel had been going back and forth about which events to include in the Fun Day for over an hour.

They'd been at it so long that Ike had made two batches of snickerdoodle cookies, Noel had his carrot cupcakes in the oven and Frank and Mary had retired to the living room, where, last Sophie Jean checked, they were napping.

"I still say we should grease each horse's back for that event." Noel was against any game he considered too easy. "Everyone can ride bareback with a dollar bill under your knees."

Sophie Jean doubted that, although she'd never tried it herself.

"Are you going to clean a herd of greasy horses when we're done?" Griff was the practical funster. "I think not."

"You'll help me," Noel said even as Griff shook his head.

"*Boys*," Sophie Jean began, then thought better of it and shifted course. "*Noel*, you heard your mother. She doesn't want any dangerous events. If kids slide off horses, they'll get hurt."

"Dad says the younger you are, the better you bounce." Ike brought a plate of snickerdoodle cookies to the table, took a seat next to Noel and then took a bite of one. "I bounce off the mechanical bull all the time."

Ike's face had the promise of good looks, like Noel. When combined with his humility and humor, Sophie Jean could understand why Ginny had a crush on him.

"Hey." Ike beamed, pointing at his cookie. "These are great!"

"A baker who bounces when he's thrown." Noel patted his brother on the back. They'd dressed as if they shared the same closet—blue jeans, black-checked button-downs. "Enjoy your bounce-ability while you can, kid."

Sophie Jean frowned at Noel. "Just because a kid bounces doesn't mean they won't get hurt."

"I'm siding with Sophie Jean." Griff took another cookie. "And before you ask why, Noel, I'll tell you. If some young cowpoke gets injured on Friday, you'll most likely be gone by next Monday, no matter what you say about staying today. Which means Bess, Sophie Jean and I will bear the blame, not you."

Noel considered Griff and Sophie Jean in turn before relenting. "Fine. I guess I'll be the grumpy old man who says, '*In the old days, we'd have greased those horses.*'"

After a round of laughter, the conversation returned to which events would be held.

Sophie Jean cleaned the kitchen while she listened. She'd never been to a Fun Day and wasn't familiar with most of the events. Listening to the foster brothers talk was enlightening but hearing their criteria for selecting events made her smile. A pole-bending race was too tame for Noel. The egg-on-a-spoon ride was too boring for Griff. Amusement seemed to be their key decision criteria, followed by, albeit reluctantly, safety.

They chose Bareback Ride-a-Buck because they liked to imagine kids riding bareback around the arena at a trot with a dollar bill under each knee. Stepping Stones also made the list, which seemed to be a timed game where participants rode to upside-down buckets, dismounted, hopped from one bucket to the other as if using stepping stones, mounted again and then galloped to the finish line. Griff and Noel also considered adding a water-carrying horseback relay to fill a tub with water. They tabled it for further discussion pending a search for tubs in the ranch garage.

"I smell cookies!" Sam entered the kitchen with Rusty at his heels as the guys were finishing up. He stopped mid-kitchen and stared at Noel and Griff. "Why are adults doing homework?"

"We're planning a Fun Day." Griff reached out to ruffle Sam's brown hair. And then he ruffled the dog's reddish-brown hair.

Sam gasped and hurried over to Sophie Jean, hugging her around the waist. "Are you gonna be my coach for Fun Day? *Pluh-eaze.*"

Noel captured Sophie Jean's gaze and repeated, "*Please.*"

"*Please,*" Griff echoed.

"*Please,*" Ike chimed in, grinning.

"I have a lot on my plate," Sophie Jean hedged. "Work. Committee meetings. The town Easter egg hunt coming up. Not to mention my mom is visiting and needs my support."

"Just tell us what you need and we'll pitch in." Mary entered the kitchen. Her short white hair was stuck up in back. Sophie Jean hurried over to smooth it in place. "You can bring your mother whenever you need to be here, Sophie Jean."

"I love your mother," Noel said solemnly. "I'll keep her entertained."

He loves my mother.

Conversation continued around her but Sophie Jean didn't hear. Her mind wandered back in time.

"I love you, Sophie Jean. You know that," Noel had said, his strong hand clasping hers. "But I have to make my mark on rodeo. Be a winner worthy of the Hall of Fame. And it'll be harder to concentrate on the circuit if you're with me."

"I'm not a princess who needs taking care of." In hindsight, Sophie Jean had ruined the effect by flinging her hair over one shoulder and pouting. She'd thought for sure that Noel would agree it was time to settle down and start a family. His career had plateaued. She'd convinced herself that, unlike her mother, love with Noel was something she could rely on. Too late, she'd realized that pressing the issue had boxed Noel into a corner. "We can make it work, Noel."

He'd slowly shaken his head. "I'll be in a different town every week. You'd just be tagging along, not working. And if you can't work, you'll never achieve your dream of owning your own beauty salon. I can't delay your goal while pursuing mine. It wouldn't be right. I'd feel guilty. And to win, I need to have one hundred percent focus on me."

"You're right," Sophie Jean said in the here and now, something she hadn't been able to admit back then.

"You'll do it?" Mary asked, beaming.

And because Sophie Jean didn't want to admit her mind had wandered back to one of the most painful days in her adult life, she agreed. "Yes."

"Yay!" Sam hugged Sophie Jean again. "All I need to do is eat my fill of cookies and then we can start practicing."

"Start?" Sophie Jean eyed Noel warily. "Start what?"

"My roping lessons," Sam said as if it was obvious.

"I can give you roping lessons, Sam." Frank shuffled into the kitchen, yawning and looking as if he'd just woken up.

The mudroom door opened and closed once more. There were whispers in the mudroom as whoever entered dropped their boots on the floor with a clatter.

And then Piper and Ginny came into the kitchen. The teenage girls' gazes landed on Ike.

"Hey," they both said. And then their faces turned deep red.

"Hey," Ike said by way of greeting. Suave with the ladies, he wasn't. He hunched his shoulders and stuffed a cookie in his mouth.

The teenage girls seemed to freeze in place, and then they bolted out of the kitchen, into the mudroom and, with what sounded like a mad scramble for boots, they ran out of the house.

"Do you know Ginny and Piper?" Noel asked Ike.

"Kinda." Ike shrugged. "They go to my school."

"*Girls.*" Sam shook his head.

"You're right, Sam. Can't live with 'em," Noel said slowly, staring at Sophie Jean. "And can't live without them."

Sophie Jean felt her cheeks heat. But she didn't have the urge to giggle. And she was too proud to bolt out the door.

CHAPTER FIVE

LATER THAT AFTERNOON, kids kept arriving at the Done Roamin' Ranch with their parents. Word had gotten out about the Fun Day and everyone wanted to learn more.

And it was those parents who gave Noel the hero's welcome he'd expected the day before. Praise for his successful career. Awe for his continued longevity. Admiration for his current point total and recent win. It took the sting out of Noel's original homecoming because they made him feel like the rodeo champ he'd worked so hard to become.

But despite that, a small voice in his head whispered, *"Those are hollow victories,"* and his gaze kept drifting toward Sophie Jean.

"Remember what we talked about, Sophie Jean." That was young cowboy Sam, staring worshipfully at Noel's ex-girlfriend.

Sophie Jean stood in the Done Roamin' Ranch arena near Noel, looking highly attractive. Blue jeans, purple blouse, straw cowboy hat. Long, touchable, dark hair spilling over her shoulders.

Warm brown eyes sparkling with warmth. Smile as bright as a ray of sunshine.

If I was retiring, I'd do something about the sparks between us. Wouldn't that be a win worth savoring?

"Pick me first," Sam said, making Noel blink back to the task at hand—winning Fun Day.

Pick one of the youngest kids first? Nope. Not happening.

"Hang on. What's this?" Noel touched the lump at the base of his noggin. He'd planned to pick the older, more skilled kids first. Sam was a mere eight-year-old.

"You're my number one," Sophie Jean told the boy. Then she smiled at Noel. "Isn't he?"

No!

"There's a lot of strategy that goes into picking teams," Noel said carefully, cool as you please.

That earned him a frown from Sophie Jean. "It's called a Fun Day for a reason, Noel."

"Yeah, because winning is fun." Noel held up a hand for Sam to high-five but the boy left him hanging.

Sam turned to Sophie Jean instead. "Does Noel have to coach with you?"

Noel's jaw fell open. He'd never been an also-ran when it came to leading Done Roamin' Ranch events. He was the Chairman of Fun, not to mention, a fierce competitor.

"Sophie Jean?" Griff gestured for her to join

him at the arena gate before she had a chance to answer young Sam.

She excused herself and walked over to join Griff and Bess. It didn't escape Noel's notice that they hadn't invited him. But before he barged over there, he had other fish to fry. Specifically, one small fish named Sam.

"Dude, we need to talk." Noel summoned the miniature cowboy closer. When Sam stood next to him, Noel gestured toward the large belt buckle at his waist. "See this? I'm a bull riding champion. A highly skilled competitor. Convince me you'll be an asset to my team. What talents will you bring to Fun Day?"

"I'm good at everything." Sam kicked up dust with his brown cowboy boot and then fixed Noel with a disapproving stare. "And I want Sophie Jean to help me be a good cowboy, not you. Grandpa Frank says she's one of a kind. And *I* want to be one of a kind."

"I'm one of a kind." Noel tapped his belt buckle once more. "Not everybody can ride enough bulls for a high score in a year to be crowned overall champion." Especially after age thirty, much less thirty-eight.

Sam scoffed. "Everybody around here has a big belt buckle."

"Not everybody." Noel rolled his shoulders back, trying to shrug off the shade thrown by Sam.

"Mae!" Sam waved to get the attention of his

stepsister, who was throwing tennis balls for the pair of Labradoodles. "Mae, over here. You can be on my team."

"Hang on. The coaches are picking teams, not the players." And Mae may have been the same age as Sam and cute as a button, but she was a wisp of a girl who practically tripped over her own two feet.

"Sophie Jean won't mind if I put my sister on my team. She likes Mae." Sam seemed so certain.

This Fun Day was shaping up to be no fun at all.

Sophie Jean's laughter drifted to Noel as clear and cheerful as early morning birdsong.

Magnetized, Noel started to walk to her side but Ike intercepted him.

"Hey, Noel…"

"Yes." Noel didn't take his eyes from Sophie Jean, not from that pretty smile or the happiness that was radiating from her every pore. He'd missed that appreciation she had for life and people. He knew he was in trouble where she was concerned but he couldn't seem to stop himself from staring.

This is why I stayed away.

"You have to help me, bro." Ike took hold of Noel's arm, bringing him back to reality.

"Help you?" Noel did a quick inspection of his kid brother. Ike wasn't bleeding anywhere that he could see. "Help you with what?"

"Piper and Ginny." Ike sidled closer to whisper, "They walk up to me and all they do is giggle."

Noel glanced over at the teenage girls in question. They were staring at Ike and tittering. He shrugged. "Get used to it. That's about par for the course of teenage infatuation."

"Par for the..." Ike stepped behind Noel, using him as a shield between himself and his fan girls. "It's embarrassing. Make them stop."

"Do you like one of them?" Noel turned to face his brother.

Ike shook his head vehemently. "I told you. I like Cindy Hidalgo. Me, Ginny and Piper used to be friends when we were kids. And that's all we are now. Friends."

"You're still kids." Noel glanced over his shoulder to find the teenage girls creeping closer, silly grins on their faces.

"Don't look. You'll only encourage them." Ike tugged Noel back around. "We were always just friends. Being with them was easy. And then... Something changed last summer."

"I bet." Noel took his younger brother's arm and directed him toward the main arena gate where Sophie Jean was. "It's called puberty. They'll get over it in a year and then you'll wish they hadn't." In Noel's high school experience, that shift corresponded with girls gaining their confidence. And then it was the teenage boys who were struck dumb and followed them around.

"A year?" Ike raised his voice and then he was the one hauling Noel farther away from the girls.

"That's torture." Ike's phone chimed with a message. He glanced at the screen, looking even unhappier. "Dad's back from town and wondering where I am." Ike glanced over at the girls, eliciting another series of giggles, and then he turned his back on them. "Can you drive me home?"

"Not just yet." The whole point of hanging around this afternoon was to pick teams. "Don't let their attention bother you, Ike. I'll fix this." Not that Noel was sure how he'd do that. "But before I take action, I need to get together with Griff and select teams."

He strode toward the three other team captains with his brother trailing behind him and the giggling, lovestruck teenage girls bringing up the rear.

"Not to worry, Noel. We've chosen the teams already." Griff rubbed his hands together, grinning as if his team had already won the Fun Day. "Sophie Jean will fill you in." He and Bess walked over to greet some of the older kids who'd just arrived but not before Griff turned and mouthed to Noel, "Loser."

Noel spun on Sophie Jean, annoyance pounding at his temples. "You picked teams without me?"

Sophie Jean's smile challenged. "You trust me, don't you?"

"Not particularly," Noel said, feeling vulnerable. It didn't help that Griff's triumphant laughter boomed out over the arena.

Loser.

"Maybe if your smile was more reassuring, Sophie Jean," Ike suggested from behind him. "I barely know you and I don't feel a lot of trust."

Sophie Jean's chin rose and her demeanor turned serious. "We're going to have *fun*. That's our charter and you two are going to help me fulfill it."

Ike and Noel exchanged glances.

"Noel, can I see you for a minute?" Mary called before Noel had a chance to learn whom Sophie Jean had picked or if he wanted to protest her selections.

Although he was fairly certain he wanted to protest her selections, even without knowing the names on their team roster.

Loser.

"We'll talk more about this later," Noel promised Sophie Jean before striding toward Mary.

Ike matched Noel step for step, all the way over to where Mary was standing on the other side of the arena fence. Ike's arms were crossed and his cowboy hat brim drawn low, as if he wanted to be invisible to his two giddy fans. But he was so tall, there was no way he'd ever be invisible.

"What do you need, Mom?" Noel asked, fighting to keep his tone and smile as light and breezy as the day had promised to be.

"Can you keep your eye on Shay and Ford?" Mary pointed out two of the kids who'd been introduced to Noel the day before. "I hear they're on your team."

What?

Ford was the sturdy kid with brown hair, whose aunt was marrying one of Noel's foster brothers. Shay was slighter than Ford but with a determined expression on her face beneath a pair of goggle-like glasses as she tossed a rope miles wide of an orange cone target. Her stepdad was another of Noel's foster family.

"Ford and Shay are five and the youngest ones out here," Mary continued. "They need a close eye on them."

"Will do." Noel nodded, shooting Sophie Jean a dark look that he hoped said: *Does our team have any capable kids on it?*

Her answering smirk said no.

And for some reason, that made Noel smile.

Ike eased in between Noel and the fence as feminine giggles filled the air nearby. "Thanks for encouraging me to bake, Miss Mary. I enjoyed it."

"My pleasure. We'll work on making burgers next," Mary assured him. "A man's got to eat."

One of several moms hanging outside the arena called to Mary. She walked over to join them, her steps shorter and less purposeful than they had been just a few years before.

Ike moved in front of Noel, invading his space.

"Dude." Noel took a step back. "What are you doing? Back up."

"I'm hiding from the girls." Ike stared at his boots, his shoulders hunched.

Noel had never hidden from a girl in his life. He gave Ike a bracing, double-shoulder shake. "Don't cower. You've got this."

Mary called to Noel, gesturing for him to join her.

"What I've got," Ike said through gritted teeth, still looking down, "is nothing."

Glancing over at Sophie Jean and then around his former home, Noel could relate.

"We need to pick teams again." That was Noel an hour later, appearing in front of Sophie Jean, poker-faced. "Griff bamboozled you. We have the youngest team *and* only five members to his six. We don't have a chance to win."

"You don't know that," Sophie Jean told Noel, not flustered in the least. She'd been waiting for him to confront her about this. But she'd chosen their team with Noel in mind. She was determined to show him he could compete for fun, not a trophy. It would fulfill a wish of Mary's and, seeing how annoyed he was, keep Noel at a distance from her.

And Griff…

Well, he'd been happy to follow Sophie Jean's suggestion, although he hadn't been thrilled to accept her demands to even up their odds during the competition to account for the age advantage of his team. She wasn't a complete fool. But that fact was something Sophie Jean didn't plan on telling Noel until later.

Noel's hat brim was pulled low. His guard was down, making him look vulnerable, more like the man she'd fallen in love with than the bull riding champion she saw on TV. "Other than Ike, our entire team is under the age of nine."

She gave him a soft smile. "It's not like we need to win. It's a Fun Day, remember?"

"Nobody ever *needs* to win," Noel said in a detached voice. "They *want* to win. *I* want to win. Or rather, I want Griff to lose."

"Of course you do." Sophie Jean had known Noel's competitive spirit, thanks to his hard-nosed father, would get in the way of the breezy nature of the event. That's why she'd undercut him on team selection. "But it's not about you. This Fun Day is about your foster mother. And Mary wants the kids to have a good time." She'd made that plain over and over again. "And everyone learns better when it's fun." She did, anyway.

Noel shifted his weight. "The kids will have a great time if we win. But the way it stands now—"

"I'm just reminding you." Sophie Jean adjusted the set of Noel's cowboy hat, only to realize she didn't have the right to invade his personal space anymore. She dropped her hands to her sides. "We're not coaches. We're just concierges of a good time for the kids."

"A concierge?" Noel's mouth dropped open.

"Of a good time." Sophie Jean nodded.

"Well..." Noel lifted his cowboy hat and ran a

hand through his dark hair. "You're saying I'm not the Chairman of Fun but the *Concierge* of Fun. That changes things, doesn't it? Implies I'm not top dog…"

Sophie Jean didn't answer. She was remembering the thick, silky feel of Noel's hair. She was itching to reacquaint herself with it. To fuss and tousle those dark locks until Noel took her in his arms and kissed her breathless.

Danger, Sophie Jean Shearer! Danger!

She tucked her hands in her back jeans pockets and jettisoned thoughts of kisses.

"Right." Noel plopped his cowboy hat back on, still looking displeased. "I shouldn't complain. It's not as if I've never shown anyone a good time."

"Have you shown anyone a good time recently?" Sophie Jean blurted.

Immediately, she regretted opening her mouth. The question was too suggestive. Too flirty. Regardless, Noel might tell her about being in love with another woman and then she'd be well and truly crushed.

"Have I shown anyone a good time recently?" Noel repeated slowly, grin taking over his features. "Of course."

Sophie Jean's heart sank past her toes.

"I present to you Exhibit A, my brother Ike." Noel gestured to the teen, who'd been shadowing Noel most of the afternoon.

"What am I an example of?" Ike asked, eyes on the swivel.

Sophie Jean gave Ike a reassuring smile, having dodged a bullet with Noel and her good-time question. Curiosity killed the cat, after all. She'd been lucky this time. "Ike, your brother claims he's showing you a good time."

"He's failing at that." Ike tipped his cowboy hat to Sophie Jean. "No offense, Noel, but… If Sophie Jean hadn't talked to Ginny and Piper, I'd be hiding in the kitchen convinced this was the worst day of my life." Although he was still as jumpy as Kiki during a thunderstorm.

"They didn't mean to make you feel uncomfortable." In fact, when Sophie Jean talked to the girls about ogling poor Ike, they were horrified he'd noticed.

"You talked to the girls?" Noel sputtered. "That was my job."

"Yeah, I asked you first but…" Ike grinned. "Sophie Jean actually got the job done."

Noel sighed wearily. "I would have gotten around to it. I was catching up with my family."

His fans, Sophie Jean thought he meant. He'd always put too much stock in what other people thought of him.

"Hey, Ike. Can you check on the younger kids?" Sophie Jean pointed toward two kids sitting in the arena dirt. "Play tag with them or something?

Mary really wants us to watch out for the young kids, like Shay and Ford."

"I already told Mary I'd watch out for them," Noel protested.

"Again, bro," Ike said, backing away from them, smiling. "Sophie Jean gets the job done." He sauntered over to where the other kids were, leaving Noel and Sophie Jean alone.

If you could call being thirty feet away from the nearest pair of ears alone. All adult eyes seemed to be upon them.

"Are we good, Noel?" Sophie Jean asked, feeling self-conscious under the scrutiny of the Done Roamin' Ranch folks. "Besides my team selections, that is."

Noel stared at Sophie Jean woodenly.

"I know that look." And Sophie Jean wasn't afraid to call Noel out on it. "You're unhappy. Why?"

"It's nothing," Noel said stubbornly, angling his gaze away.

"It's something. Tell me." Sophie Jean took a step closer to Noel, forgetting her need for space while lowering her voice. "You always feel better after you vent some steam, either by talking or riding a bull."

He scuffed his boots across the arena dust before looking her in the eye. "I don't always feel better by venting." Noel's gaze brushed tenderly across her face. "Especially when what I need to vent about…is you."

"*Me?*" Sophie Jean squeaked. Almost immediately, she tried to recover her composure and put distance between them. "If you really want a different team, I can ask Griff to reshuffle. The kids on our team will be disappointed but—"

"That's not it." Noel was staring at her so intently, she felt her internal temperature start to rise. "You've replaced me."

That threw Sophie Jean for a loop. "As a coach?"

"No." His gaze fell to her lips. "If you must know…" His voice was gruff. "… I'm jealous."

"But I… I'm not dating anyone." Sophie Jean hadn't wanted to admit that. It was none of his business, after all.

But he's jealous!

A part of Sophie Jean reveled in that fact.

"I'm not jealous of your love life," Noel said in a low voice that tore at Sophie Jean's heart. "I'm jealous because you've replaced me. Here. At the ranch. With my foster family. With Ike. And probably even in Clementine."

"Don't say that." Sophie Jean settled her cowboy hat further back on her head, settled her cowboy boots deeper in the arena dirt. "Your family loves you. My being here doesn't change that."

"They all turn to you." He lifted a hand to the back of his head, sliding his fingers into the hairline. "Even my kid brother."

"Noel, you're tired. Maybe even injured and—"

"Is Noel injured?" Mary called from across the arena. She had the hearing of a cat.

"No, Mom. I'm fine." But Noel squinted when he looked Mary's way, as if it was painful for him to focus with the sun in his eyes.

"You're not fine," Sophie Jean whispered. "And I haven't replaced you here. No one can replace you."

Not even in my heart.

Noel stood with his back to his mother and insisted, "I'm fine." Ignoring everything else she'd said.

But not the chemistry between them. The dry spring air practically sizzled with it. Their gazes were caught.

Sophie Jean's breath became ragged under his continued scrutiny and her mind wandered through memories of kisses, snuggles and tender touches. Suddenly, she was struck by a deep, profound sense of loneliness. Tears welled in her eyes.

Kids ran by accompanied by two bounding Labradoodles. Adults at various places in and around the arena called to children, to Frank and Mary, to each other. And still, Noel's gaze held Sophie Jean trapped in limbo between the idyllic days of the past and the stance she should take in the present. That his love wasn't a sure thing.

"Take a picture, why don't you?" Sam ran past, pausing to make googly eyes at Noel and Sophie

Jean before stumbling back into a run with the pack of kids. “Hey, Max. Wait up.”

The two Labradoodles raced after Sam. And Sophie Jean’s detachment, when it came to Noel, seemed to run along with them.

“Fine?” She blew out a breath, mind returning to the topic at hand, not jealousy or memories of smooches. “I know you, Noel. Your arms and legs seem to work all right. But you’ve been wearing your sunglasses inside. Having your head kicked like a soccer ball rattled your brains, didn’t it?”

“*Noel*,” Mary said in a louder, sharper voice, one that demanded answers. “Are you injured? I can take you inside.”

“No need, ma’am.” Noel smiled at Mary over his shoulder. Then he turned back to Sophie Jean, unsinkable smile still in place. But even with his sunglasses on, Sophie Jean could tell his smile didn’t reach his eyes. The top half of his face was rigid and immobile. “I need you to stop talking about injuries, Soph. For the rest of the week.”

Oh, he’s injured, all right.

Sophie Jean tsked, suddenly feeling empowered enough to let his use of an old endearment slide. “I’ll stop bringing it up if you stop talking about needing to win this Fun Day.”

They stared at each other in silence for a moment.

Sophie Jean’s mind whirled around unbidden feelings—*of love and tender moments*—and memories—*of whispered endearments and kisses that promised forever.*

"All right. The Concierge of Fun is here," Noel deadpanned, breaking into her thoughts. "At your service. Are we good?"

"Okay." That was probably as much of a concession as she was getting out of him today. "You're my assistant coach, then."

"Yep. I'm the Concierge of Fun," Noel repeated, looking rigid, from his stance to his shoulders to his jaw.

"Bro, how many lariats do you have on the ranch?" Ike trotted over, boots kicking up arena dust. "Everyone on our team needs one to practice."

"Even you?" Noel asked woodenly.

Ike rolled his eyes. "Yes. Even me. I'm on your team, remember?"

"How could the Concierge of Fun forget?" Noel smiled that fake smile. "Come on. I'll show you where the ropes are kept."

The pair of Emersons walked toward the barn together. They passed Griff, who was walking the other way and carrying a bale of hay and a black plastic sheep's head. He set the hay bale on the ground, then shoved the plastic sheep's head in one end so that the hay bale served as the sheep's body. Sophie Jean had learned to rope with the same setup. She'd started with orange cones, then fake sheep and finally worked her way up to fake cattle with horns. All on the ground before moving to horseback, and then live targets.

It had been a slow progression, like her love for Noel.

But I made it work.

"How are you doing, Sophie Jean?" Mary called from across the arena, breaking Sophie Jean from her reverie.

"Fine." It wasn't lost on Sophie Jean that she was hiding behind the same mantra Noel had used since returning home. But she wasn't hiding a physical injury. It was the scars on her heart she wanted to disguise. They were at risk of reopening.

Things weren't going well between her and Noel. She'd expected awkwardness, not jealousy over her place here or latent attraction. Her thoughts were a jumble. Her heart a mess.

When it came to Noel, she didn't know where she stood.

Or if it mattered.

CHAPTER SIX

"ARE WE READY to rope yet?" Noel sat on a hay bale and eyed the plastic sheep head. Like his father, he wasn't much of a roper and didn't want to admit he had little to add to this Fun Day practice.

"We're going to start with the basics." Sophie Jean didn't even turn around to answer him. "*Swing wide. Thumb down. Wrist up.*" She demonstrated proper roping technique for their five team members. "Good. Repeat. Focus on your motion. Noel, that includes you."

Noel dutifully mimicked what Sophie Jean was doing, pretending to throw, pretending to be part of the team, pretending not to be entranced by the power and grace of her movements.

Griff had decided it was a good idea to focus on a different event in each of the six practice sessions before the Fun Day on Friday. Today was roping. And the kids on Noel and Sophie Jean's team were working on their rope twirling motion, swinging six feet of rope tail, not a loop, around their heads. Sam had his tongue sticking out of one corner of his mouth. Ike's expression was just as intense, minus the tongue.

On the other side of the arena, Griff's team was roping metal calf targets with a depressing amount of skill.

Loser.

Noel tried to roll the tension from his shoulders the echo of Griff's taunt caused. He had to face facts: *We're going to mess this up big-time.* "We should throw now."

"Not yet," Sophie Jean replied sweetly.

It was her and her alone who was teaching the kids. Frank was over giving pointers to Griff's team, who'd skipped a tutorial of the basic hand-and-arm motion and gone straight to roping. It was so basic out here that the parents of the participating kids had gone inside the main house where they were probably enjoying cold glasses of iced tea, cookies and large slices of cake. Even the dogs had gone inside.

Noel would like to call it a day, too.

Movement at the other end of the arena caught Noel's attention.

Piper and Ginny each held an end of the same lariat and turned it like a jump rope. For Griff.

He's the Concierge of Fun. Not me.

But after a moment, Noel grinned.

Griff is a slacker wasting time on fun!

Maybe things weren't as bad as they seemed.

Still grinning, Noel lay back on the hay bale,

tipped his hat over his face and hugged the plastic sheep head like a teddy bear. He was tired. His eyelids heavy. But he heard Sophie Jean's voice as clear as a bell.

"Fantastic," she said. "Now, let's take hold of the Hondo—" the lariat knot "—and pull the rope through to make our loop." She seemed to be helping their team members with their ropes because there was a pause filled only with the soft sounds of cowboy boots walking slowly on arena dirt. "Yes, that's right, Ike. Oh, Sam. We want a big loop to start but not that big."

Noel squinted in Sam's direction. The kid had pulled most of his rope through the Hondo, leaving nothing to hold on to. Noel closed his eyes once more.

"Now," Sophie Jean continued. "Hold the Hondo in your throwing hand and the coiled rope in the other." There was another pause and the sound of her footsteps, slow and deliberate. "That's right. Now, we're going to extend our arms like a T. And that's how much length you need to throw with, the distance from one hand to the other. The rest will be in a coil of about four loops. Okay?"

Noel couldn't remember being taught to rope with such meticulous attention to detail. He was pretty sure he'd copied whatever Chandler did to learn.

"Good. We're ready to practice that motion we learned. *Swing wide. Thumb down. Wrist up.*" Sophie Jean had the patience of a saint. "Don't throw yet. Get used to the feel of the loop."

"My arm is tired," Ford complained.

"If your arm is tired, you're doing it right," Noel called to the group. He remembered that much about roping.

"Just a little longer on technique, Ford," Sophie Jean promised. "And then we're going to rope Noel."

"Woo-hoo!" Sam cried.

"What?" Noel sat upright too fast, making his head spin and his hat nearly tumble off. He raised the plastic sheep head in the air. "This is our target."

"But it's so much more fun to rope you." Sophie Jean's smile was angelic. "And you are the Concierge of Fun."

"What's a con-surge?" Sam asked.

"Me." Noel tapped his chest. "I'm here to serve up fun and laughter."

Sam scoffed. But he hoisted his lariat and spun it around his head, tongue sticking out.

"Ropes down," Sophie Jean commanded. "The last motion we need to review before you rope Noel is the release. That's how you aim." She pretended to whirl a lasso, pretended to release a rope and then kept her arm extended, pointing at him. "Where you point your hand is where your rope will go."

Ike pantomimed a rope-throwing motion that was pretty decent. "It's like throwing a baseball."

It was the first time Noel had any inkling his brother knew how to play another sport. Noel made a mental note to hunt up his baseball glove and invite Ike for a catch.

"Yes. It's exactly like throwing a baseball." Sophie Jean nodded. "Keep pointing at Noel after you release. If your empty hand isn't pointing at him after you throw, your release is either too early or too late."

The kids all went through their throwing motion, lassos at their feet. But they were just as impatient to get to the main event as Noel was.

"Can we rope Noel now?" Ford asked, drooping.

"Yes, you can." Sophie Jean moved out of the way. "Fire when ready."

"*Fire?*" Noel caught Sophie Jean's smile and the accompanying come-hither gesture, which he translated to mean it was time for the Concierge of Fun to leap into action. *Finally.* "Come on, guys. I dare you to rope me."

Ropes whirled.

Ropes flew.

None hit Noel.

"Not even close." Noel chuckled.

Ropes were gathered, dragged through the arena dirt.

In no time, ropes whirled once more.

Ropes flew once more.

A couple bounced off his boots. One bounced off his hat.

His team chattered happily. Noel laughed.

"I almost got him," Ike said excitedly.

"We're not playing horseshoes," Noel taunted. "Close doesn't count. You have to rope me."

"Hang on. Team meeting." Sophie Jean gathered their team of five and whispered instructions Noel couldn't hear. "Okay. Try again."

Noel took up his position again and stood tall "Ha! You can't rope me. No, sir."

Ropes twirled.

Ropes flew in the air.

Someone's rope bounced off Noel's nose. Another struck his Adam's apple, albeit with no force. A third knocked his hat off.

"Great job!" Sophie Jean clapped her hands. "Again!"

"Hey." Noel rubbed his scraped nose, then his throat. "I think it's time to switch to the sheep head." He held it up.

"Nope. Stay where you are, cowboy," Sophie Jean commanded.

Sam was already swinging his rope around, tongue sticking out the side of his mouth.

"Stay?" Noel stuck his tongue out at Sam, prompting the kid to throw, an effort that swung way wide. "Why?"

"Why?" Sophie Jean laughed, looking joyful enough to kiss. "Because these kids are having fun."

Lo and behold, so was Noel.

WHEN NOEL AND Ike got home, Dad was angry.

"Where have you been?" He met Noel and Ike at the front door, broad features pinched in displeasure. "We've got a training schedule on the weekend, Ike. You can't go taking a flyer just because your brother is back in town. Get in the barn and warm up."

"We practiced already." Noel tried to take the wind out of Dad's full sails. "Roping, mostly. That's enough for one day."

"Roping?" Dad pointed out Ace in the pasture. "Without your horse?"

"Yeah, Dad." Ike eased past him into the house. "We focused on the basics. It was fun. I'm going to shower." He disappeared down the hallway. "Will dinner be ready when I'm done? I'm starved." A door closed and latched.

"Fun?" Dad shook his finger at Noel. "You're a bad influence. He's fifteen. Time to get serious."

"Can we not do this now?" Noel was exhausted from a concussion and in no mood to argue.

"I see it now." Dad moved aside to let Noel in the house. "I see everything."

Noel wasn't feeling his father's clarity. But he glanced around anyway, not pleased with what he could see.

The living room was small and filled with oversize brown leather furniture. A man cave. There were no decorative pillows, no well-worn quilt or soft afghan over sofa backs. There was just a big bookshelf filled with belt buckles, trophies and photos of Noel holding the prizes he'd won over the years. There were no baby pictures. No photographs of Noel or Ike as gap-toothed kids standing in front of a Christmas tree. No family photos.

Noel couldn't see himself growing old in this room. The man who lived out his life here would be stuck in the accolades and achievements of the past.

That's Dad's bailiwick, not mine.

"There's something wrong with you, Noel," Dad was saying, having closed the front door. "You never take a break mid-rodeo season unless you're injured." Dad looked Noel up and down. "And you never come home, regardless. Haven't since Sophie Jean dumped you. Not even for Christmas."

"Dad..." Noel's head throbbed harder than it had when he'd argued with Sophie Jean earlier that day about her team selections. "You're reading too much into things."

"Are you feeling your age?" Dad demanded in a loud voice that nearly shook the house. "Have you lost your nerve?"

"I'm as nervy as ever." But it was clear Noel had lost something. Sophie Jean came to mind. Her laughter. Her unexpected skill with the rope. The way she looked at him sometimes, as if remembering the good times and wanting a do-over. "It's like a mausoleum in here. Why don't we get a dog?"

"A dog?" Dad scoffed. "Don't tell me you're thinking of retiring?"

"It's not on my radar." Noel sank onto the couch, eased back and lowered his straw cowboy hat over his face. The lights inside, dim as they were, were still too bright. "I'm just saying this house is empty. There aren't even any pictures on the wall."

"What's wrong with you?" By the sounds of it, Dad was standing in front of Noel. "Have you been watching renovation shows in your hotel room? I trained you to be a coldhearted winner."

As if I could forget.

From the early days of mutton busting at the county fair, Dad had seen Noel had the ability to hang on to an animal, even if he'd been terrified back then, having fallen and been stomped on early on. Repeatedly. Dad didn't give up on Noel. By the time Noel was twelve and qualified for riding small bulls, Dad had him coming home every day after school to lift weights and ride the mechanical bull.

His mother had already left them at that point. Nothing that didn't benefit a future as a bull riding champion was allowed. No after-school activities. No football games, no school dances. He couldn't even hang out with kids his age at the Tasty Freeze for ice cream. Instead, Noel and Dad had traveled every weekend to junior rodeos, far and wide. It had been a lonely time. Dad wouldn't let Noel make friends with anyone on the circuit. Everyone he competed against was the enemy.

Noel came to believe he only had two enemies—the bull he was riding and his father. It was when he was fourteen that he realized something had to give. And so, he'd run away, only to be brought back. To be punished. To be forced to listen to long rants Dad called lectures. On how to hang on like a man. On how to be cutthroat. On how to be feared by others and respected when he showed up at a rodeo. Dad had sucked all the joy from Noel's life. There hadn't been a Concierge of Fun, much less a chairman.

"Are you listening to me, Noel?"

"No." Noel's body was heavy, his defenses weak. "Give it a rest."

"Rest is for also-rans. The Emersons are winners. And winning requires sacrifice." The strength of his father's conviction was disheartening.

Because I sacrificed a future with Sophie Jean to win.

Worst decision of my life.

That stung to admit. Reluctantly, Noel removed his hat and sunglasses. He ignored the out-of-focus view of his father and soldiered on to the point. "Your anger isn't about me. It's about Ike. About him not following your rules. There were good, professional cowboys helping Ike rope today." Noel decided to keep Sophie Jean out of the conversation. "Ike showed promise." He'd roped Noel several times. His younger brother was as coachable as his foster father had labeled Sophie Jean.

"But he's not going back tomorrow," Dad said firmly. "We have a routine we follow here."

"Your routine is killing his spirit." Noel kept himself from saying more, from making this about himself and the past. "I'm taking Ike back to the Done Roamin' Ranch tomorrow. He's learning *and* having fun." Then Noel said something he shouldn't have. "If you recall, my skill and confidence in all things cowboy really took off when I lived there." When he'd been allowed to be a kid. Maybe there was something to what Sophie Jean was trying to achieve at Fun Day.

Noel quickly dismissed that thought.

Dad's complexion turned ruddy.

Too late, warning bells went off in Noel's foggy brain.

"Roping is secondary for Ike. We're this close to everything clicking on the bull." Dad held his thumb and forefinger nearly touching. "*This close.*"

"Or he might never get it, Dad. And that's okay, too."

His father made a grumbling noise and headed toward the kitchen. "Emersons are winners. And winners don't take time off. Or give up when times get tough."

Times were tough. Not just for Noel, but for Ike. And something inside Noel was dropping anchor here, countering everything Dad said, and urging him to stay.

"YOU LOOK LIKE you've been dragged through the dirt." Mom was in the kitchen when Sophie Jean made it home that night. Not that she was cooking. Mom stood at the refrigerator with the door open, inspecting its contents. She closed the door to greet Sophie Jean, looking teary-eyed. "I thought you were baking today. Why aren't you covered in flour?"

"I was baking. Then I spent the afternoon teaching kids roping skills for a Fun Day the Done Roamin' Ranch is hosting." Sophie Jean set down a plastic container with snickerdoodle cookies and carrot cupcakes, then picked up Kiki and gave her cat a cuddle. "Somehow, I ended up agreeing to coach with Noel."

They weren't exactly coaching together. Noel had taken his role as the Concierge of Fun seriously. He'd done no coaching today. And Sophie Jean could handle that. At least, until it came to preparing the kids for mutton busting. She'd never ridden a sheep and had no advice to give other than to hang on.

Unbidden, the image of Noel being bombarded by ropes returned. He'd tried being stoic. He'd tried being cocky. He'd tried taunting. And those playful taunts… That's what finally got the kids to put it all together—their technique, their aim—and they'd roped Noel. Even Shay and Ford.

Much to his surprise. And hers.

Sophie Jean smiled. Noel expected their team to

lose. Badly. He was in for a surprise bigger than ropes falling around his shoulders when he learned Griff had agreed to spot them several seconds on two timed events and had given them other advantages.

"I bet you'd have more fun if you had someone special in your life and were coaching a kid of your own." Mom may have a broken heart but she was consistent in her post-breakup messaging—that a happily-ever-after was something Sophie Jean should aspire to. "Then you might keep more food in your kitchen than nuts, string cheese and lettuce."

"Don't forget the bananas," Sophie Jean said absently, imagining the shocked look on Noel's handsome face when she finally told him about Griff's concessions. Now, that would be fun.

Kiki purred loudly in Sophie Jean's arms, happy to be her spoiled fur baby. It never lasted for long, however. Any moment now…

The fluffy calico leaped from Sophie Jean's arms to the floor, where she turned her back to both humans in the apartment and gave a mighty tail twitch.

"Cat dinner gets priority, then." Sophie Jean washed her hands before moving to the cupboard for a fresh can of cat food.

"And how is Noel?" Mom managed a wan smile. "Still mighty fine?"

That's the way Sophie Jean used to describe

him when they were dating. She'd liked everything about Noel except his unrelenting competitiveness and desire to win, even if that was what made him successful on the circuit.

Mom turned off the oven, sniffing lustily. She drew a steaming tray from the oven, then faced her. "You still love him, don't you?"

Sophie Jean gaped at her mother, who was placing the piping-hot ready-made lasagna on the counter. "Yes… No… I don't know. How did you…?"

"You're my baby. I know you like the back of my hand." Mom flashed Sophie Jean the back of her left, ringless hand. There was a tan line left where her wedding ring should have been.

"You took off your wedding ring?" Sophie Jean asked.

"I left it when I left *him*." Her mother's expression crumbled. She started to cry.

"What's wrong?" Sophie Jean wrapped her arms around her. "Do you want to go back?"

"No. I thought my marriage was fine. I thought I'd finally found my soulmate. But I was wrong." She sobbed louder. "Five divorces. I was so certain the other marriages were just practice for Byron. What is happening to me?"

"Life," Sophie Jean told Mom, drawing her into a hug. "Life happens so fast. It doesn't take much to sever a tenuous bond." She knew that from experience.

Mom's sobs turned into hiccupy tears. "You're

saying…Byron's and my love…wasn't strong enough…to go the distance?"

"No. I…" Yes. Yes, she was. But that wouldn't help anything. Sophie Jean switched tactics. "If it's any consolation, Noel's love for me wasn't strong enough to last forever, either."

It was no consolation. Mom kept crying until Sophie Jean was tempted to join in.

CHAPTER SEVEN

"YOU'LL LIKE THIS PLACE, Sophie Jean." Vickie Taveras opened the door of a retail space in Clementine on Monday morning. "It has potential to be your dream salon."

Vickie was a real estate agent. She considered every building within Sophie Jean's price range to have potential.

"Didn't Walt Eichel used to own this place?" Sophie Jean stepped out of the bright spring sunshine and glanced around the inside of the building. Her spirits sank.

Walt used to own the gas station next door. He must have used this building as storage. Junk had been stacked throughout the space higher than Sophie Jean's head. There was a narrow trail through it from the front of the shop to the back. It was an eclectic collection of rubbish. There were tires and toys. Boxes and bulging plastic bags. Spider webs and layers of dust.

Sophie Jean quaked inside. "I hate spiders."

"I know how it looks." Vickie headed toward the back door with confident steps, perhaps heedless of Sophie Jean's reluctance to dive in. Perhaps not. "But that's why it's competitively priced. Elbow grease always equals a lower price tag. Plus, you could have a rummage sale to help finance your remodel. It comes as is."

"I'd have to sort through Walt's things to host a sale." That sounded daunting. "And make several dump runs." That sounded exhausting. "And what if I don't like this space after all that work?" That sounded demoralizing.

"Walt's family said there were pictures of this place from when it was newly built hanging about. If we can find them, they should give you a better idea of the potential here." Vickie disappeared through a doorway. "Found them! Walt hung them on the bathroom wall." She stuck her head back out, every strand of her shoulder-length blond hair in place while Sophie Jean's felt like hers was standing on end. "Come on. Take a look."

Sophie Jean picked her way carefully through the junk to reach the bathroom at the back. A spider web clung to her face and she shuddered as she wiped it off, wishing she'd worn her cowboy hat.

"See?" Vickie pointed at a black-and-white framed picture of what might have been the inside of the building decades ago. It was hard to reconcile then to now. "It used to be a barbershop. That means there are sinks or plumbing in the main space."

Sophie Jean wasn't convinced.

"When I said I could take on some DIY, Vickie,

I meant *some*." There was a pit in Sophie Jean's stomach just thinking about all the work that would need to be done before she could open. And she couldn't imagine any beautician wanting to rent a station from her without significant work being completed first. Salons had to be beautiful. And, although not necessary, Sophie Jean wanted hers to be efficiently laid out, too. "My only hammer skills involve inserting picture hooks in walls. This place..." It would need a variety of trades—from painters to plumbers to electricians.

"I think you should give it a chance." Vickie took gentle hold of Sophie Jean's shoulders. "We've been looking for years now and you always have an excuse not to buy. Nothing is perfect, Sophie Jean. Not love and not dreams. *You* have to shape your dream to the limited options in Clementine."

"Uh..." The brown state of the toilet water was enough to send a sane person running. But Sophie Jean couldn't seem to form as much as a single syllable to argue.

"And this is what I mean by giving it a chance." Vickie turned Sophie Jean around and guided her out of the bathroom. "We'll tell Walt's family that we aren't interested without inspections. There's no way an inspector can do his job to certify utilities and the structure without the removal of some of the items stored here."

"Some?"

"Or most." Vickie waved Sophie Jean's concerns

aside. "The point is that you'd be amazed at what a motivated seller can do for you." Vickie sounded so upbeat. She always seemed so together, being a single mom who was running her own business. "Now, there's another location I want to show you. Let's get some fresh air and check it out." Her cell phone rang and she hung back to answer it.

Sophie Jean practically ran out to the sidewalk, brushing cobwebs, both real and imagined, off her face and arms.

A cowboy coming out of Doc Nabidian's office across the street caught her eye. New blue jeans. New black cowboy hat. Familiar, attractive face.

"Noel?"

He stopped when he heard her voice and turned a worried expression her way.

"Bad news?" Sophie Jean's heart went out to him.

Noel shook his head, masking the worried facade with a weak smile as he walked across the street to join her. "I'll be fine."

It didn't escape Sophie Jean's notice that Noel had changed his qualification of the word *fine* from present—*I'm fine*—to future tense—*I'll be fine*. He didn't have a clean bill of health yet. She wanted to be supportive but there was something about him denying being injured since he'd arrived back in town that made her feel chippy. "You'll be fine someday? You said that the time a bull smashed your leg in the start chute," she reminded him.

"And also when a bull flattened you like a rolling pin and cracked your ribs. Not to mention the time—"

"Hold on. I'm still upright, aren't I?" Noel knocked his cowboy hat upward and set his cowboy boot tips temptingly near hers.

"Lucky you." Sophie Jean removed Noel's sunglasses, making him squint. He might even have swayed. She called him all sorts of names in her head while she hustled to prop him up against the wall of Walt's storehouse. Then she eased his sunglasses back on and apologized. "I can't believe you aren't taking better care of yourself. You should be at home in a dark room."

"I'm being as careful as I can," Noel said stubbornly, never having been a good patient. "I've just been to the doctor and I'm taking a break from competing. If that isn't self-care, I don't know what is." His cell phone chimed with a message. He checked it quickly, then shoved it back into his jeans pocket, scowling. "I appreciate your concern."

"Do you?" Sophie Jean asked, curious and welcoming of the distraction from her salon search woes. "You're annoyed."

"Not at you." Noel shook his head. "Team bull riding is all the rage. And there's someone forming an expansion team that wants me as their head coach. They just texted, requesting a meeting. Again."

"You should be flattered that they're so persistent." Sophie Jean was proud of him. All his hard work had paid off. "I bet those opportunities are few and far between."

Noel rolled his shoulders back. "That's what I told them when I turned them down—I'm honored, but no. I'm still a competitor with gas in the tank."

"And yet, they continue to hound you with offers of money, increased fame and the chance to get more wins on your quest for a nook in the Hall of Fame." Not to mention a job where he no longer had to risk life and limb. Sophie Jean wanted that for him.

"You make it sound like turning them down is a mistake." Noel's words rang with a goodly dose of masculine pride. "I'd be hitching my wagon to the skills of other, as yet to be named, bull riders."

"And we both know your aversion to being hitched," Sophie Jean blurted. She covered her mouth and offered a mumbled apology.

Noel waved it off. "You know how hardheaded bull riders can be. I doubt they'd listen to me." He scoffed. "I can't even get the kids on our team to listen to me."

"It's not as if you've tried," Sophie Jean gently pointed out.

"I'm just the Concierge of Fun. The barely needed assistant coach. You said so yourself." Noel's mouth worked as if he was tussling with whether or not to say more.

He was twisting her words. "What I meant was that you're good at fun, Noel, as long as there's no competition involved," Sophie Jean said softly, gently touching his arm. "But these kids…" She struggled to find the right angle.

Noel found it for her. "They need the fun I found at the Done Roamin' Ranch, not the competitive drive my father instilled in me." At her nod, he slid a hand to the back of his head, looking away. "I get it. I'm…not the best role model."

"That's not true." Sophie Jean's heart melted at the pain in his words. "The best role models are the ones who admit they aren't perfect."

His gaze returned to her, warm and appreciative. "What are you doing over here?"

"Looking at potential spaces for my salon." Sophie Jean shivered, brushing her arms again as if cobwebs still remained. "Vickie takes me out once a month."

Noel peered inside. "Oh. Didn't you tell Vickie you're afraid of spiders?"

"Why should I? Everybody's afraid of spiders."

Noel smirked at her, a reminder that he'd been the bug killer in their relationship. And the biggest supporter of her dream to be a boss. "Spiders or no spiders. That's a project in there."

"Now you see why I haven't opened my own salon. It's hard to find something I can afford in Clementine and have the resources to renovate." The words felt like a flimsy excuse, especially when Noel knew she was risk averse and she knew he embraced his fears every time he sat on a bull. "But enough about me. Tell me more about this concussion of yours." That's what it had to be.

"I'll be fine."

"I wish..." Sophie Jean bit her lip. She'd been about to admit she wished he'd confide in her. Despite a broken heart and a long absence, she'd missed him. His sharp wit. His sense of humor. His ability to make any stranger feel like a friend and all his friends feel like family.

"You wish?" Noel prompted when she didn't expand on her thought.

Sophie Jean put on a brave smile and gave him a different wish. "I wish the perfect space for my salon would be just around the corner."

"I can fulfill that wish." Vickie joined them on the sidewalk, turning to lock the door. "Long time, no see, Noel. Didn't think you lived here anymore."

"Why not? I own a ranch within the county limits." Noel eased himself away from the support of the building's wall.

"Kinda feels like that's your dad's place." Vickie didn't look up to catch Noel's frown. Her head was bent as she checked her phone, tapping at the screen before shoving it into her black leather tote. And then she smiled brightly at them both. "Sophie Jean, have I told you how much I like your outfit today? Those boots are radiating girl-boss vibes."

"Thanks." Sophie Jean stared at her high-heeled

boots. She liked them because they made her look taller and feel attractive. She hadn't thought about girl-boss vibes. But the idea intrigued her.

"All right. Back to fulfilling Sophie Jean's dream of business ownership." Vickie hitched her tote bag higher on her shoulder. "I've got another hidden gem to show you this morning. It's more expensive than this place but it isn't loaded with someone else's junk. You'll see the potential the moment you step through the door."

Sophie Jean contained a smile because that, too, was what Vickie always said—*You'll see the potential the moment you step through the door.*

"Are you coming, Noel?" Vickie didn't give him a choice. She hooked her arm through his. "We could use another opinion."

"Sure." He shrugged.

Sophie Jean frowned at them both, not having been asked if she wanted Noel along. Not that they noticed.

Noel was already charging forward with Vickie, leaving Sophie Jean behind, which was probably not where girl bosses should be.

"HAVE YOU SHOWN Sophie Jean a lot of places?" Noel asked Vickie as they walked past brick-front buildings in an old part of town. He glanced behind him to check on Sophie Jean. She was lagging half a block behind them.

Vickie nodded. "I've been showing Sophie Jean

properties for years now. Nothing suits her. There's always a reason to cross buildings off her list."

"It's a scary thing to start a business of your own," Noel allowed, thinking of all the caveats Sophie Jean had put forth over the years to keep herself from owning her own business. She was scared to take a chance on something that wasn't a sure thing.

"Being your own boss can be daunting." Vickie began an inspiring recital of her hard-won travails establishing her real estate business while juggling the demands of being a single mother.

Noel glanced back at Sophie Jean again.

She was dragging her feet in that pair of fancy high-heeled black cowboy boots. Her blue jeans accented her curves. A flowing, flowery black blouse flattered her torso, decorated by the tangle of pendants hung from various lengths around her neck. Her long brown hair was held in a smooth ponytail caught below one ear. Her eyes and lips were highlighted with colors that were as vibrant as her personality.

She's beautiful, inside and out. She deserves every wish, every dream.

Sophie Jean had shared those dreams with him, along with her fear of risking everything she'd saved for on something that wasn't a sure thing. She couldn't understand how Noel repeatedly put everything on the line for eight seconds and a chance at prize money. He'd told her nothing in life was a sure thing. But risk… That wasn't in Sophie Jean's DNA.

"I'm coming." Sophie Jean made a shooing motion toward Noel with her hand. "Don't wait on me."

Would we still be together if we'd agreed to wait out my rodeo run?

He thought so. But now, there seemed too much water under the bridge. "Why hasn't Sophie Jean found anything?" Noel interrupted Vickie when he turned back around. "Is money holding her back?"

"No, sir," Vickie's cell phone chimed with a message, which she promptly scanned and deleted. "She always finds a flaw. Either she doesn't like the layout. Or the location is too far from downtown. And then, a lot of buildings in the historic district have brick walls, which aren't conducive to adding electrical or plumbing. At least, not in an attractive way."

"That must be frustrating." For both Vickie and Sophie Jean.

"Not really. Being a real estate agent is about finding compromise." Vickie laughed a little, as if this was an understatement. "The thing about Sophie Jean is… Well, I shouldn't say."

"Go on. I'm still Sophie Jean's friend and want the best for her."

Vickie gave Noel a searching look. "Well… Sophie Jean has her heart set on the Cozy Clip but

Helga isn't ready to sell. Anything else I show her…isn't the Cozy Clip."

Noel nodded. "She grew up in that salon. It's where her heart is."

"I know." Vickie sighed. "But sometimes, you have to set aside what the heart wants in order to move forward with your life."

"Tell me about it." That's the sacrifice he'd made, stuffing down his love for Sophie Jean to prove something to himself and the world. Something vital. His self-worth. He had no idea who he'd be if he retired and he resented the owners of the Tulsa Travelers for putting that thought in his mind. "Maybe Sophie Jean needs to hit the pause button and really think about what she wants."

"I take Sophie Jean out on tours once a month," Vickie countered good-naturedly. "She gets enough pauses. If I didn't like her so much, I'd have dumped her as a client long ago."

They arrived at Dr. Salter's dentist office. A large for-sale sign had been affixed to the front wall above the mulberry bushes.

Noel peered in the empty windows. "When did Dr. Salter retire?" He'd been cleaning Noel's teeth since he was a kid.

"Dr. Salter worked up until the day before he died," Vickie said in a hushed tone of voice. "His family sold his practice to Dr. Simi. But Dr. Simi has a nice new building on the edge of town. That leaves this place empty." Vickie unlocked the door and turned to call Sophie Jean. "This building has everything you need. Electrical plugs everywhere. Plumbing everywhere."

"Walls everywhere," Noel murmured, glancing inside.

He knew from experience that there were three patient rooms in back, plus a bathroom and Dr. Salter's office. A countertop separated the reception area from the waiting room. A door led to the rear rooms. Noel had never been to a salon that was closed off as much as this building was. It would never hold up to Sophie Jean's standard set by the Cozy Clip.

Noel stood aside for Sophie Jean to enter. "No spiders in sight."

"Good. But…wow," Sophie Jean whispered. "I haven't been in here since last summer for my teeth cleaning. It makes me feel sad to be here."

Vickie moved into the lobby. "Let's use our imagination. You could take down the counter here to make space for hair stations. It's got great light. A little paint. Some luxury vinyl plank flooring. Add some plants. Can you see it?"

"I'm trying." Sophie Jean opened the door from the lobby to the rear of the building. "I'd need to convert two of the exam rooms into one rinse room. I'd also need a storeroom with a sink for mixing hair color."

"Or…" Vickie followed Sophie Jean. "You could rent each of the exam rooms to other technicians.

Then you could work in the area where the receptionist used to be as the star of the show."

"It's so big." Sophie Jean bit her lip as she glanced around the space. She looked overwhelmed.

Noel felt the same way. "It'll be pricey. This is a gut job even with existing modern plugs and plumbing."

"You said you wanted a small retail space," Vickie pointed out, smiling past their objections. The woman was a trooper. "This has room for a friendly little shopping area."

Sophie Jean didn't seem convinced.

"How about I take you for a coffee, Sophie Jean?" Noel had no idea where that came from. He'd planned to spend the morning reviewing the ranch accounts with his father before going over to the Done Roamin' Ranch with Ike. But frankly, spending time with his father was as appealing as having a cavity filled without novocaine. He'd gladly put that off. "You know I'm a good listener, Soph. You can tell me all about the choices you've seen for your salon."

"We could use a new perspective," Vickie said, as if she had skin in this game, too. Which clearly, she did. "I'll let you two talk it out. Let me know if you want to pursue anything." Vickie ushered them out, locked up and left, leaving Noel and Sophie Jean alone.

Noel looked at Sophie Jean, fully expecting her to refuse his offer of coffee. "Well?"

"A new perspective?" Sophie Jean sighed. "Okay, Noel. Let's go get a coffee. But we're going Dutch." She marched off.

Because she had a strong independent streak? Or because she didn't want it to appear they were getting back together? Both statements could be true. And both could disappoint the man who still loved her.

Noel stopped in his tracks, gobsmacked.

I still love Sophie Jean.

He didn't just miss her company or long for the familiar, heart-pounding feel of her touch. He loved her. She was the piece that was missing from his days, his life and his ranch.

I still love Sophie Jean.

This was going to ruin everything.

CHAPTER EIGHT

SOPHIE JEAN CHOSE Betty's Bakery to have coffee with Noel for several reasons.

First off, the small bakery's windows faced north. Since Noel had a concussion, the dim light would be good for his head. Second, it wasn't as popular as Clementine Coffee Roasters, so their appearance would be less likely to cause a fuss. And finally, Sophie Jean hadn't eaten this morning and Betty's Bakery made a tasty breakfast sandwich—egg, blue cheese, onions, sausage, garlic flatbread and red peppers. Yum! But it also left a person with nasty bad breath.

Which will make me highly unkissable.

They placed their orders separately and Sophie Jean chose a small table in the corner, one of just four in the entire bakery. She let down her guard, smiling despite the morning's setback. Her coffee was hot. The pleasant aromas of fresh baked goods filled the air. And it was nice to watch Noel without anyone watching her watch him.

He made small allowances for that equilibrium-challenging concussion—a wider stance, chin up, one hand on the tall bakery case. No one would suspect he was injured. And that made her feel sad. Someone should know. Someone should care.

Noel came to sit across from her with a large coffee and an apple fritter on a plate, which he placed between them. "Just like old times."

When they used to meet here for breakfast while he was in town.

Too late, Sophie Jean realized her error. Noel must think she'd chosen Betty's Bakery for nostalgic purposes. "I don't want to get back together." One severe case of heartbreak was enough for her.

"Huh." Noel sipped his coffee, smiling softly. "I guess I should learn how to rephrase things. I remember coming here fondly. Just like I remember our time together. Fondly. And you. Fondly."

Sophie Jean took a big piece of apple fritter and stuffed it in her face.

Noel grinned.

"What's…so…funny?" Sophie Jean managed to ask without choking on a mouthful of sugary pastry.

"Whenever I asked you something too personal, you'd eat. It's nice to know some things never change."

This is a walk down memory lane that I shouldn't have taken.

Sophie Jean's breakfast sandwich was delivered piping hot. She couldn't very well gobble it down. She had to wait for it to cool. But she was regretting agreeing to have coffee with Noel because they weren't talking about the obstacles to making her dream of owning a salon a reality.

Why did he offer to have coffee with me?

She searched his face for clues. Sophie Jean stared at Noel's features for so long that she noticed a gray hair beneath his cowboy hat brim. She pointed to it.

"All the stress from your career is giving you gray hair, Noel."

"Being a bull rider doesn't give me gray hair." Noel reached a hand behind his head, presumably where a lump was.

Sophie Jean rolled her eyes. "Well, I know it's not me making you worry."

"Really?" Noel lowered his sunglasses and stared at her over the rims with those blue eyes she loved so much.

He worries about me.

Funny how that made her heart beat happily. But it wasn't funny how she'd let a smile slip through her defenses. She sobered. "Even if I was on your list of worries, I'm willing to bet that I'm close to the bottom."

Noel shoved his sunglasses back in place and looked away. "You'd lose that bet."

Again, her heart skipped to a happy beat. Again, she tried to ground herself in reality, recalling the wreck she'd been after he left town that last time. She'd cried buckets, canceled client appointments, spent a week in her dark apartment until her friends came to drag her out into the world again.

"I can prove I know what you worry about, Noel." Sophie Jean poked her breakfast sandwich but it was still too hot to eat. She tore off a small piece of apple fritter instead, using it to emphasize her talking points. "I heard your father purchased one of Jo's well-trained roping horses for Ike using your money. You've got to be worrying about how to make that horse earn its keep. Or if Ike will be good enough to compete on it."

Noel's cheek ticked.

"And I also heard your father bought a fancy new gate for your ranch." Sophie Jean popped the apple fritter piece in her mouth because being with him alone required the bolstering that junk food and caffeine provided.

Noel's lips compressed into a thin line.

While Sophie Jean chewed, she let him stew on that. But when he didn't confide anything, she swallowed and added, "I also heard that your dad bought a new truck and wants to buy Ike a new truck for his sixteenth birthday."

"A new truck? For a new driver?" Noel made a growly noise. He removed his cowboy hat and ran a hand over his face. "Do you cut my father's hair? Is that how you know this?"

"No." Sophie Jean allowed herself a sad smile. There was no joy here. He should know what was going on in his own family. "Your dad's girlfriend is one of my clients."

"My dad doesn't..." Noel smashed his cowboy hat back on his head. "He rides Ike hard every minute of the day. When does he find time to have a girlfriend?"

"Iona works nights at the post office in Friar's Creek. They go out to breakfast while Ike's at school." Sophie Jean glanced over toward the Buffalo Diner. "In fact, there they are now."

Noel turned to look toward a couple walking hand in hand down the sidewalk from the direction of the diner. "I know her. She's got a couple of boys in junior rodeo."

"Yep. Ropers. That's where she and your dad met. In the stands at a junior rodeo."

Noel turned back to her, expression grim. "This is bad for Ike."

"Why? Your kid brother doesn't strike me as the type to begrudge your dad a little happiness."

"That's not what I meant." Noel's voice was cold. Hard. "My father is just as competitive as I am. And he wants Ike to find his niche in rodeo. If Iona's boys are any good at roping, Dad's only going to pressure Ike more." Noel tore a piece off the apple fritter, frowning deeply. "You know how intense my father can be. And Ike's already admitted he's thought about running away from home because of it."

"Oh, no." Instinctively, Sophie Jean reached across the table for Noel.

He hesitated before accepting that little comfort, threading his warm fingers between hers.

"Do you mind if I tell Ike he's always welcome at my place if things get too contentious at home?"

"I'd like that, actually," Noel spoke slowly, staring at their joined hands. "You always assume winning is what drives me inside, Soph. But there are all kinds of reasons why winning is important to me. Winning this Fun Day will give Ike a much-needed boost of self-confidence. That'll help when he has to deal with Dad without me around."

"Noel Emerson." An attractive woman in her twenties approached. She was wearing appliqued blue jeans, featuring large sunflowers, and a stylish, bright yellow top. She carried a bulky yellow leather tote and had a resolved shine to her eyes when she looked at Noel. "Babe, you're a hard man to track down. You know you can't run from me forever." And then she leaned over and kissed Noel on the lips.

Sophie Jean nearly fell out of her chair.

THIS...

This was just one more reason why Noel didn't want to join the Tulsa Travelers. Bill Krantz's daughter Anya was too much trouble. Period.

Noel pushed her lips away from his, intending to explain to Sophie Jean in no uncertain terms that Anya considered kisses a replacement for a handshake greeting. He suspected Anya used those lip-locking salutations to knock cowboys back on their heels.

She'd certainly done that today, with both Noel and Sophie Jean, who was currently rushing out the door of Betty's Bakery, leaving her breakfast and coffee behind.

A fire lit in Noel's belly. An angry fire.

Anya took Sophie Jean's seat but no way was she ever taking her place in his heart.

"What are you doing here?" Noel demanded.

"What am I doing here?" Anya smiled, unfazed by Noel's frosty tone. "I'm trying to close a coaching deal with a talented man who'll make the Tulsa Travelers near impossible to beat." She gathered her long blond hair over one shoulder, looking far too pleased with herself. "If the mountain won't come to Anya, Anya will come to the mountain. You haven't answered my calls, emails or texts. Your business manager told me you were here."

Noel's business manager handled all his endorsement deals. Noel made a mental note to remind Warren that he valued his privacy.

"I told you I'm a bull rider, not a coach. I don't know how to say this any plainer. I'm not interested in signing on with you." Noel got to his feet, gripping his coffee cup as tightly as he held on to his temper. "Now, if you'll excuse me, I have other business to attend to." Like finding Sophie Jean and explaining away this fiasco.

"Hang on, honey." Anya snagged his empty hand with surprising strength, holding him in place, at least temporarily. "You haven't heard our latest offer." She named a figure that was shockingly high.

Despite his best intentions, Noel hesitated.

Anya's smile grew. "Now, see? I knew we could come to an agreement. Welcome to the team. I've drafted a press release to announce your retirement. I'll send it over for your review."

Team... Retirement... Loser...

The words washed over Noel like a cold bucket of water.

"I don't do teams." He yanked his hand free and headed for the door. "And I'm not retiring."

"Not yet anyway." It was maddening how his refusal didn't sink in. The woman looked intelligent but she didn't seem to understand the meaning of no, thanks. "I brought more numbers to show you this is a good deal for you on multiple levels. I'm here all week. Or as long as you're here. See you around."

"Not if I see you first." Noel sounded like a scared kid. Felt like one, too.

But that didn't stop him from quickly striding out of the bakery as if he'd just been told his house was on fire.

SOPHIE JEAN FLED Betty's Bakery.

But she couldn't outrun the prickly-skin feeling of cowardice.

It all happened so fast.

The beautiful woman. The proprietary kiss.

How did I not know Noel had a girlfriend? He held my hand as if...

She waved at Iona as her client drove past.

Now Noel thinks...

Sophie Jean didn't know what he thought. Maybe that she was crushed he had a girlfriend because of the way she'd fled.

I'm not crushed! It's been four years!

But her heart clenched, denying that statement. She wasn't over him. Didn't matter how many times she told herself otherwise. The proof was in the pudding. All she could do was stop the damage.

Sophie Jean rounded the corner where the Buffalo Diner was located and jaywalked across the street, heading toward the Cozy Clip. She wasn't working but it was open today and she'd parked behind the salon.

The Cozy Clip was almost directly across from Clementine Coffee Roasters, which was doing a brisk business.

Her friend Jane came out to the sidewalk, carrying a coffee and wearing a pair of blue scrubs. Her short blond hair ruffled in the breeze. She waved. "I just got off my shift at the hospital. See you at the library fundraiser meeting later?"

"Yes, ma'am." Sophie Jean waved back before darting into the Cozy Clip. She paused at the door to take a deep breath, to soak in the vibes of familiarity and steadfastness.

This place is home.

The Cozy Clip was mostly open plan. There was a small waiting area separated from the workstations by two low bookshelves displaying hair product. There were four beautician stations, one cone dryer and one nail station. Beyond that, a small hallway led to a double-sink rinse room, a hair color mixing room where they stored supplies, a restroom and a rear door that led to the parking lot out back.

It was here that Sophie Jean had learned the intricacies of hairstyling, how to mix hair color ingredients and how good a little bit of pampering did a person. It was here she got used to the smell of perm solution and nail bonding agent. She associated the Cozy Clip with laughter and a sense of community. It was here that Sophie Jean never doubted she belonged.

A few beauticians were working—Lainey cutting an old cowboy's hair, and Twila touching up a woman's gray roots. Mom and Helga were talking at the nail station in back.

"Hey." Lainey straightened and greeted Sophie Jean. She was a slender brunette who'd taken up taxidermy last year, claiming it was more like hairstyling than most people would think. "I saw you walk by with Noel earlier."

"Are you getting back together?" Twila asked without looking up from her work. She was a grandmother who scheduled her shifts to end when school let out every day.

"Yes, I walked with Noel. And no, we're not getting back together." Sophie Jean hustled her way toward the rear exit. "He's moved on. And so have I."

Or I thought I had.

But seeing him kiss someone else…

Her entire body mourned.

I won't cry.

She charged between the hair stations instead.

"Where are you off to in such a rush?" Mom asked as Sophie Jean barreled by. Her nose was red, as if she'd been fighting tears, too.

"I've got some volunteer meetings to attend. See you later." And then Sophie Jean burst out the back door afraid that her intention to protect her heart from another devastating break had failed.

"DAD." NOEL PULLED UP short at the sidewalk in front of the Buffalo Diner, holding up a hand to block out the strong morning sunshine. Sophie Jean was nowhere in sight while his father was about to climb into his truck. "How did your date go?"

For once, his father was speechless.

"I saw you with Iona." Although Noel didn't see her anywhere now.

"I'm a grown man," Dad said in a gruff tone of voice, clinging to his truck door. "I'm allowed to date."

"But you're not allowed to buy Ike an expensive roping horse to impress your girlfriend." Noel probably could have tossed that as a lob instead of throwing a line drive at his father. And Noel might have gone easier if he wasn't mad at Anya and taking it out on the first person he came across.

Dad stood stone-still, as if in shock.

So, Noel kept riding the anger wave. "You can't live vicariously through your kids."

"I don't." Dad came alive. "I want you both to succeed. You can't get ahead in this world without outworking the other guy. Don't complain about my methods. You haven't done so bad for yourself."

"I do well enough to support you," Noel said forcefully. Oh, he should have kept right on walking. This wasn't going to end well or help Ike. But frustration swept Noel along with the tide. "I pay you a salary."

"It's nothing less than I deserve," Dad steamed. "I raised you. I sunk money into you. Money that helped get you where you are today."

"So, I'm your retirement portfolio, am I?" Noel managed a mirthless laugh, ignoring the little voice in his head that said it was time to cut his losses and bail on this ride. "Whatever happened between us, I don't want to repeat the mistakes you made with me with Ike."

"What are you saying?" Dad demanded, red-faced.

"Take your foot off the gas where Ike's concerned." Noel used his coffee cup to emphasize his message, holding it up toward his dad. "Don't deprive him of a childhood the way you did me."

"This world is filled with quitters," Dad sputtered. "I won't let your brother be one of them."

Noel spotted Jane, one of Sophie Jean's friends, at the corner. She might know where Sophie Jean had gone. "We'll talk about this later, Dad."

His father didn't answer.

"Hey, Jane." Noel flagged the blond nurse down. "Do you have a minute?"

Jane turned…stared at Noel, then past Noel. And then she sprinted his way, shoving her coffee at him as she passed. "Call 911!"

"Why?" Noel juggled both their coffee cups before turning in the direction she'd gone.

To find her kneeling next to his father, who'd collapsed on the curb.

And there was blood.

CHAPTER NINE

SOPHIE JEAN ARRIVED at the library's conference room for the fundraiser meeting still breathless from her mad dash away from Noel and his new girlfriend. She tried to smile at the mostly older women gathered there, the oldest of which was the head librarian, Leigh Rawlings.

Leigh had been dragged into the computer age kicking and screaming. She had an old card catalog cabinet behind the check-in desk. Presumably, it still held the cards folks used to use to look up where books were shelved. Leigh was also a caller, not a texter. She telephoned everyone meeting reminders. And she printed out hard copies of meeting agendas and minutes. And when she tried to get a point across, she often referenced the classics.

Sophie Jean claimed a chair at the empty end of the long table, setting her purse on the chair next to her to reserve it for Jane when she arrived. The meeting wasn't scheduled to begin for another ten minutes. Sophie Jean had time to check her cell phone for messages or to doomscroll on social media, but what if Noel called or texted?

Chicken that she was, Sophie Jean found her cell phone in her tote bag and turned it off.

It's better this way. I have deniability if Noel tries to call and explain or ask me if I'm okay.

News flash: *I'm not okay!*

Sophie Jean's leg bounced nervously under the table. Jane still hadn't arrived and neither had Mary, Noel's foster mother. There were now nine minutes until the meeting was scheduled to begin. A lifetime in Embarrassed Ex-Girlfriend Years.

The conference room was sparsely furnished. Book covers printed as large as posters were framed and hung around the room—*Pride and Prejudice*, *39 Steps*, *Death on the Nile* and others. There was a machine in the corner that made coffee and tea using pods, a reminder that Sophie Jean had left her coffee and her breakfast back at Betty's Bakery.

Unable to sit still any longer, Sophie Jean stood. "Can I make coffee or tea for anyone?"

Several women took her up on the offer. Sophie Jean turned the machine on, prepared four cups with various amounts of sugar and creamer and waited for the brewing light to come on.

"Being in love was nice." Carla Tucker patted her short, white, naturally curly hair. "Intense and contentious at times. But now that I'm in my eighties and single, I'm happy with my cat."

"Does your cat give you love bites?" Sophie Jean asked, thinking of Noel's love metaphor and how Kiki hadn't fit.

Carla grinned. She was one of Sophie Jean's regular customers and a ray of sunshine. "No love bites, but she brings me lots of dead mice every spring."

Several women laughed, including Sophie Jean.

The coffee machine's ready light flashed. Sophie Jean loaded it with a pod and set it to brewing.

"If Harry ever leaves me, I'm going to find myself another man, not a cat." That was Bonnie Durango, retired schoolteacher, avid gardener and devoted community volunteer. "If I do find myself single someday, I'll go for a younger man with muscles."

"Dare I ask?" Grinning, Carla leaned closer to her friend. "Why the need for muscles?"

"To mow my acreage." Bonnie tittered. "Harry takes two days to recover from mowing our three acres. He barely gets out of his recliner during that time. And the only thing he wants to watch when he's exhausted are John Wayne movies. Now, I love John Wayne as much as the next person, but I prefer him in small doses."

That brought another round of laughter.

The women continued their lively discussion while Leigh passed out printed agendas and previous meeting minutes.

"Sophie Jean, are you staying for the Easter egg hunt meeting?" Leigh asked in the hushed tones of a career librarian.

"Yes, ma'am." She was willing to hide out here all day, staying for Bonnie's gardening club meeting if she must to try and regain her composure. The gardening club was one of the few local organizations Sophie Jean hadn't clicked with. She could barely keep the potted geraniums outside her apartment door alive. "Can I help you with something at the next meeting, Leigh?"

"I hope so. Our Easter Bunny backed out for Sunday." Leigh tsked, easing past Sophie Jean to pass out agendas down the other side of the conference room table. "We need to find a replacement to fill the costume. It's made for someone tall. You know all the young men about town. Can you find us a replacement?"

"I'll ask around," Sophie Jean promised, delivering a coffee to Carla while the next cup brewed.

"How about you, Sophie Jean?" Carla accepted her coffee with two hands. "You've had one great romance. Are you ready to dive into the relationship waters again?"

"No, ma'am." An image of that woman kissing Noel came to mind, hurtful as it pressed down on her chest. "Couldn't handle the heartbreak." Couldn't even handle meeting Noel's new number one.

A few of the women made commiserative noises.

"You can't let worst-case scenarios guide your life choices, Sophie Jean, whether it's dreams you're working toward or a relationship of any kind," Leigh said in her low-pitched librarian's voice. "You should read *Pride and Prejudice*, followed by *The Old Man and the Sea*."

"Why?" Sophie Jean handed Bonnie her coffee.

"Because the theme of *Pride and Prejudice* is in the title. We all have our pride and our prejudices, large and small, meaning we're a work in progress. Now, *The Old Man and the Sea's* theme is perseverance." Leigh was in lecture mode. The mood in the conference room sobered. "Book themes aren't just for literature class. They exist to inspire us in our lives. Perseverance. That's what you need to make dreams come true. Keep reaching for the stars when times are tough, never stop growing and changing and look to the bright side when you feel like giving up."

"It's the growing and changing that gets harder as we age," Bonnie said in a voice that sounded like she'd had trouble persevering in the past.

"Oh, Leigh. Can we update your reading list?" Carla gave a woeful shake of her head. "I never could finish *The Old Man and the Sea*."

"I heard someone made it into a musical." Bonnie brightened. "I do so love musicals. *Annie* is my favorite."

Leigh plopped the remaining papers at the head of the table. "Bonnie, if you launch into that song about the sun coming out tomorrow, I may just have to ban you from the library."

"Why?" Bonnie half smiled. "There's hardly anyone in the library this morning."

"Don't take offense." Leigh took her seat at the head of the table before answering, letting the gurgling coffee machine fill the silence, at least temporarily. "But you can't sing in here, Bonnie, because your pitch wanders like a steer lost on the open range."

They all laughed, even Bonnie. Probably because it was true and she owned it.

Carla's phone pinged multiple times, as did Leigh's, making Sophie Jean so twitchy that she almost dropped Leigh's tea.

"Oh, no," Carol said. "I just got a message from Jane. There's been an emergency. She's at the hospital and won't be able to make it."

"And here's one from Mary." Leigh slid on her readers and peered at her screen. "Steve Emerson had a heart attack. Jane found him collapsed on the street."

"She says Noel was there when it happened," Carla added, scrolling down. "Lucky for Steve. I didn't think Noel ever came back to Clementine."

"He doesn't." Sophie Jean gathered her purse, needing to be at the hospital to support Noel regardless of whom he was dating. "I'm sorry. But I need to go."

"We'll send you the meeting minutes," Leigh promised. "Just don't forget to find us an Easter Bunny."

RUSH. RUSH. RUSH. Wait. Wait. Wait.

Noel sat next to his father's emergency room bed, shell-shocked. Nothing this morning had turned out the way he'd expected. But nothing was as earth-shatteringly bad as his father's collapse. He hadn't even seen it happen. He would have walked away if Jane hadn't spotted Dad sprawled on the pavement.

"I did *not* have a heart attack," Dad insisted for what had to be the tenth time. He had leads stuck on his bare chest and was connected to a machine that tracked his heart rate, among other things. "Haven't been sick in years. I had a little heartburn after breakfast, sure. Can't drink two cups of black coffee the way I used to. And then I tripped on the curb during our argument. But now… Now, I'm fine." For all his bluster, Dad looked small in that bed. Small and scared.

Made Noel wonder how many times he'd looked like that after a serious rodeo injury. Too many, if he had to guess.

Noel leaned forward in his chair. "Dad, you *did* have a heart attack. That's why you face-planted on the sidewalk." His father had a bright red goose egg on his forehead that rivaled the size of the one on the back of Noel's head. "The doctor confirmed that there were high levels of troponin in your blood." Some tests couldn't be refuted.

The clock on the wall above Noel ticked. He glanced up at it, squinting to make out the time. The small emergency room cubby had nothing but a curtain at the foot of the bed to look at. Beyond that curtain, people hustled about, used medical terminology he had no clue about and brought in one patient after another, if the sound of stretchers rolling past was any indication.

Rush. Rush. Wait. Wait.

Who knew Clementine had so many medical emergencies?

"I feel fine." Dad fidgeted in the bed. Then he reached toward Noel. "Give me my shirt. I'm going home. Ike's not going to train if I'm not there."

"No. Frank and Mary are bringing Ike here." Noel expected them at any minute.

Dad made several blustery noises. "I don't need folks to hover over me. It was nothing. A blip, that's all. Like a…a backfire from a truck engine."

"A backfire is an indication something is wrong with the truck engine, Dad." Noel eased his shoulders back. The chair he was in wasn't designed for comfort.

"It was a blip," Dad repeated staunchly. "Nothing to worry about."

"Is that why you wouldn't let me call Iona? Because you think it's nothing serious?" Noel reached to the back of his head, touching that lump. "If it was me lying there, I'd want my loved ones near me." Sophie Jean came to mind.

"That's the difference between you and me, Noel. I'm fine, and I'll be fine by myself. At home." Dad's dark, bushy brows slammed low. "Don't call Iona. She works the graveyard shift. This isn't worth waking her up for. Not when I'm fine." He was like a broken record.

Noel suddenly realized how frustrating it was to hear *I'm fine* when you knew someone you cared about wasn't fine at all.

I owe Sophie Jean an apology.

For so many things.

He'd do it as soon as he could. They were biding their time here until a bed became available in the cardiac ward, plus additional tests could be run, to hear if the cardiologist wanted to do an angioplasty and, if necessary, to do a procedure, like insert stents into Dad's arteries to prevent more heart attacks. Or death.

Noel drew a deep breath. His thoughts were grim and had been since he'd seen his father on the ground.

"My will is in the safe in the barn tack room," Dad said out of the blue.

"Your will?" Stunned, Noel rocked back in his chair. "I thought you were fine."

Dad wouldn't look at him or speak. But his jaw thrust out and he gripped the bed rails. The machine he was hooked up to began to beep faster.

"You're not dying," Noel said more firmly. "You'll be right as rain when they release you." He wasn't going to let his father walk out of here without a doctor's approval and a treatment plan. Noel handed Dad his cup of water. "Drink. The nurse said you should hydrate and stay calm."

Dad sipped, breathed deeply. And then he turned an intense stare at Noel. "You were right earlier. I've been a bad father."

Noel was stunned. Shocked silent, maybe for the first time in his life. A minute passed. "We don't have to do this now, Dad. I lost my temper before. I said things I shouldn't have. I'm sorry."

His father shook his head. "No. I pushed you when you were a kid. That's because no one pushed me and by eighteen, I was behind the other bull riders in skill level. I wanted you to understand that you could make something of yourself with hard work and dedication." Dad blew out a slow breath. The machine he was hooked up to beeped at a more regular rhythm. "When you turned eighteen and headed out on your own, I didn't know what to do with myself. I felt I'd done what I'd been put on this earth to do."

"As I recall, you fell in love, got married and had a kid." Noel tried for a bit of levity but was afraid he sounded cutting. Inaction was hard for Noel to endure. "Why don't you close your eyes and try to rest?"

"My second marriage..." Dad stared at the ceiling, ignoring Noel's suggestion. "That might not have been the brightest thing I've ever done. But I got Ike, so I don't regret it. He's going to amount to something someday, too."

"Whether he does so in rodeo or not," Noel said evenly, shifting in the chair. It was giving him a knot between his shoulder blades. Or maybe that was from this conversation.

"When I get out of here, I'm going to get a job as a ranch hand somewhere," Dad said as if he hadn't heard Noel. "I need to pull my weight."

"You do pull your weight. You have a job," Noel reminded him. "You're my ranch foreman."

"*Caretaker* of your property." Dad fidgeted once more, touching each of his electronic patches in turn, a worrisome frown on his broad face. "That ranch could be a showstopper. Make everyone envious of what you've accomplished."

"All I need it to be is home, Dad." A place where his family would always have a roof over their heads. "I don't need to keep up appearances." It wasn't as if anyone was truly interested in his win record or his trophies. Young Sam had told the truth: *Everyone has a big belt buckle around here.*

Dad made a grumbly noise, ready to go another round. But a nurse interrupted, yanking the curtain open and ushering Ike in before pulling it shut behind him.

Ike's face was pale and his eyes wide. He sat down on the foot of Dad's bed, looking like he might cry.

"I'm fine," Dad reiterated gruffly. "Be home by supper."

"Don't believe a word Dad says, Ike. Can you keep an eye on him? I need a coffee." Noel waited for a nod from Ike, then hurried out the door and down the hall toward the cafeteria, passing through the crowded waiting room to get there.

"Noel," Mary called to him, rising from a chair.

"Noel," Sophie Jean echoed, entering the waiting room through the wide double doors.

They were a sight for sore eyes.

Noel held out a hand to each woman.

They rushed forward and hugged him.

This… This was the family Noel wanted. Folks who'd be here when he needed them.

"How is he?" Mary asked. She listened intently as Noel quickly explained what had happened.

"How are you?" Sophie Jean asked when he'd finished.

"I'm fine now." He managed a smile. "Can you call my dad's girlfriend, Soph? He's refusing to do it himself." His old man was vacillating between being a macho man and believing he was on death's door. "You mentioned she was one of your clients."

"She is. I can do that." Sophie Jean dug her cell phone from her purse while she moved toward the door.

"What can I do?" Mary asked.

"Grab a coffee with me." Noel had a feeling it was going to be a long day. And no matter how many hospital stays he'd endured alone, the reason for this visit shook him to his very core. He didn't want to be on his own.

Sophie Jean didn't see much of Noel after getting in touch with Iona. He was busy sitting with his father and waiting for diagnoses and next steps, coming out occasionally to give those gathered to support the Emerson family an update before returning to his father's bedside. Thankfully, the prognosis was good. No more heart attacks had happened since.

Sophie Jean knew Noel and his father had a complicated relationship. She was proud of Noel for standing by him.

Midafternoon, Sophie Jean went home to change into her ranch grubbies and then headed over to the Done Roamin' Ranch for a Fun Day practice session. She and Griff decided the teams would train together. Today's practice event was stepping stones. They turned ten empty five-gallon buckets upside down and set them a foot apart in the middle of the arena.

"Before we add horses to the mix, you've got to walk across the buckets without falling off," Griff told them.

"Piece of cake." Ford, the youngest of the lot, snapped his fingers, hopped up on the first bucket and promptly dumped it and himself into the dirt.

"Are you all right?" Sophie Jean helped the boy to his feet, brushing him off.

Ford gave her a thumbs-up and limped to the back of the line.

"Everyone's so serious," Griff said quietly, standing next to Sophie Jean.

"That's because someone's dying," Sam said in a loud voice, causing a few of the kids to gasp.

"Nobody's dying," Sophie Jean said just as loudly as Sam. "Noel's dad is—"

"*Dying*," Sam reiterated dramatically. "I heard my dad on the phone. He said heart attack." Sam clutched his chest dramatically and fell to the ground, trying to play dead although Rusty came over to lick his face, making Sam giggle. "Stop, Rusty. We can't have fun when someone dies."

Sophie Jean went over to stand near Sam, resting her hands on her knees as she caught his eye. "I hate to burst your bubble, Sam. But most people live long lives after having a heart attack."

"Really?" Sam brightened.

"Are you sure?" Ford looked worried. He inched closer and took Sophie Jean's hand. "My mom said people die of a broken heart all the time."

Sophie Jean exchanged a glance with Griff, who shrugged.

She extended her free hand and helped Sam to his feet. "Actually, a broken heart is different than a heart attack, Ford. You can't die of a broken heart." Just saying that out loud reminded her of Leigh recommending she read *The Old Man and the Sea* to learn more about perseverance. But didn't that end poorly? And didn't it imply that you should stick in a relationship that wasn't working for the wrong reasons? She'd much rather reread *Pride and Prejudice*.

"My favorite aunt had a broken heart last Christmas." Ford's brow was wrinkled. He looked like he didn't want to be proved wrong in front of the older kids. "She said it hurt something awful."

"I can vouch for that," Griff said, chuckling. "I've had a broken heart myself."

"Me, too," Sophie Jean felt compelled to admit. "Broken hearts are painful."

"But it's a different kind of hurt than a heart attack," Griff explained.

"Does it hurt like when you have a sliver in your finger?" Ford held up his forefinger, which had a bandage on it.

Sophie Jean nodded, thinking how adorable Ford was.

"Or does it hurt like when you fall off the fence railing?" Sam asked, although he backpedaled almost immediately. "Not that I ever fall off anything."

"Yeah, right?" Ginny chuckled. "You fell off the other day trying to hop on Shirley."

The group all whinnied on cue. Smiles emerged.

"But it hurts, right?" Ford just wasn't ready to let this go. "Hearts breaking or…attacking."

"It hurts but then you heal." Sophie Jean nodded, looking around at the kids with what she hoped was a reassuring expression. "You heal and you move on."

I've got to try harder at moving on.

"How do you know you'll get over a broken

heart?" Ginny asked in a low voice. "It's not like a doctor can make it better."

"That's why you have friends and family around to pick you up and dust you off." Griff chuckled. "All right. Enough of question-and-answer time. Who's ready to take on the stepping stones?"

Everyone raised their hands.

And even though Sophie Jean laughed and smiled with the rest of them as they took turns balancing on overturned buckets, she had to admit that there was a certain truth to Griff's words.

Someone would be around to help Sophie Jean heal if she allowed herself to love Noel again and he broke her heart a second time.

The question was: *Am I courageous enough to risk my heart breaking again?*

She didn't think so.

CHAPTER TEN

DAD DIDN'T WANT to spend the night in the hospital alone.

Oh, he didn't say as much. But he was nervous. Noel could tell. He'd confessed to a long list of poor parenting decisions he'd made over the years. And somehow, the conversation always looped back around to Dad's firm opinion that he hadn't had a heart attack and was fine.

"Who needs a procedure? Not this cowboy," he'd said after he'd been assigned a room and given dinner. "We should all head home."

"If we don't stay the night with him, Dad might take a runner," Ike predicted to Noel in a low voice.

Noel nodded. He thought so, too.

So, Noel and Ike spent the night in Dad's hospital room—Noel in the too-short recliner, Ike on the too-short padded window bench. Both were uncomfortable, not to mention the nurse came in every few hours to take Dad's vitals. And, of course, Dad had to talk to the night nurse, who happened to be Jane, Sophie Jean's friend and the woman who'd stabilized him until the ambulance arrived.

"I have fantastic blood pressure, don't I, Jane? Who needs a stent? Not this cowboy!" Dad was nothing if not consistent in his denial of any health concerns.

And every time he'd make such a statement, Jane would say, "Your numbers are good now, Steve, but Dr. Mullins knows what he's talking about. Trust him."

Her argument didn't calm Dad's fears. He'd scoff and get quiet.

When Jane came around at six Tuesday morning, Dad was getting a little jumpy and Noel's head felt heavier than a blacksmith's hammer. Even his eyesight was poor. He had to hold his phone close to his nose to read anything on the screen. Finally, he gave up, which was probably for the best since he'd been checking his drop in the rodeo rankings.

"I think I'm ready for some good strong coffee and my clothes, Jane," Dad said, sitting up.

She chuckled, logging into her portable computer on that desk she wheeled from room to room. "Steve, cardiac patients don't get anything but decaf and you can't have that or breakfast until after your angiogram." She smiled at Noel. "I can get you a coffee, Noel."

"Please," Noel croaked. His mouth was dry, the result of too much caffeine yesterday and not enough water. But he'd need more coffee to get through the next few hours.

Over in the window seat, Ike put a pillow over his head. "Wake me up when the procedure is done and we can go home."

Predictably, Dad took that as an opening. "We can go home now."

"We're not going anywhere." Noel rubbed his eyes. "How many stents do you think they'll put in, Jane?"

"None." Dad crossed his arms. "I'm fine."

"I don't know, Noel." Jane put a blood pressure cuff on Dad's arm. "But families always enjoy taking a guess."

"Six," Ike said in a muffled voice.

"None," Dad reiterated. "I'm fine. Perfectly fine."

"Three," Noel guessed, feeling ornery. He wasn't good with sleep deprivation at the best of times. Add in a concussion, a tortuous reclining chair and a father intent upon making amends, and the past twenty-four hours felt like torture. Since coming to the hospital, he'd seen a side of his father he'd never seen before—a remorseful man (when it came to parenthood), a tender man (when it came to his girlfriend), a desperate man (when it came to a potential procedure).

A figure entered the room with a stethoscope around their neck.

Noel's buggy eyes couldn't make out who it was

but he assumed it was Dr. Mullins. He wiped a hand over his face. "Maybe the doc can tell us how many stents he thinks you'll have, Dad."

"That's not my specialty." A familiar voice. Followed by a familiar face coming into focus. A reassuring smile accented by middle-age lines on his face.

"Doc Nabidian." Noel sat up straighter. He'd just been examined by him yesterday morning. "What are you doing here?"

"Making the rounds. Heard Steve was in here. Thought I'd stop by to check." He peeked at Jane's computer screen. "Imagine my surprise when I walked in and found I have two patients I can check on."

Ike sat up, looking groggy. "I'm fine, Doc." And then he lay back down, replacing the pillow over his head.

"Ike, I meant your brother. Noel is under my care." Doc came around the bed to reach Noel in his chair. "You should have your sunglasses on in here. Fluorescent light isn't kind to concussions."

"Aha!" Dad cried gleefully. "I knew it. That's the reason you came home midseason."

"I'm good as gold." Noel worked the kinks out of his back as though the doctor was here on a social call, not to examine him. "Tell him, Doc."

"Hold still, Noel, and I'll weigh in." Doc Nabidian flashed a penlight at Noel's eyes.

Noel flinched. The world went out of focus more than usual. Nausea crept up his throat.

"Not good as gold just yet." The doctor slid a hand around the back of Noel's head, tenderly probing the lump. "At least your contusion is down. After your father's angiogram, you need to go home and rest in a dark room. All this activity is extending your recovery time."

"Noel has a concussion?" Ike sat back up, hugging the pillow. His dark hair stuck up every which way. "Should he be driving? I have my learner's permit."

"I'm fine," Noel insisted, clinging to the chair handles as the world came into a fuzzy sort of focus. He'd stayed over in Austin after the accident for a few days until the local doctor had approved him to drive.

"Fine?" Dad laughed. "That's what I've been telling you and you didn't believe me. I guess we both need to be better patients."

Noel nodded reluctantly as Doc Nabidian turned his attention to his father.

"You know what this means? I'm driving us home." Ike was just as gleeful as their dad. "Hand over the keys, Noel."

"No." The nerve of the kid.

"Now, Noel." Ike got to his feet. "I know which rib is your ticklish one." He held out his hands, ready to administer tickle torture.

"I wouldn't try that," Noel growled, verbally

stopping his brother's advance. "I have a razor at home and I'm not afraid to take it to those two whiskers you're so proud of."

Ike gasped.

"Oh, let him have the keys," Dad said between taking deep breaths for Doc Nabidian. "The last thing we Emersons need to be known for is causing a ruckus in the hospital. We're winners. Did you know that, Doc?"

The doctor nodded, wrapping his stethoscope around his neck. "You've only told me that a hundred times over the years, Steve." He was a good sport as well as a good doctor. "But if you need to tell me again, I'm here to listen."

Dad froze. Blinked. Then smiled. "I have a one-track mind."

"You think?" Doc Nabidian quipped.

They all laughed.

It was the strangest thing. If anyone would have told Noel he'd be sitting with his biological family, laughing and shooting the breeze over spring break while he recovered from a concussion, he'd have told them it would be a warm day in the North Pole before that happened.

But here they were.

And he kind of liked it.

WORD TRAVELED FAST in Clementine, at least where the services of a known and beloved nail technician was concerned. Sophie Jean's mother had nail appointments booked from eleven o'clock until five in the afternoon on Tuesday.

But that wasn't what the beauticians in the Cozy Clip were obsessed with on Tuesday morning. That was Sophie Jean, Noel and a blond mystery woman rumored to have stormed into Betty's Bakery on Monday morning and kissed the socks off Noel.

"Is she Noel's girlfriend?" Lainey asked while applying highlights to a client's hair, juggling a brush and strips of aluminum foil. Her station was between Sophie Jean's and the nail station. "Noel's fiancée? His wife?"

"I don't know," Sophie Jean said, not for the first time. She was doing a Brazilian blowout on her friend Tillie and had to raise her voice to be heard above her blow-dryer.

Not that anyone listened to her, including her own mother, who'd tried to pry the same information out of Sophie Jean when she came home last night after Fun Day practice.

"Do we have an update on Steve?" Sophie Jean asked, trying to change the subject. No one took the bait.

"Maybe she's a cowgirl on the circuit with Noel," Helga speculated, trimming the dry ends from a client's hair. She had a station across from Sophie Jean. "What do you think, Charlene?"

"I heard Noel dumped her in Betty's Bakery and chased after you, Sophie Jean. And that's when Steve had his heart attack," Mom said from the nail station in the corner, not bothering to raise her head as she applied polish to a client's fingernails.

"Didn't Noel explain who she was to you, Sophie Jean?" Twila was touching up the roots on a client's red hair. "That must have been awkward."

"He doesn't owe me any explanations," Sophie Jean insisted and they hadn't had time alone at the hospital if he'd wanted to clarify his relationship status. "Not dating him, remember?"

Not that anyone other than Tillie listened. "I remember," she said with a supportive smile.

The front door to Cozy Clip opened. Everyone turned to greet the newcomer.

But no one said a word.

Noel's girlfriend hesitated under their scrutiny just inside the door. She looked city-cowgirl chic in a short, fringed brown leather skirt, white embroidered blouse, white cowboy hat with brown embroidery on the brim and white, high-heeled cowboy boots with silver leaf embellishments.

Sophie Jean experienced a stab of outfit envy, even though she hadn't slacked off in the wardrobe department today. On the off chance she'd see Noel, she'd worn a shiny turquoise blouse, turquoise bangles and earrings and a black suede miniskirt with her going-out turquoise cowboy boots.

"Hey, ladies." The blonde recovered her chutzpah and smiled. It was a pretty smile accented with an enviable shade of red lipstick. "I'm Anya and

I need a trim." She held up the ends of that blond hair, which looked to have been poorly colored. "I hear Sophie Jean comes highly recommended. I don't have an appointment but I was hoping she could squeeze me in."

Sophie Jean forced herself to smile. "I'm sorry but I'm—"

"She'll fit you in," Helga overrode Sophie Jean. "We just need to shuffle things around a bit." She crossed the center of the salon to stand next to Sophie Jean with the smile of a gossiper suddenly handed the news flash of the decade. "Trims don't take long."

Sophie Jean turned off her blow-dryer. "Helga—"

"I can finish Tillie's blowout," Twila offered, sweet as sugar. "My client is going under the dryer now." She hustled the redhead from her station to a chair beneath the dome dryer.

"I'll move," Tillie said, surprisingly disloyal for having chosen Sophie Jean as one of her bridesmaids for her wedding.

"Wouldn't want to turn away a woman in need of a trim," Mom said, having put down her nail polish brush to study Anya, which allowed her client, Sophie Jean's real estate agent, Vickie, to turn and stare.

Helga ushered Tillie over to Twila's station. "See? No problem at all."

I have a problem.

But Sophie Jean wasn't going to run the way she had when Anya kissed Noel yesterday. Deep down, she was as interested about this woman as everyone else.

"Give me a minute to tidy my station." Relenting, Sophie Jean quickly swept Tillie's hair on the floor into a bin. All too soon, she was escorting Anya to her station, sitting her down and covering her with a plastic drape decorated with pink hearts. She removed Anya's fancy cowboy hat and hung it on a nearby hat tree that already had a few client cowboy hats on it. "How much are we taking off?"

The salon was quiet. For all Twila said she'd finish Tillie's blowout, she was brushing her hair, not running the blow-dryer. And from the curious expression on Tillie's face, she was willing to lengthen her salon time if it meant learning more about the woman everyone in town was talking about.

"Half an inch should do it." Anya studied Sophie Jean in the mirror, gnawing on her bottom lip.

Sophie Jean was getting mixed messages here. And standing this close, Anya seemed a bit flustered even, which she had not noticed yesterday morning.

"Half an inch isn't very much." Sophie Jean clung to her smile as she began lifting Anya's locks and letting them fall over her back. Anya had thick, over-processed dry hair. "Are you sure you want a trim? The length suits you. Some low-lights would look good in your hair, though." It was a bright, brassy blond that was unlike any natural human hair color.

"A trim," Anya said firmly. "Half an inch."

Sophie Jean relented. The customer always had their way at the Cozy Clip. "Come back to the bowl and I'll wash your hair."

"No need," Anya blurted, with a nervous smile. Yes, nervous. Her gaze darted everywhere and she couldn't seem to sit still. "Can't you just use a spray bottle to wet the ends?"

Sophie Jean tested the texture of Anya's thick hair once more. "A spray bottle misting isn't ideal for cutting long hair."

"Then this is a test of your skill, isn't it?" Anya's smile challenged.

The expressions on their audience's faces hardened. Mom's was especially dark. The salon crew would most likely report to the gossip grapevine that Anya was as unlikable as a cactus in a room full of balloons. But Sophie Jean wasn't fooled. Anya was playing some sort of game. And she was anxious about the facade the woman was trying to pull off.

Is this for my sake? Or Noel's?

"Well?" Anya asked.

"I'm confident of my skill." Sophie Jean channeled some of Leigh's quiet librarian authority into her voice. "I can't say I'm as confident of your colorist's skill. Your hair has all the signs of overprocessing."

Someone gasped.

If I was a cat, my tail would be twitching a warning that my claws would be flexed next.

The other beauticians seemed to hold their collective breath.

Anya hesitated a bit too long before defending herself. "I like my hair color. It's a bold choice for a bold woman. It says I can get things done."

Again, Sophie Jean was under the impression that Anya was trying to pull off a charade. But she retrieved a spray bottle and her scissors, deciding to confuse Anya with kindness. "You made the right choice with your lipstick."

"Thank you." Anya caught Sophie Jean's eye in the mirror. "I'm curious about your...relationship with Noel."

"That's none of your business." Sophie Jean battled with her catty instincts. The words coming out of Anya's mouth sounded off, like a cover band doing a poor job of singing a popular song. That made Sophie Jean want to be kind. But some of the words themselves...

Them's cat-fighting words!

Sophie Jean sprayed a lot more water than she needed on Anya's hair before bending down behind her client's head and starting to work.

"Did Noel tell you about...me?" There it was again. That hesitation.

There was more going on here than met the eye. And Sophie Jean doubted she'd have answers in the short time it took to give Anya a trim.

"Sophie Jean?" Anya said when she didn't answer. "Have you heard about me or the Krantz family from Noel?"

"Nope. I don't know why he would tell me. We're just friends." Sophie Jean very carefully clipped half an inch of Anya's hair from the ends. No more. No less. "Are you someone important enough to bring to meet his father?" Oh, that was putting the woman on the spot. Anya hadn't been at the hospital yesterday and Sophie Jean was curious.

Kiki would be proud that I'm flexing my claws.

Someone in the salon chuckled. It might have been Sophie Jean's mother.

"I like your style," Anya admitted unexpectedly.

"Thank you?"

"That said, I just want to be clear," Anya continued in a loud, girl-boss voice that Sophie Jean envied even if she suspected it was all for show. That tone said the speaker took action. That tone said the speaker wouldn't take ten years or more to open their own salon…or whatever their dream was. "Sophie Jean, you don't want to be the one standing in the way of Noel making his mark on the world."

Like I could.

Sophie Jean managed to laugh. "Noel is definitely driven by winning and no one in Clementine has ever been able to stand in the way of that."

Her client went quiet, leaving Sophie Jean to her work. And she made quick work of the trim.

"There you go." Sophie Jean whisked the drape off Anya when she was done. "Half an inch."

The wisps of blond hair on the floor proved she'd met that standard.

"Hmm." Anya drew locks of blond hair over her shoulders. "It hardly made a difference, did it?"

"You'd see more of a difference with some lowlights." Sophie Jean held on to her patience, her smile and her composure as she handed Anya her expensive cowboy hat.

The younger woman took her time finding the right slant of that hat on her pretty head. "How much do I owe you?"

"Fifty dollars," Helga said, a twinkle of mischief in the elderly salon owner's eyes.

Anya looked taken aback, opening her mouth as if prepared to argue.

"That's the going rate for emergency services," Twila added, turning on the blow-dryer, while flashing a troublemaking smile of her own.

"And given the split ends Sophie Jean chopped off, it was an emergency," Lainey chimed in, pointing at the hair on the floor.

I love these women.

Anya paid in cash but not without a good bit of huffing and puffing. And when she left—without giving Sophie Jean a tip—those in the salon gave a collective sigh.

"Thank you, ladies," Sophie Jean told them.

"We take care of our own," Helga reassured her.

"It helps to have a strong boss leading the way," Mom said from the back. "At the Cozy Clip, we're a family."

Which was probably one of the reasons why Sophie Jean couldn't find the courage to open her own salon.

CHAPTER ELEVEN

"I DON'T THINK heart patients are supposed to have wild rides the day they receive three stents." Dad was still floating on a drug-induced cloud a mere four hours after his procedure on Tuesday morning.

Noel couldn't believe they'd sent him home so soon.

"You're tougher than you feel, Dad." Ike was floating on a cloud of a different kind. He'd driven Noel's truck home. And even though he'd been too heavy on the brake and had forgotten to signal a couple of turns, Noel could tell Ike thought he was ready to drive solo.

Noel didn't share that belief but he wasn't about to start a debate when the three of them were getting along relatively well.

"We need to get Dad inside, Ike, give him his meds and tuck him into bed." Noel was tired, patience with people in general worn down to the nub. He was used to having time alone each day after competing, either in his truck or when he retreated to his hotel room. "It'd help if you could feed the stock."

"Can do." Ike hurried ahead to open the front door, disappearing inside, probably to put his cell phone on a charger.

Dad leaned heavily on Noel's arm as they followed at a much slower pace. "You're going to have to take over Ike's training until I'm cleared for activity. Should be a week. Two tops. You can start tomorrow. I'll sit in a chair and—"

"That's not happening, Dad." So much for the repentant father he'd been during his hospital stay, the one who admitted he pushed his boys too hard.

"Sure it's happening. We agreed on things." His father stopped, staring at Noel, confusion in his eyes.

"Agreed? On what?" Noel's sleep-deprived, concussed brain couldn't recall what had been agreed to other than Dad staying in the hospital and having a procedure.

Dad's chin came up. "We've spent the past twenty-four hours working out our differences. You understand me. I understand you." Frustration bled through those words, sharp and cutting. The old Steve Emerson was back. "Together, we agreed we're going to create a rodeo dynasty."

Oh, Dad was definitely still floating in outer space. "Slow down, cowboy. Why don't we talk about this tomorrow?" When Noel would make it very clear that he'd agreed to no such thing.

Ike ran out the door and headed for the barn. Ace and Pie whinnied for him, trotting along the pasture fence, eager for their hay flakes, Ike's company or both.

Noel's kid brother looked so happy. So carefree. The way a kid his age would look if he wasn't forced to over-train in a sport he had no passion for. Noel wanted his brother to have that weight lifted. But in order to do that, Noel had to hold some hard conversations and make some hard decisions.

My family needs me.

But to stay… That meant quitting.

"Come on, Dad." Noel moved his old man forward. "The doctor said to go slow. Let's take tomorrow one step at a time. Meds and rest. I promise we'll talk about training schedules tomorrow." Or not.

Noel might break that promise and whisk Ike over to the Done Roamin' Ranch when Iona showed up in the morning to help out. There, Ike could dabble more in roping at his pace and without someone intent upon a family dynasty dogging his every move.

TUESDAY AFTERNOON, SOPHIE JEAN drove through Noel's fancy new ranch gates feeling her confidence draining.

Oh, she'd spent the rest of her shift smiling at clients and listening to her coworkers retell the story of Anya and Sophie Jean, making it sound more like a boxing match than a haircut. She'd left at three, gone home and made a comfort casserole.

And then, when it was time to head to the Done Roamin' Ranch, she'd turned the other way, toward Noel's place, casserole on her passenger seat.

Why am I here? What am I going to say to Noel?

She didn't know. It wasn't as if she had a right to ask him about Anya. But she couldn't turn around now. She had a warm casserole in her passenger seat and Iona had arrived ahead of her, if only just.

Iona waved at her as she got out of her car.

Sophie Jean gave a weak wave in return, parking next to Iona's sedan. On the bright side, she wouldn't have to knock on the door. Iona opened it and went right in.

Sophie Jean took her time collecting her macaroni and tuna casserole. She took so much time that Iona stood in the doorway, waiting for her.

"They're all asleep," Iona whispered as Sophie Jean approached. The woman's short, spiky blond hair and bright, boisterous personality were the opposite of Steve Emerson's tightly wound one. It was always a surprise to think they'd been together for over a year. Iona took the casserole from Sophie Jean and whispered, "Thanks for coming. I took the night off to make sure Steve's taken care of. Got my mom to stay the night with the boys." Who were twelve and thirteen.

"That's so nice, Iona," Sophie Jean whispered back. "I just stopped by to drop this off. I need to skedaddle, though."

"Don't leave yet." Iona moved into the house, dragging Sophie Jean in her wake.

Sophie Jean hadn't been inside Noel's house since they broken up. It almost looked the same. Noel's black cowboy hat hung on the rack. His keys and wallet sat on the table nearby, although the framed picture of them celebrating a win at a rodeo was no longer there. In the living room, the pillows she'd bought for Noel's couches were gone. The cozy quilt and afghan, also missing.

He erased me.

A lump formed in Sophie Jean's throat.

At least, there's no picture of Anya.

Meow.

"I'm going to make a fruit salad." Iona beckoned to Sophie Jean from the kitchen pass-through. "Can you make cookies?"

"I didn't bring anything to bake with." And she had to get to Fun Day practice. But Sophie Jean closed the door behind her, nonetheless.

"I brought baking ingredients." Iona smiled reassuringly. "But I've been told your cookies are better than mine."

Sophie Jean entered the kitchen. "Who would say that?"

"Steve." Iona hugged Sophie Jean briefly. "If he remembers that after all these years, I figure your cookies would be a better surprise than mine. Besides, we're practically family. Everyone says you and Noel are getting back together once that blond woman leaves town."

Sophie Jean rolled her eyes. "The gossips are having a field day talking about Noel's love life."

"Could be worse." Iona moved to the counter and began unpacking her groceries.

"Worse? How so?" Sophie Jean walked slowly around the kitchen, taking stock. There were traces of her here—the horse-shaped salt and pepper shakers, the matching spoon rest, her brightly colored mixing bowls in the same cupboard where she'd left them. She felt better.

"Sophie Jean." Iona shook her head. "It would be worse, for you at least, if Noel married that woman." She pinned Sophie Jean with a knowing stare. "She doesn't seem like she'd find much happiness in our little town. You know it's true."

Sophie Jean nodded. "There is that."

She texted Griff, letting him know she wouldn't make it to Fun Day practice. Then she got busy making snickerdoodle cookie dough, all the while worrying about Noel. Was he taking good care of himself? Was he resting peacefully? Once she had the cookies in the oven, she crept down the hall to Noel's bedroom and peeked in.

It was dark. The blinds were closed, curtains shut and the door to the master bathroom closed. Only a sliver of light shone in the room.

Noel stirred in bed.

Sophie Jean knew she should back out and close

the door. But she was worried about Noel, worried enough to gently whisper his name. "Noel..."

The figure in the bed rolled over. "Noel sleeps across the hall now."

"Mr. Emerson? Oh... I..." Sophie Jean gripped the doorknob, body heating with embarrassment, mind consumed with the urge to flee. "How are you? Iona is here, too. We're making you some food. Give a shout if you need anything." She closed the door quickly and hurried back toward the living room.

Iona stood at the end of the hallway, wiping her hands on a dish towel. "Is Steve still resting?"

"Yep."

Iona smiled, eyes sparkling with mirth. "Did you go into the wrong room?"

"Yep."

The older woman's smile morphed into a grin. "I can finish the cookies for you if you want."

"Yep." And with that, Sophie Jean made her escape.

NOEL STUMBLED OUT to the kitchen in the middle of the night, moving by the moonlight coming through the open living room and kitchen windows. Hunger had awakened him.

He opened the fridge, hoping there were some leftovers inside. He found a bowl of fruit salad next to a familiar casserole dish. He smelled tuna fish.

Noel straightened and looked around, pulse racing. “Sophie Jean?”

No one answered.

The refrigerator light from the open door revealed cookies in a clear plastic container on the counter near the stove. Colorful mixing bowls were in the sink.

Sophie Jean came to check on me.

Fool that he was, he’d slept through her visit, not hearing a thing.

But she came to check on me.

Heartened, Noel stood in the kitchen for a few minutes, eating some fruit salad. Then he took a cookie and went back to bed, determined to get better quickly. Because the only way he was winning Sophie Jean back was if he was on top of his game.

SOPHIE JEAN AND her mother walked to work on Wednesday morning. It was only a few short blocks from her apartment to Main Street and the Cozy Clip.

Sophie Jean yawned.

Her mother sniffed as if she was fighting tears again. She was at her most fragile when she had nothing to do with her hands.

“Are you okay?” Sophie Jean clasped Mom’s hand. “Did Byron call?”

“Yes.” It took her mother several more sniffles before she could continue. “I didn’t answer. Or check voicemail.”

"Why not? Maybe he wants to get back together. You still love him, don't you?" She'd certainly cried more than Sophie Jean could remember her doing over any of her other spouses.

"What if he wants to serve me divorce papers?" Mom put a hand to her throat. "I'd just die."

Definitely sounds like love to me.

"Mom, you were married for five years." It wasn't a record for her but it was a long time. "Maybe you should try talking to him instead of running away and shutting him out."

Her mother shook her head.

Sophie Jean thought her mother could use a bit more perseverance, compromise and personal growth when it came to pride, strategies to face the hard moments in her life. But Sophie Jean kept from suggesting Mom read *The Old Man and the Sea.* "You never told me… Why did you break up?"

"He said… He said…" Mom's voice was a thin thread. She sucked in a breath and tried again. "Byron said he didn't care what I made for dinner. He said I could pick anything from the freezer to microwave." Mom's voice increased in volume, as if she was working up to the greatest slight of all. "He said it all tasted the same to him. And you know…" One lusty sniff followed another. "You know I only cook frozen food. The oven and the microwave are my friend. Life's too short to cook from scratch."

Sophie Jean had to bite her lip because she had a very different perspective.

"Byron hates my cooking." Mom sobbed. "Five years. He's been eating my meals for five years and he never said anything until now."

"Aw, Mom." Sophie Jean drew her mother into a hug at the corner of Main Street. "What Byron said… That's something you say when you're tired and don't care what you eat. He probably didn't realize how that sounded to you."

"No. It's a deal-breaker to him." Her mother shuddered and released a wail, right there on Main Street.

A cowboy who was heading into the Buffalo Diner paused and glanced their way.

"Mom, you could have told him that he was welcome to take over in the kitchen, right?"

She ignored Sophie Jean. "Byron is going to ask me for a divorce. I just know it. And that's why when he left on Saturday morning, I packed up and left after him."

"You just know he wants a divorce?" Sophie Jean held her mother at arm's length. "Do you know what I know? Byron knew you had no passion for cooking long before he asked you to marry him."

Mom's nose thrust into the air. "That's not true."

Sophie Jean nodded. "It is. He told me that didn't matter when he asked me if he could marry you." That was six years ago.

"Byron asked your permission to marry me?" Mom hiccupped. "That's so sweet."

"That's your Byron." Sophie Jean dug out a tissue from her tote and carefully wiped her mother's face. "And I know something else, too."

"What's that?" Mom gave her a brave smile. "Is Noel going to ask me if he can marry you?"

"No." Sophie Jean held up her hands. "What I want to say…very gently…very kindly…as your favorite daughter…"

"My *only* daughter." Mom blew her nose.

"You don't talk about your feelings, Mom." In that respect, her mother was like Noel, locking everything emotionally important deep inside. "I don't think I've ever heard you talk about your feelings. The really meaningful ones."

"I talk about my feelings." Her mother drew herself up. "I tell you *and* Byron that I love you all the time."

"I'm not talking about those feelings," Sophie Jean said gently. "I'm talking about your feelings toward Grandma Oswald. I bet you haven't told Byron you don't cook because she was practically a chef and that discouraged you from being in the kitchen."

Mom drew a shuddering breath, eyes wide.

"It's okay to admit you aren't good at something, Mom. And it's better to admit to your loved ones *why*."

"My mother was good at everything," Mom said in a numb voice. "Nothing I did could match her."

Sophie Jean slung her arm over her mother's shoulders and drew her onward. "Grandma Oswald was good at many things. But there are two things you're better at, Mom."

"Two things?" Mom tried to laugh. "That can't be possible."

"Yep. Two things." Sophie Jean had noticed this a long, long time ago. "Grandma Oswald was horrible at giving manicures."

Mom smiled softly. "That's one."

"And she gave up on having a relationship after just one try."

Mom was silent all the way to the Cozy Clip.

CHAPTER TWELVE

"YOUR BLT IS READY." Coronet set a plate, with a sandwich cut diagonally and French fries, on a corner booth table right as Sophie Jean walked into the Buffalo Diner for lunch Wednesday. "What can I get you to drink?"

"Just water, thanks." Sophie Jean had ordered ahead. She slid into the booth and went right for a French fry. It was hot and salty and just what she needed on a splurge day. She sank back in her seat. She'd been crazy busy this morning and this was the first chance she'd had for a moment of solitude.

Anya slid into the booth across from her in a hot pink business suit, bringing along a mug of coffee and a smug smile.

Hot pink suit aside, Sophie Jean hadn't even realized the woman was in the diner. Before she could say anything, the diner owner returned.

"I'm assuming you were invited to join Sophie Jean," Coronet said as she placed a water glass on the table. She gave Anya a stern glance.

And she wasn't the only one. Several people

turned their attention from their food and conversation to stare disapprovingly.

"It's okay, ma'am." Anya smiled all around, waved all around, looking totally unfazed by the collective condemnation sent her way. "Sophie Jean and I… We have things to discuss."

That was news to Sophie Jean. And put her calm-seeking lunch plans at risk. But she figured putting up a fuss would only kick up more fodder for the gossips.

So, Sophie Jean waited for Coronet to leave and most of the diner patrons to return to their business before saying to Anya, "We have nothing to discuss." She channeled her inner kitty cat, frowned and made a shooing motion with her hand. "Move along."

Not surprisingly, Anya ignored Sophie Jean. "I'm trying to hire Noel. And I need your help."

"Listen, whoever you are," Sophie Jean began in a hard voice that sounded nothing like Leigh's even librarian tones. "I have a client in another thirty minutes. I need to eat and I need to keep my nose out of Noel's business."

"You eat and I'll talk." Anya dragged a thick pile of papers from a bulky bright yellow tote and dropped them with a thud on the Formica tabletop. She leaned over the substantial stack. It had row upon row of numbers in small print that made Sophie Jean's eyes cross. And then Anya whispered, "My father bought the rights to a professional bull rider expansion team. We start competing next year. Dad's the owner. I'm the manager. And we need a coach."

"Noel's not interested." Sophie Jean picked up half her sandwich and took a bite. But the salty goodness just didn't hit the spot. Because now she was interested in what Anya had to say.

"Let me prove to you why Noel working for us is beneficial to both parties." Anya slid on a pair of reading glasses, then flipped through the pages in front of her as if looking for something. "I'm a numbers person. Statistically… Noel is an outlier for his age. He's still winning enough to stay in the rankings and his injury rate historically has been low."

Sophie Jean attributed that to Noel's dedication to training, keeping in shape and knowing the quirks and habits of bulls on the circuit. She took another bite of her sandwich.

"But after age thirty-eight, the numbers don't lie." Anya placed a sheet of paper in front of Sophie Jean and tapped the middle of the page. "At that age, bull riders are more likely to incur severe injuries, which means increased recovery time, which means fewer wins, which means they are no longer at the top of their game and will quickly lose their qualification to be a professional rider, at least, at the top level." She tapped the page again, then returned it to her stack. Anya continued to lean forward, continued to whisper, continued to look as if the information she was imparting had life-or-death consequences. "There's also a bleaker outcome. The last rider of Noel's caliber to turn thirty-nine while still active on the circuit broke his neck. The guy before that suffered a punctured lung. And the bull rider before that had internal injuries so bad, the hospital assumed he'd been in a car crash."

Sophie Jean set her sandwich down, having lost her appetite.

This could happen to Noel.

But Anya wasn't done. "The statistics are bad enough to make any bull rider consider retirement before they turn thirty-nine."

"There's your problem. Bull riders aren't exactly known for being..." Sophie Jean didn't want to trample on anybody's dreams. "...logical."

"If you ask me, they have cotton stuffed between their ears." Anya straightened her piles of paper. She smoothed a hand over the top page. "All my life, I've loved a handful of things. My dad, our ranch, rodeo and numbers. Numbers are the most reliable of my favorite things. They don't lie."

"Have you been doing this long?" Sophie Jean selected a French fry. "Crunching numbers like these?"

Up until that point, Anya had looked open. Honest. Unlike the woman who'd come into the salon yesterday with half-truths and bad acting. But Sophie Jean's question about her credentials had Anya closing herself off.

Sophie Jean considered the woman's obvious naivete, the admission of a recent team buy-in and her gut feeling that Anya was in way over her head on something. And Sophie Jean came to a conclusion. "You've never done this before. Worked with rodeo numbers, I mean. For elite riders."

"Rookies come in all professions," Anya said defensively. "Admittedly, I've only been doing this for a few months. We received a ton of data from all the knowledgeable sources to help us decide which bull riders we want on our team. I've been going through it and the results are shocking for men in their thirties."

"That's pretty much common knowledge." Sophie Jean ate her fry. "Is that the essence of your pitch to Noel? That sooner or later, his age is going to catch up to him?"

"When you put it that way, it doesn't sound so brilliant." Anya swiped a French fry. "I did do additional analysis of the team coaches on the circuit. Granted, it's a qualitative sample size given team bull riding hasn't been around all that long. But I was able to compile a profile of the characteristics of winning coaches. And Noel fits the profile."

Sophie Jean could believe it. "He didn't mention any of your analysis to me."

"Wouldn't let me get to that part of the pitch," Anya muttered, stealing another French fry.

They ate in silence for a few minutes, during which time Sophie Jean studied her pretty seatmate. Anya was a contradiction. Intelligent and confident at times, playing at being a siren the next. And then there'd be those flashes of vulnerability.

Sophie Jean decided she needed to know more. "Can I ask…? Why do you dress…in such bright colors?"

"Good question." Anya picked up her phone and scrolled through what felt like several screens, not that Sophie Jean could see. "This is why." Anya turned her phone screen toward Sophie Jean. "This is me and my dad. My mom died when I was five. Dad raised me like he would have raised a son. I never wore a dress until this year."

The photo showed Anya wearing torn-up blue jeans tucked into scuffed, boring brown boots, and a T-shirt with stains on the front. She wore glasses with square black frames and had her dirty blond hair in two ponytails. She looked to be no older than Ginny and Piper in that photo.

"Cute," Sophie Jean said, since it felt like she should comment.

"You don't have to be nice. I'm a tomboy and a nerd." Anya set her phone face down on the table. "No fashion sense whatsoever. I double-majored in college. Statistics and finance. My goal was to use those skills to help my dad better manage the ranch. I started by doing a cost-per-head-of-cattle analysis crossed by acreage usage."

That was all gobbledygook to Sophie Jean.

But Anya's eyes were bright, as if she was in her

element. "Led me to the conclusion that leasing some of the land would help us offset costs. Found some gold prospectors looking to lease land. They struck a vein last summer. And our cut was substantial." She beamed with pride. "Still is."

"Enough to buy a stake in a professional bull riding team," Sophie Jean guessed. "But that doesn't explain the makeover. Did someone suggest it?"

"No. I..." Anya leaned forward, lowering her voice once more. "I went around to some of the big rodeo events with my dad last fall. He said he wanted me there because I'll own the team after he's gone. But looking like I did, like just another ranch hand, I was invisible."

"Overlooked, you mean."

Anya shrugged. "Same difference. After just a few weeks, it felt like my dad started to overlook me, too. He was beginning to believe that the mother lode had been found on our land and would provide endless funds, despite me telling him the likelihood of that happening was low. He used to be wise with his money. Stingy even. But now..." Anya wiped her cheek as if a tear had spilled over. "You know, there are lots of people around rodeo who are ready to take advantage of folks who have money and don't quite know what to do with it. I couldn't let that happen to Dad."

Sophie Jean nodded. "Your father needed your protection."

Anya nodded.

"So the makeover was your idea." Sophie Jean sat back in the booth. The more Anya talked, the more she liked her. The young woman took action.

"Yes, the makeover was my idea. And a side of myself I always wanted to explore. But I couldn't venture down that path alone." She sipped her coffee. "I went into one of those fancy boutiques in Dallas and bought several outfits the nice salesladies put together for me. I spent a fortune on shoes and accessories. Then I went back to the hotel with a box of hair color, a bag of freshly purchased makeup, and created the new me."

She really should have let a professional do her hair. But Sophie Jean was curious. "How'd that work out for you?"

"My disguise? Not quite the way I expected." Anya rubbed her nose. "I got more bigwigs to shake my hand. But they still wouldn't listen for long. I needed to up the ante." Anya's brow furrowed, as if she was remembering the obstacles she'd faced, as if she still faced them now. "When Dad and I finally got a meeting with Noel and he tried to dismiss both of us, something came over me."

"Lust?" Sophie Jean murmured absently.

"Rage. I kissed him."

So that kiss at Betty's Bakery wasn't the first time.

A bolt of jealousy stole all Sophie Jean's words. Or at least, the polite ones. She frowned.

"It was inappropriate," Anya went on, not seeming to notice Sophie Jean's upset. "But that smooch was a miracle. For the next few minutes, Noel and my father were speechless. I was able to start my pitch. Told him we wanted to hire him as our coach, stroked his ego by reciting his accomplishments. Dropped an initial salary offer. And before I could follow up with hard data about how a transition to coaching could be life-changing and lifesaving, he walked away."

"Sounds like Noel."

"And he's been walking ever since."

Sophie Jean nodded. "He told me as much."

"Which is why I came up with a new approach." Anya gestured toward Sophie Jean. "You."

"I politely decline." Although she gave props to Anya for coming up with another idea. That woman was going to make her dreams come true long before Sophie Jean ever did.

"You care for Noel," Anya went on evenly. "And he cares for you. Don't deny it. I saw you holding hands. And he was furious that I lip-bombed him at the bakery."

"Maybe he just didn't like his personal space invaded by a relative stranger." There were rules to social engagement for a reason.

"I admit, I went overboard. I owe him—and you—an apology." Anya tilted her head to study Sophie Jean. "You don't have a lot of confidence in yourself, do you? If a man looked at me the way Noel looks at you, I'd… Well, first I'd let him see my nerdy side to make sure he wasn't just blinded by my disguise. And if he still looked at me like I hung the moon, I'd make sure he made smart choices—have adequate health insurance, wear his seat belt, stop riding bulls when the odds began to turn against him."

Sophie Jean considered Anya for a moment, and then laughed.

Hurt, Anya stuffed her stack of facts and figures into her tote with jerky movements. "I knew this was a long shot."

"I'm not laughing at what you said." Sophie sobered, trying her best to repress her chuckle. "I laughed because I didn't expect you to be…you."

"Weird, you mean. Or nerdy? Too reliant on numbers in a sport that relies on gut feelings?" Anya slid toward the end of the booth seat. But she stopped and stared at Sophie Jean as if she'd nearly forgotten to convey the most important of all her facts. "I think I know the answer to this but…which is more important to Noel? Winning? Or the challenge of riding a huge, angry beast?"

"Winning," Sophie Jean breathed shakily. She could see where Anya was going with this.

"That's too bad." Anya shook her head and got to her feet. She was wearing an incredible pair of hot pink cowboy boots today. "When winning drives bull riders, the probability of injury is three times worse."

Sophie Jean's breath caught in her throat.

Noel…

Dear, sweet, infuriatingly stubborn Noel…

He'd rather kill himself than stop trying to win.

Unless she and their Fun Day team could teach Noel that winning wasn't the best or only thing in life.

"WHO'S THIS BEAUTY?" Noel asked Sophie Jean when he arrived at the Done Roamin' Ranch for Fun Day practice Wednesday afternoon. He'd made sure to arrive early, having slept nearly twenty hours and woken up feeling better than he had in over a week.

Almost good enough to take a bull for a winning ride. For sure good enough to take a stab at winning Sophie Jean back.

It was just Noel and Sophie Jean, plus the dapple-gray draft horse she led. No ranch hands were around. No kids ran about. Not even Frank and Mary leaned on an arena rail. Which was great. Noel was eager to explain Anya's presence and boundary-breaking behavior at Betty's Bakery to Sophie Jean. But of all the things he wanted to say, Noel knew intuitively he shouldn't lead with that. And that's why he decided to begin by talking about something innocuous, like the weather. Or in this case, a very large, very fine-looking horse.

"Hello, Noel." Sophie Jean had a thoughtful expression on her pretty face as she led the large horse into the arena. “This is Shirley, the horse the kids were talking about.”

The mare whinnied.

“She likes the sound of her name,” Sophie Jean continued, still in an absent tone. “Whinnies every time. Don’t you, Shirley?”

The horse whinnied again.

The dapple-gray mare walked proudly. She wasn’t a plodder. She was a prancer, as if she knew all eyes were on her and enjoyed the attention. It was no wonder everyone was enamored with her.

Noel smiled. “Are you going to hitch her to my mom’s wagon? Or is someone going to ride her?” The draft horse had a bridle on but no saddle and he’d forgotten what was on today’s practice schedule.

“We’re going to use her to practice the bareback ride, Noel. Some of our team were afraid they’d bounce off during that event, so I thought I’d bring Shirley—”

The horse neighed.

“—out to build their confidence.”

“Great strategy.” She was smart and organized. He’d always respected that about her. “About Monday morning—”

“Where’s Ike?” Sophie Jean interrupted, still avoiding Noel’s gaze.

“He went inside to say hi to Mary and Frank. I think he was hoping to have a snack.” His teenage brother was a bottomless pit where his stomach was concerned. “About the other morning—”

"And how's your dad?" Sophie Jean cut him off again.

"My dad is fine. All he can talk about is Ike returning to his bull riding training schedule." Noel tipped his hat back for the first time in over a week and took a good long look at Sophie Jean. "Took a solid hour of negotiation to agree to give Ike a vacation this week."

"So, your dad's back to normal, then."

"It seems so, but—"

"That's good."

Sophie Jean faced him squarely, the way folks did when they were determined to make a point. "Your dad pushed you so hard that you had a love-hate relationship with rodeo."

"That's not true. I love rodeo." Kinda. Sort of. Most days.

"No, Noel." Sophie Jean wasn't bending on this. "You love winning. It doesn't matter what it is, as long as you come in first." Sophie Jean looped the reins over Shirley's neck, climbed up the arena rails and then hopped on the mare's back and picked up the reins. Sophie Jean stared down at Noel, her face lined with disappointment. "It's so clear to me now."

"That's good because nothing's clear to me." Especially the point she must be building to.

"I was talking to Wade in the barn. He just retired from bronc riding and he can't stop talking about the void in his life." She pressed her straw cowboy hat more firmly on her head before giving Noel a look he couldn't decipher. "The love in his voice when he talked about his sport..."

"I love Wade as much as any of my foster brothers," Noel said, floundering when it came to the purpose of this conversation. "But it sounds like he's been trying to garner your sympathy."

"No, Noel. He's dealing with grief over retiring. He's talking through his feelings." Sophie Jean gave Noel the smallest of smiles, so small it could almost be termed pitying. "You only ever talk about your belt buckles and point totals on the circuit. Since you've been back, you haven't even done that. If you've lost passion for bull riding or have finally begun to feel your age, you should seriously consider Anya's offer."

No.

"Well, I..." Noel touched the significantly smaller lump on his head. He wasn't sure what to say. If this conversation was any indication, his hopes of winning Sophie Jean back seemed out of reach.

Sophie Jean stroked Shirley's long neck. "You told me you had mixed feelings about rodeo as a kid. That's why you were always running away. Because you felt like you were being forced into it. When we broke up, I thought it was an excuse to prove to your father that you were dedicated to the task he'd set for you."

"I was thirty-four when we broke up." Noel

rubbed a hand around the back of his neck. "I wanted to prove that I was worth something to… to myself."

"You were worth something to me," Sophie Jean said in a voice filled with regret. She turned her gaze toward the stock paddocks behind the barn and the pastures beyond. "You didn't have to win anything for me to value you. But you knew you'd honed your skill. You knew you had a good chance to succeed if you jettisoned all the distractions in your life. But there was no enthusiasm in your voice when you told me."

"Because I was crushed that we were breaking up," Noel protested, albeit weakly, because something about this conversation was making him physically ill, something about the truth deep down that he hadn't wanted to face, something involved with the loneliness of life on the road and the hollow victory when he won lately. "Because I was trying to do right by you."

"I didn't want you to do right by me." Sophie Jean's features were pinched, as if she was trying her best to hold something back. But what? "I wanted you to fight for me. *For us.*"

Noel laid a hand on her jean-clad knee. "I want to do that now."

Tears welled in her eyes as she stared at him. "Long-distance relationships don't last," she whispered. "We tried. And I…" Sophie Jean swallowed thickly. "I don't want to try again if everything is the same."

Noel felt empty inside, probably because his heart seemed to have lodged itself in his throat.

"You haven't changed. You still keep everything important about your life hidden. Your situation hasn't changed. You'll be back on the circuit before you know it. And I…" Sophie Jean's breath caught and her gaze sought his. "I don't think I believe in romantic love anymore. I'm not worth fighting for."

"That's not true."

"*Noel*," she said in that call-you-out tone of hers. "How do you plan on fighting for me? Will you retire? Will you share your feelings with me?"

Noel's mouth went dry.

Shirley flicked her tail, swatting him.

Even the horse knows I have to give up something to get Sophie Jean back.

And still, he didn't speak. He couldn't. Everything inside him—all his goals, all his sacrifices, all the bad parts of his childhood—was knotted, twisted, tangled. Who would he be if he wasn't Noel Emerson, champion bull rider?

No one.

His hand fell away from her knee.

Sophie Jean gave a brisk nod and sat taller on Shirley's back, as if bolstering herself for what happened next. "The kids will be here soon." She cleared her throat. Finally, she looked at him, expression all businesslike, and leaned over from atop

Shirley, holding out her hand. But not to shake or touch him. "Do you have any money?"

"Did I lose a bet I've forgotten about?" Noel reached for his wallet, anyway, still trying to find his balance in this conversation and in his life.

"I need bucks to put beneath my knees when I ride Shirley." The draft horse whinnied on cue, eliciting a smile from Sophie Jean. "Can't have the kids try something I haven't." She made the gimme gesture with her free hand.

Luckily, Noel had a couple of one-dollar bills to give her. He paused, money in hand, thinking about the note he kept tucked behind his driver's license.

This is what she wants. To know all the chinks in my armor.

He closed his wallet and handed her the money.

Sophie Jean tucked a dollar bill under each knee. "Let's see if we can do this, girl." She cued Shirley into a slow trot around the arena.

Sophie Jean looked small and delicate riding the huge gray. The draft horse had a gentle gait, which, when combined with Sophie Jean's good form, made the pair look like they were floating on a cloud. As they came around the other side of the arena, a smile was on Sophie Jean's face, full and beautiful.

If only they were on the same wavelength and she smiled like that for him.

Horse and rider came to a stop in front of Noel.

"Your turn." Sophie Jean plucked the dollar bills

from beneath her knees, then hopped off Shirley and stumbled.

Noel kept her from falling. "Whoa, girl. That's a big height to jump from."

"You're right." Sophie Jean laughed, staring up at him. "My feet are tingling."

"I've got you," he reassured her, repeating, "I've got you. Now and always."

They stared into each other's eyes. And all Noel could think about was kissing her.

She licked her lips.

And oh, how badly Noel wanted to sweep her into his arms. He'd kiss her until neither one of them cared how or why Noel made his living.

"Are we riding Shirley?" Sam cried, bolting into the arena and eliciting a whinny from the gray draft horse.

Rusty, the reddish-brown Labradoodle, trotted after Sam, a green tennis ball in his mouth. He bit down on it, making it squish.

"You guessed right, Sam." Sophie Jean backed away from Noel, regret in her eyes. "We're riding Mary's pretty mare. But Noel's going next."

The only thing Noel wanted to do next was kiss Sophie Jean.

I ALMOST KISSED NOEL.

That would have been a mistake. Noel didn't want to think beyond his next bull ride. Didn't want to open his heart to her. Didn't want to reach for something more.

He simply stood next to her, quietly radiating discontent.

"I can't wait to ride S-H-I-R-L-E-Y." Sam hopped around like a frisky bunny. Rusty pranced around him, wagging his tail and squishing his slobbery tennis ball. "If you don't make S-H-I-R-L-E-Y whinny, you get to ride her first. Those are Grandpa Frank's rules."

"That's because he's afraid Mary's horse will tire of the name game," Sophie Jean told Sam, trying not to pay attention to the cowboy standing next to her. "And your grandma, Mary, finds such joy in her horse recognizing her name."

"Sophie Jean, you know everything that goes on around here." Sam kept hopping. His dog kept prancing. And Noel kept brooding.

"People like to talk to me," Sophie Jean turned her away from Noel. "I'm a good listener."

"My teacher says I talk too much," Sam piped up, leaving Sophie Jean wondering what Noel had been about to confess his love for. Sam wrested Rusty's ball from the dog's mouth and threw it over the arena rails.

The dog raced off. He sure had some strong feelings. He *loved* to chase that ball, carrying it almost everywhere, like a badge of honor. You couldn't pay that dog to fetch. He'd do it for free until the day he died. Unlike Noel, who'd only ride bulls as long as he won something.

"You're nice to everyone, Sophie Jean." Sam stuck his head through the rails as he watched his dog run down the bouncing ball. "And that's why you're one of my favorite folks." He glanced back at Noel. "You need to take your turn riding, Noel, or give it up to the next in line."

"I'm going. I'm going." Noel grabbed hold of Shirley's gray mane and then leaped onto her back.

"Wow." Sam stared up at him, admiration for Noel in his eyes for once.

"Here." Sophie Jean thrust the dollar bills at Noel, not quite meeting his gaze, afraid he might see that she, too, was awestruck. "Your mounting technique is impressive. Let's see how you do on your ride, though."

"This gal and I are going to do great." Noel tucked each dollar bill beneath a knee and then clucked his tongue to give Shirley the go-ahead.

The draft horse headed off at a slow, grand trot. Noel sat tall on her back.

Sophie Jean drew Sam to her side, needing a little emotional support. "That was nice of you to let Noel have his turn, Sam. I know you wanted a ride."

"I'll tell you a secret." Sam turned his face up toward hers. "I don't want to ride without the other kids watching me."

"You don't need people watching you to have fun or practice a skill," she gently reminded him.

"I know. But it's better with an audience." He gasped and looked toward the rise that led to the highway. The sound of tires on gravel filled the air. "And here they come!"

Sure enough, trucks came over the rise and pulled into the ranch yard. Rusty trotted over to greet them, his green tennis ball in his mouth.

Noel completed his bareback lap on Shirley with both dollars still in place.

"My turn." Sam danced as enthusiastically as his energetic, young Labradoodle.

Noel smiled when he hopped off Shirley. "This is what I imagine it'd feel like to ride a tame bull."

The two bills fluttered to the ground on either side of Shirley.

Sam scurried to pick up the one closest to him, then darted under Shirley to retrieve the other dollar bill. A few seconds later, he was coming back under her to stand in front of Noel. "My turn. Pick me up."

"Please," Noel urged.

"Please *and* thank you." Sam clutched a dollar bill in each hand and turned his back to Noel. "Toss me up on Shirley."

The horse whinnied and looked around at Sam. But she didn't move a hoof. She was a sweetheart, worth every pretty penny Frank had paid for her.

Noel lifted Sam onto Shirley's back and handed him the reins.

"I'm gonna be so good at this." Sam tucked a

dollar bill under each knee. And then he waved at the kids approaching the arena. "Look at what we get to do today!" And with a quick kick of his heels into Shirley's broad gray flanks, the draft horse took off at a fast trot.

While two dollar bills drifted slowly to the ground.

CHAPTER THIRTEEN

NOEL WAS TRYING to keep up the facade of the Concierge of Fun. But his heart wasn't in it. The promise of the day had shattered because he'd been unable to choose love over glory once more.

He watched Sophie Jean help Sam up on Shirley for another practice round. She had the patience of a saint when it came to those kids, alternating between helping their young squad work on their roping technique and helping them up on Shirley to practice their bareback riding. She'd make a fantastic mother.

Or she would have if he hadn't shredded her tenuous belief in love.

Ike moseyed over to stand next to Noel. "What's up between you and Sophie Jean?"

"Nothing."

"Do you need me to talk to her for you?" Ike managed to ask that with a straight face.

"No."

"Are you sure?" Ike grinned, stroking those two whiskers on either side of his mouth.

"Yep." Noel gestured for Ginny to join them. She was riding a palomino mare bareback.

"What are you doing, Noel?" Ike whispered urgently.

"You'll see." Noel gave his brother a grin that felt very real.

"Hey, Uncle Noel?" Ginny brought her horse to a stop in front of him, avoiding looking at Ike. "What's up?"

"Didn't you have something you wanted to ask Ike?" Noel turned toward his brother, glad the teenage girl had talked to him earlier.

"Yeah." Ginny tipped her cowboy hat back and met Ike's gaze with only the barest of pink color blooming in her cheeks. "Ike, I was wondering if you would want to—"

"No!" Ike cried, waving his arms as if he were calling a runner safe at first. "I don't date yet. I—I—I… I'm not allowed."

Instead of dying from embarrassment, Ginny sniffed, as if she couldn't be bothered with the likes of Ike. "I'm not asking you on a date. I was going to ask if you wanted to try and be team roping partners next season on the high school rodeo team because I think you could be really good. But forget it." And then she rode off with perfect form and those dollar bills firmly in place beneath her knees.

"Ugh." Ike pulled his cowboy hat down over his red face. "Can we go now?"

"Nope. You need to apologize for the misunderstanding first." Noel clapped his brother on the back. "Cheer up. At least, you know someone finds your roping skills to have promise. We'll make use of Ace yet." That was a ray of sunshine in an otherwise disappointing afternoon.

Soft laughter from behind Noel had him and Ike turning.

His foster mother approached the arena railing. "Ike, honey. You've gotta let a woman finish her sentence."

"I know that…now." Ike heaved a sigh and strode off in Ginny's direction.

"Noel, I'm so glad you put together this Fun Day. I'm enjoying myself immensely." Mary extended her hand through the rails toward Noel. "How's your father?"

"Better." Noel took her small, calloused hand in his. He turned her palm over, inspecting it closer. "What are these calluses from?" They looked recent and suspiciously like the ones he had on his palm from bull riding. "Have you been on a bull?"

Mary scoffed but she looked away, as if hiding something. "I've been busy. Riding horses. Driving the riding mower. Digging in the garden." His mother gestured back toward the main house. Its flower garden was in bright bloom on either side of the porch steps. Yellow daffodils and red tulips waved in the breeze. "I like my life and my home a certain way. That means work."

"You should retire."

"I'll retire when Frank retires from the rodeo stock business." She gave Noel's hand a gentle shake before drawing her hand back and resting it on the rail. "Although at the rate you're going, you and Frank will retire at the same time. Stubborn. The two of you. You both love what you do, I suppose."

"You think so?" Her opinion felt different from Sophie Jean's. And…perhaps…his own.

"I think…" Mary's smile was comforting beneath the brim of her straw cowboy hat. "I think you found something you're good at and that gives you the sense of belonging you were always looking for. But I'm here to tell you that belonging is earned by knowing, not accolades. You became family here when we got to know you, when you opened up about your fears and what makes you tick."

There was a deeper meaning in her words, just as there had been with Sophie Jean's. But this time, the message struck home.

"Thanks, Mom." He went off in search of Sophie Jean.

SOPHIE JEAN SAT on a bench in the Done Roamin' Ranch's barn after the kids had left, taking a quiet moment to relax and rehydrate before she returned to her apartment as the supportive daughter of a woman whose life was in an uproar.

What I wouldn't give for a boring day.

She closed her eyes, breathed deep and tried to focus on the positives of the afternoon.

The kids had a good time, no one got hurt and I didn't kiss Noel.

She had mixed feelings about that last item. Up was down and down was up where Noel was concerned.

"Tired?" a familiar voice asked, loudly enough to be heard over the chatter of young cowboys and cowgirls climbing into trucks in the ranch yard but soft enough that it felt like Noel's question was just for her.

"No." Sophie Jean didn't open her eyes. "Do I look tired?"

"You look..."

Sophie Jean opened her eyes and stared into Noel's steady blue ones.

"Beautiful," he said.

Her breath caught. And when she was able to fill her lungs again, she said, "You shouldn't say things like that to me." But her pulse galloped happily through her veins. She closed her eyes, clutching her water bottle and trying to distance herself from Noel and her inconvenient feelings. She needed distance, physically and emotionally. "Why don't you want to coach a bull riding team? It could be your second act. You could coach for decades instead of riding a few more years."

"Nobody wants the Emerson brand of coaching,"

Noel said slowly. "It's hard on a man, body and soul. Besides, I'm not retired and I don't do teams."

"Except for Fun Days." Sophie Jean glanced at the Done Roamin' Ranch grounds through the open barn doors. "And as part of the Done Roamin' Ranch crew—"

"I was never a part of the working crew," Noel cut her off. "And my dad didn't let me join the high school rodeo team."

It seemed as if he had more to say, so Sophie Jean stayed silent.

"You were right. About what you said earlier. Winning… It's important to me." His voice. So gruff. So…personal. "I love being good at bull riding. And maybe I'm more clinical about my sport than others but…when I win, people…*stay*."

"Noel…" Sophie Jean frowned. "You can't believe that."

He stared at his hands.

"You…" Sophie Jean's mind raced in circles, unable to process what he was trying to tell her. "I don't understand."

"When my dad first put me in bull riding competitions as a kid, I didn't win. My mom left soon after and—"

"She didn't leave because you didn't win."

Noel's expression hardened. "My dad said that's one reason why she left and… She left me a note confirming it."

"You never told me about a note." What else

hadn't he told her about? Had she known him at all? Or just the aspect of Noel he wanted her to see?

Noel drew out his wallet and then a faded, folded sheet of pink paper from behind his driver's license. He stared at it a moment and then handed it to Sophie Jean.

She opened the small note and silently read: *Noel, following your current path means you'll never amount to anything.*

"When did she give you this note?" Sophie Jean asked, studying the short, taut lines of the letters. There was no softness. No swirls. But no hurried strokes, either. Sophie Jean couldn't get an impression of his mother from her handwriting or her message.

"I found it under my pillow after she left," Noel said quietly. "It had been a bad week for me. Dad dragged me to a rodeo when I had a cold. We lost. Every bull I rode slammed me into something. A fence. A crash barrel. A pick-up man's horse. I heard about all my mistakes, on repeat, all the way home. When we arrived home, my mother was gone and there was this note."

"I think you're taking this wrong," Sophie Jean began. "She could have meant something else." Like stopping his father from dictating the rest of his life, possibly something she'd been unable to do.

Frowning, Noel plucked the paper from Sophie Jean's hand. "I know what she meant." His icy tone brooked no argument. "I hadn't been winning and she left."

"Or—"

"She thought I wasn't worth the effort, Sophie Jean." Noel's voice rose. "Dad said as much when I showed him the note."

"Have you ever considered the fact that your dad was bitter over his wife leaving him?" Sophie said gently. "He could have projected the way he felt about his wife onto your relationship with your mother."

"No." Noel's gaze was piercingly blue, angrily blue. "I'll provide one last bit of proof about why I put so much stock into winning." He drew a ragged breath. "You left me when I was on a losing streak."

"I didn't leave you." Sophie Jean stood, ready to defend that fact to the bitter end. "You chose rodeo over me. You… You chose *winning* over me. You put too much importance on awards and earnings as a way to value your self-worth. I love… *loved*…you for you. Not for the belt buckles, the prize money or the accolades. Don't you see?" She desperately wanted him to. "If you can't move beyond that…"

We can't try again.

His lips formed a grim line.

A line Sophie Jean couldn't cross.

So she left him. And this time, it felt as if it was for good.

NOEL SANK DOWN onto the bench Sophie Jean had just vacated, dropped his cowboy hat beside him and leaned his back against the barn wall.

Before Noel had time to put more thought into Sophie Jean's words, someone cleared their throat in the tack room.

Noel's foster father poked his head out, an apologetic smile on his thin face. "I didn't mean to eavesdrop. I was cleaning Shirley's bridle."

"But you heard." Not a question. Noel sighed. "Go on. I know you have thoughts." And he respected his foster father enough to listen.

Frank walked over to sit on the bench, handing Noel his cowboy hat before claiming a spot next to him. "The only thoughts that should matter are yours."

Slowly, Noel told Frank what Sophie Jean had pointed out in the arena earlier.

Frank didn't interrupt. He just let Noel toss all his thoughts into the air.

"Can't make a living if I don't win," Noel said matter-of-factly. "Doesn't matter what I believe about winning." He had his father and brother to support.

"There's a lot more to unpack here than winning and losing." Dad leaned forward, hands clasped, elbows resting on his knees. "Recognizing who you are deep down inside is key. All you boys came here with painful pasts. And some of you bandaged that pain without sorting out the source." He gave Noel a significant look.

"I know where it comes from…this need of mine to win." Noel shrugged and said simply, "The note. Everything after that just confirmed that belief."

"Beliefs serve to protect old wounds, which is good. But…" Dad began, which would have set Noel's mind at ease if his foster father wasn't adding a qualifier. The older man stared at his cowboy boots. "When I was eighteen, everybody told me I'd stopped growing. My boot size was eleven. And my attitude toward life was… Well, let's just say I had a way of finding trouble."

Noel smiled.

"As I got older, my feet grew." Frank chuckled. "I'm an eleven and a half wide today. But my attitude toward life is different. Now, I can spot trouble—usually before it gets out of hand—and I try to head it off at the pass."

"You've changed." Noel nodded.

"Life will do that to a person. Change you physically, emotionally, mentally." Frank tapped his temple. "In some ways, you get stronger and braver. In others, you feel more vulnerable." He rubbed a spot over his heart.

"You're afraid to lose Mary," Noel guessed, thinking of her battles with cancer and how frail she looked.

His foster father pressed his lips together and nodded, perhaps unable to speak.

"I'm afraid to lose…everything," Noel admitted quietly. "And everyone." If he stopped riding. If his bank account and investments were bled dry.

"Winning isn't going to make anyone in your life love you any more than they already do," Frank said softly, staring at his hands. "Mary and I…your foster brothers…even Sophie Jean. We all love you, win, lose or draw."

"I know that…on some level. But in here…" Noel tapped a spot over his heart. "In here, I feel better about myself when I win. And I know—*I know*—people see me differently when I win. I know…if I give it up, things will change." And not for the better.

Dad considered Noel's words, and then said slowly, "Could it be…that you've been conditioned to feel that way by your father's managing your rodeo career from an early age? And now, when that belief no longer serves you, you can't let it go because it's almost like a habit?"

It was Noel's turn to ponder in silence. To challenge the way he looked at the past and the lens he examined life through, his future through.

Dad laid his palm on Noel's shoulder. "Think on it. You might surprise yourself."

"And I might not," Noel allowed.

Because old habits, even mental ones, died hard.

SOPHIE JEAN'S RED geraniums looked perky and well-watered on either side of her apartment door.

She wasn't used to that. Or used to having the specter of Noel in her head, stubbornly unable to see her arguments and be the man she knew he could be.

To be fair, Sophie Jean wasn't entirely sure she could be the woman Noel deserved. As he'd so astutely pointed out days ago, she'd had four years to achieve her dream and hadn't made any progress.

Sophie Jean opened her unlocked apartment door and dropped her purse and keys on the entry table. "I'm home."

"Dusty, dirty and tired, as always." Mom sounded far too chipper. "Anya brought us dinner."

"Anya?" Sophie Jean spun around.

"Hey." Anya sat in the sole living room guest chair, a wingback antique that used to be Granny Oswald's. Sophie Jean had it recovered in a flashy gold, which, with the flashy young blond sitting in it, made it look like a throne. "I thought I'd make up for disrupting your lunch today, Sophie Jean."

Kiki sat in the bedroom doorway, flicking her tail and staring daggers at the intruder, who clearly hadn't won her over.

Sophie Jean tugged off her dirty cowboy boots. "Anya, has anyone ever told you about personal boundaries?"

"You did. At lunch. When you questioned my lip-bombing tactic." Anya smiled brightly. Unfazed.

"I don't think those were my exact words," Sophie Jean allowed.

"Oh, I'm pretty good at reading people. You didn't need to expand the point." Anya gestured toward Sophie Jean's mother. "Charlene was just telling me what's been making her so teary-eyed."

"Not in so many words," Mom murmured.

"Really?" Sophie Jean stared at her mother, the woman who wouldn't willingly talk about the root of her emotions. "You talked to Anya?"

"Yes. About my back," Mom said, making a show of rubbing her spine. "Can't sleep on a sofa the way I used to."

You are such a fibber!

Sophie Jean bit back a smile.

"Tell me about it." Anya nodded. "Hotel beds are just as bad as couches." She got right to the point. "Did you talk to Noel, Sophie Jean?"

"I did but I didn't enhance your sales pitch, if that's why you're asking." Sophie Jean went over to inspect the bags of food on the small kitchen table. "Mexican food. My favorite." There were three different entrées, each labeled and in its own box.

"Anya is so thoughtful." Mom came to stand next to Sophie Jean, her back to their guest and a smirk on her face. "I said I'd repay her by doing her nails tomorrow."

"Charlene is the nicest person I've met in Clementine aside from you, Sophie Jean." Anya came to the table and sat down. She changed out of that hot pink business suit and now wore impractical black velvet slacks with a white blouse and those fabulous pink cowboy boots. "If nothing else, I'm learning a lot about people. I hear there's going to be a Fun Day on Friday at the Done Roamin' Ranch."

"Yes, there is." Sophie Jean took a box with cheese enchiladas inside, wondering if Anya had ever had any real friends. "The kids are really looking forward to it. We have practice every afternoon."

"If you need a helping hand, I can come by," Anya offered. "I'm a good roper."

"Best leave the roping to the professionals," Mom said, taking the steak fajitas. "Like Sophie Jean."

Anya had been in the process of opening the box with the vegetarian burrito. She stopped at Mom's words and stared at her. "You don't think I have skill?"

Mom chuckled, seemingly oblivious to the nerve she'd struck. "Not with boots like that, you don't."

Sophie Jean stopped trying to hide her smile. "Funny thing about appearances, isn't it, Anya?"

Anya nodded. "They can sometimes backfire."

CHAPTER FOURTEEN

THURSDAY MORNING, NOEL and Ike led their saddled horses into the large, empty pasture behind the Emerson Ranch barn, each with a lariat hanging from their saddle horn. Dad was setting up roping targets for them to practice with nearby.

The spring air was brisk and promised another sunny day. And for the second day in a row, Noel wasn't squinting like a mole outdoors. Given the restless night he'd had, that was surprising.

Dad was in a much better mood, a changed mood since his heart attack. Part of that was the continued presence of Iona. She'd spent a lot of time here since Dad was released on Tuesday.

Noel and Ike had taken advantage of Dad's lighter mood. Surprisingly, Dad agreed to Ike taking a break from bull riding training, although it was clear Dad hoped by Easter Sunday that Ike would have settled on something. Either bull riding or roping. Choosing neither wasn't an option.

Noel believed roping was the way to go if Ike chose anything. The trouble was that Ike had a late start. Ropers in junior rodeo had begun competing in the sport long before he had. But Ginny's request for him to be her roping partner proved that Ike had some talent. It was just that they hadn't put that talent on horseback.

Today was the day.

There were other things that needed to happen today. Noel had thought a lot about Frank's, Mary's and Sophie Jean's opinions that his thinking about winning…bull riding…life…needed to change. Noel suspected he needed to talk things through with his biological father to leave his fear of losing, and losing everyone he cared about, behind.

But not this morning.

"Have you ever roped from horseback?" Ike swung into the saddle on the tall black gelding, slouching like a greenhorn.

"I have. And there's a reason that's not my career path." Noel mounted up, then gestured at Ike. "Here's a tip. You never slouch in the saddle unless you want your body language to tell your horse that he's the boss. Not you."

Ike sat up taller.

Beneath Noel, his horse Pie shifted and pawed the dirt, ready to run.

"Good." Noel shifted the reins, his weight and his legs until the horse stilled. "And while I'm giving out tips…you need to employ the same ideas that Sophie Jean taught you about roping. Which means…"

"Start with baby steps and use good technique. Sophie Jean preached a lot about relying on mechanics." Ike rolled his shoulders back. "I never had my own horse before. I used to ride Pie around the pasture but I think he thought he was in charge. We just went wherever he wanted to go and when he thought we'd ridden enough, he took me back to the gate."

"You've got a long way to go if you want to be Ginny's roping partner," Noel teased.

Ike's cheeks ruddied. "I apologized and admitted I thought she was taking a big risk asking me. I know I've got lots of catching up to do. Ginny told me she'd take me riding next week. I just have to ask Dad." Ike patted Ace's sleek black neck. "I have a good feeling about roping. I think Ace and I are going places."

"Going places." Noel grinned. "Don't go riding him into town and visiting to the drive-through at the Tasty Freeze. That horse is an expensive investment. In your future, if that's what you really want."

"How did you know I wanted to ride Ace to the Tasty Freeze?" Ike laughed. "It's scary how you and I think alike."

Noel nodded but it was the similarity in the way their father was raising them that made him worry.

"I'm ready," Dad called in his loud, authoritative voice. "Let's go."

Noel had the strongest urge to gallop away, despite being thirty-eight and his own man.

That's what Frank would call triggering.

One look at Ike's taut, closed-off expression and Noel could see he felt the same way.

"We're not ready yet!" Suddenly, Noel had questions for his baby brother. "We've got to warm up the horses. Come on." Noel cued Pie into a fast walk. And when they were far enough away from their father that he couldn't hear, Noel asked, "Why didn't you go with your mother when Dad and Delilah broke up?"

"She didn't ask. My mother was gone when we got back from a rodeo one weekend. Didn't even say goodbye. Still stings."

This was sounding decidedly familiar.

"And that was four years ago?" Right after Noel and Sophie Jean broke up, and Noel left town.

"Yeah. She came by at Christmas last year with her new family," Ike said stoically. "Hadn't seen her in years. It was awkward. But now I know how you feel."

The wind kicked up.

Noel held his cowboy hat on his head. "I didn't get holidays with my mom." He didn't even know where she was today.

"No. I mean, my half brother is two. Big age difference. Like you and me."

They really were living parallel lives. Noel cued Pie into a slow gallop.

Ike did the same with Ace. For all his brother said he didn't have much experience riding, he didn't bounce in the saddle. They reached the end of the pasture and came to a stop.

"Why did Dad and Delilah break up? When I

left, they seemed fine together." Not that Dad had been living with Noel back then. And not that Noel had spent much time with Dad. But he hadn't heard of any discord.

"Looking back… There was tension," Ike said slowly. "Arguing. Honestly, I'd just go to my room and put my headphones on. Sometimes, I wish I knew more but you know how Dad is when it comes to talking about anything personal. He'd rather bark commands than talk about feelings."

I'd rather ride a bull than talk about anything meaningful.

"Boys! We're burning daylight." That was their father, unfazed by his brush with death, trying to squeeze productivity out of every minute of the day. It was barely ten in the morning.

Ike seemed to hesitate. "Look, Ike," Noel began, wanting to put things in perspective for his brother. "This session is about you. It's not about winning or pleasing Dad. It's about finding something you love and have a talent for."

"O-kay." Ike drew out the word.

"Boys?"

"We're coming, Dad!" Noel shouted back. "But let's make this interesting. If you don't hit a target on horseback, you have to clean my truck, top to bottom."

"What?" Ike wasn't pleased.

"I'm kidding. After all, I'm the Concierge of Fun and I've heard you learn best when you're laughing." Noel cued Pie into a gallop, imagining Sophie Jean's approving smile.

THE SALON WAS QUIET.

Not that it wasn't full. There was a client in every chair.

But Anya sat in the seat at Mom's nail station in the back and she'd been talking nonstop for thirty minutes. No one spoke. Everyone was riveted. Even Sophie Jean, who was giving Coronet a trim.

"I've only ever driven a truck, Charlene. I'm a country girl, through and through. If I got behind the wheel of a car I'd probably be a menace, driving like I was in a demolition derby." Anya had let her guard down. And the flow of words was nonstop. "Just got a new model. It has Wi-Fi and everything. When I park, I can stream movies."

"Your truck has a television?" Mom asked, head bent over Anya's nails. "What will they think of next?"

"I always thought a microwave would be nice." Helga joined the conversation for the first time, turning off the shears she'd been using on the back of a cowboy's neck. "Out here, it can be miles and miles between towns. I'd like to be able to make a bag of popcorn if I get hungry."

"What a great idea." Anya wore another bright outfit today. Her yellow jeans and white fringed top were going to be the talk of the town. "Has anyone seen the truck Noel drives?"

"Looks like he drives a normal truck to me," Sophie Jean murmured, combing the length of Coronet's white hair in back to make sure it was straight. She'd suspected Anya would manage to loop the conversation back around to Noel and was hoping she wouldn't get sucked into it. Thinking about Noel… Talking about Noel was just too sad.

"One truck looks like another to me." Coronet caught Sophie Jean's eye in the mirror. "Does Noel's truck drive itself? Wouldn't trust that feature."

"I'm not asking what kind of truck Noel drives." Anya tried to turn around but Mom held her still. "Has anyone seen Noel's truck around town? I don't know where he hangs out."

No one gave Noel up.

"Did I cross a personal boundary, Charlene?" Anya asked Mom. "Folks got real quiet."

"Were you planning on waiting for him to make an appearance somewhere?" Mom asked her, still bent over her nail work.

"And steal another kiss?" Helga prodded.

"Shameful," Coronet whispered.

Sophie Jean took pity on the unknowing Anya. "I think Anya has a business opportunity to discuss with Noel. He can't ride bulls forever." Much as he might want to.

"That's right," Anya said enthusiastically, launching into an explanation of her father buying a professional bull riding team.

"Sounds like a sweet deal for our hometown

hero," Coronet said, apparently won over. At least, for now.

Sophie Jean plugged in her blow-dryer. "Most folks might think so." She selected a large round brush, ready for the topic to move on from her ex-boyfriend. "But you know Noel. Always marching to the beat of a different drummer."

Coronet laughed. "You say that like it's a bad thing."

"Nope. Just making an observation." Sophie Jean turned on the blow-dryer, discouraging more conversation about the man she'd given up on.

"WHY DON'T YOU come with us to the Done Roamin' Ranch?" Noel suggested to his father after lunch on Thursday afternoon. "It's bull riding today for the older kids, plus roping practice, of course."

"No, thank you." Dad sounded adamant.

They were both in the barn. Noel was checking his bull riding gear. Dad was oiling the mechanical bull. They'd been working nearly an hour without talking. It was an awkward silence, mostly because Noel wanted to broach the hard subject of the past. Dr. Mullins, the cardiologist, didn't want Dad getting upset. And since his father was easily upset, that meant tiptoeing around him, especially when Iona wasn't about.

"First time I've seen you touch your riding equipment since you've been here." Dad wiped excess oil with a rag. "Your head must be feeling better."

"It is." Noel gathered his courage and risked upsetting his father. "Why did my mother leave town?"

Silence.

"She didn't want us, Noel," Dad finally admitted without looking up. "Remember, she wrote you a note that said you were on the wrong track."

"You wrote that note." Noel had stared at it long and hard last night after his conversations with Sophie Jean and Frank. It was the only explanation that made sense. "Did you pay Mom off? Is that why she left and didn't look back?"

"I didn't write that note." Dad sounded annoyed. He turned his back completely on Noel. "And I couldn't afford to pay her back then."

That threw Noel off. Until he thought about his father's phrasing. "*Back then?* Did you promise her a payoff later? If and when I won?"

"You have an overactive imagination, son." It was hard to tell if his father was lying when his broad back was to Noel and his head was down.

Maybe he hadn't written that note. "Was I so bad that she washed her hands of me completely?"

That got Dad to turn around and face him. "She was a city girl, Noel. A rodeo fan, sure, but she never took to life in Clementine."

"Why is that hard for me to believe?" Noel wondered aloud.

"Because you'd prefer to believe that she couldn't

love a headstrong boy like you." Dad gulped and grabbed at his chest.

"Are you okay?" Noel moved closer, studying his father for signs of distress.

"I'm fine," Dad said hotly.

"Let's both take a breath, then." Noel patted his father on the shoulder.

Dad stiffened.

Noel immediately shifted into emergency mode. "What's wrong?"

"I just..." Dad swallowed thickly. "You haven't touched me since..." He blew out a breath. "I can't remember the last time."

"I didn't think..." Now it was Noel swallowing jagged emotions. "I didn't think you were the hugging type."

"*We* used to be the hugging type," Dad said in a gruff voice. "When you were a kid."

"Whoa." Ike entered the barn. "No one told me we were having a family meeting."

A part of Noel wanted to tell his brother to come back later. It felt like Noel and his father were making unexpected progress in their thorny relationship. But that wouldn't be fair to Ike. They both needed a better relationship with their father.

"We're talking about our family dynamic, along with why Dad is single." Noel figured a little humor was called for. Certainly, humor was up Ike's alley the same way it was his.

Dad frowned at Noel. But surprisingly, he didn't

frown for long. "I suppose it's time to clear the air. Your mothers both left because I'm a hard man to live with." Dad picked up the rag and oil can, turning his back on his boys to put the cleaning supplies on a nearby shelf. "Noel's mother was eighteen when we married, too young to handle Noel or me. Or the combustion that was Noel and me together. A clean break was necessary."

That rang true.

Dad turned and leaned on the back of the mechanical bull, looking as if he needed the support. "Ike's mother assumed we'd live a different life since Noel was on the circuit. She kept waiting for a windfall. None came."

"I didn't even comp you tickets to the rodeo," Noel realized.

"I didn't know this," Ike said, stroking his two whiskers as if they'd filled out to a full mustache.

"I didn't want to badmouth your mother." Dad looked at each of them in turn, his normally hard facade…unusually soft. "Either one of them."

"But you knew we needed a mother figure," Noel surmised. "You let me stay at the Done Roamin' Ranch."

"And you let Mom visit this Christmas," Ike said.

Their father nodded. "Like I said. I'm a hard man to live with." His voice was roughened with emotion, his eyes filled with the same. "I'm proud of the pair of you. You boys deserve better than the likes of me."

"I think we made out all right," Noel said, just as gruffly as his father. He slung an arm over his kid brother's shoulders. "Don't you think so, Ike?"

"Most days," Ike said, grinning. "I'm kidding, Dad," he added when their father looked horrified. "Come over here and give your boys a hug."

Dad moved slowly around the mechanical bull and off the crash pads.

"What?" Noel teased. "Are you thinking we're going to change our minds? Get over here, Dad!"

Finally, it was just the three of them in a tightly linked hug, one that brought tears to all their eyes.

"I'm sorry," Dad said when the embrace ended. "I'm trying to do better with you both. And Iona."

"Iona is a class above you, Dad," Ike joked.

"That she is." Dad winked at Ike. *Winked.* "Do you have a problem with me being outclassed?"

"Nope." Ike leaned back, holding up his hands in surrender. "As long as you don't mind me asking out Cindy Hidalgo when I get my driver's license."

"Cindy Hidalgo?" Dad scoffed, exhibiting a rare bit of humor. "She's out of your league, son."

"*Dad.*" Noel rolled his eyes.

"Dad!" Ike cried. "Since when do you know who Cindy Hidalgo is?" For once, Ike showed some backbone where their father was concerned. He had his hands on his hips and was frowning.

"She's Iona's niece. A real go-getter." Dad's expression softened, although whether it was because he knew something Ike didn't or because

Iona was involved wasn't clear. "President of her class. Volleyball captain. Played varsity basketball as a freshman."

"She sounds tall," Noel noted under his breath.

"She sounds out of your brother's league unless he puts more effort into his grades or starts winning at bull riding or roping." Dad chuckled and slapped his thigh. "Now there's motivation for you."

"Winning isn't the way to a woman's heart," Noel said, possibly too harshly.

"'Course not," Dad replied, surprising Noel.

Still frowning, Ike turned toward Noel. "Aren't we supposed to be at the Done Roamin' Ranch soon?"

"Yep." Noel decided it was time to make an exit. "Sure you don't want to come along, Dad?"

Their father shook his head. "You boys head on out without me."

"But you'll be there tomorrow?" Ike asked, heart in his eyes. "For the competition?"

"I'll think about it. Maybe if Iona wants to go," was all Dad would say, flooring Noel.

Ike and Noel left him in the barn. The day was bright, the air filled with flitting birds and bugs and…truths. Hard truths the likes of which Noel always avoided facing.

"That was…unexpected." Ike grinned. He pinched Noel's arm.

"*Ow.* What was that for?" Noel rubbed his arm.

Ike laughed. "I just wanted to make sure I wasn't dreaming."

"Pinch yourself next time." Noel tried to pinch his brother back but the scarecrow-limbed teen darted away.

"Dad's wrong about Cindy. Girls like me," Ike said to Noel as they approached Noel's truck, still walking yards apart.

Noel grinned. "I've seen that firsthand." With Ginny and Piper fangirling him.

"I'm talking about girls from my class," Ike muttered, catching on.

Noel laughed. He wondered if in a few years Ike would realize there was more to appreciate about Ginny than friendship.

"You're one to talk." Ike veered toward the house. "You lost Sophie Jean and she's awesome."

"Hey. I'm a work in progress." If he had any hope of winning Sophie Jean back, he had to make some changes. "Is your stuff in my truck?" He hated being late, plus he wanted to see Sophie Jean. He wanted to try talking through some of the hard, tangled feelings inside him.

"My gear's in the house." Ike darted inside.

And so was the food. Ike had to microwave a couple of frozen burritos before he was ready to go.

As they left the ranch and turned onto the two-lane highway, a fancy silver truck slowed and signaled a turn. It was Anya.

Noel muttered, "You've got to be kidding me."

Ike glanced over his shoulder. "Hey, that lady driving that truck was waving at you."

"Yeah. I know. She's trouble." Noel gunned it, speeding down the two-lane highway toward town. It was one thing to gather the courage to face the woman he loved and bare all his insecurities and another to face a wild card of a woman who wouldn't take no for an answer.

Ike turned around to look out the truck's rear window. "She's following us."

"Or maybe she's going to give up and stop in town because she realizes I'm busy." Like that would ever happen. Anya was determined. She would have made a good bull rider.

Ike leaned forward in his seat, glancing out the side mirror. "That lady is still following us."

Noel could see that in the rearview mirror, could feel annoyance balling in his chest.

"What does she want?"

"Me."

Ike took a moment to stare at Noel. "We should have Sophie Jean talk to her. She got Ginny and Piper to give me space."

"No."

"Big mistake, bro," Ike said, grinning. "I'm telling you. Sophie Jean makes everything right."

Noel gave a brisk nod. Because that… That he could agree with.

CHAPTER FIFTEEN

THE DONE ROAMIN' RANCH cowboys were training bucking bulls when Sophie Jean parked in the ranch yard later that afternoon.

Her heart crept up her throat when she saw a cowboy with a compact build get thrown off a large bull. She couldn't get out of her truck. Her hands gripped the steering wheel.

Noel wouldn't be stubborn enough to ride with a concussion, would he?

The thrown cowboy rolled to his feet and removed his crash helmet. He was blond.

Not Noel.

Sophie Jean sagged over the steering wheel with relief.

That man...

Noel hadn't been far from her thoughts all day.

Sophie Jean hopped out of her truck.

"Wanna ride a bull, Sophie Jean?" Chandler called from astride his large bay when she got closer. "You don't have to stay on for eight seconds. We're just reinforcing chute etiquette to our bucking stock. Tornado Bill misbehaved at a rodeo last weekend." Tornado Bill and his brother Tornado Tom were the meanest and most requested bulls the Done Roamin' Ranch provided to the rodeo circuit.

"No, thank you." Sophie climbed the rail and took a seat across from the chutes. "The kids are going to be here soon."

"We'll be done by then," Chandler reassured her, adding, "Thanks for coaching Mae and Sam. They're having a blast."

"Me, too." She smiled. It wasn't a lie. She had fun with the kids. It was Noel who stressed her out.

"Sophie Jean!" Sam ran from the main ranch house clutching a napkin in one hand. He climbed up next to her. "Grandma Mary is making fudge today. I brought you a piece." He held out his hand. The napkin opened, revealing a smashed square of what smelled like peanut butter fudge.

"We'll share." Sophie Jean broke off a piece and popped it in her mouth. "It's so good."

"I know, right?" Sam gobbled his share. "Are they gonna be done soon? Rusty wants to come out." His dog enjoyed barking at the bulls, which was dangerous for both Rusty and whoever was riding the bull.

"They'll be done soon. But Rusty still needs to stay inside. The older kids are riding young bulls today for practice."

The sound of vehicles approaching had Sophie Jean turning toward the ranch yard. Noel's truck pulled in. A fancy silver truck parked next to him. The sun was out today and there was some glare on the windshields but Sophie Jean thought she caught a glimpse of a woman with long blond hair and a white cowboy hat.

The arena chute flew open. A bull and rider leaped out.

The rider might have lasted two seconds before being thrown off. But he quickly got to his feet, laughing. Sophie Jean would never understand why any type of roughstock rider would laugh when their ride was done. She'd be down on her knees sending up a prayer of thanks.

"I do not want to be a bull rider," Sam said, on the same wavelength as Sophie Jean. "I'm going to be a roper. The best roper anyone's ever seen."

"That'll take a lot of hard work, Sam. But I bet you'll make that dream come true."

"That's not a dream, Sophie Jean. That's a goal."

And oddly enough, the boy's words made sense. It was just a slight shift in a way of thinking.

Sophie Jean glanced over her shoulder at Noel, reminded of her goal when she'd agreed to coach: *Teach Noel that competition was more about fun than winning.* She wondered if she was making any headway.

NOEL WASN'T HAPPY that Anya had followed them to the Done Roamin' Ranch. This place was sacred to him. His sanctuary. Even now, a glance to the arena where there were bucking bulls made him feel like home.

Made him miss bull riding, too.

"Noel, you're a hard man to find." Anya set her white cowboy hat on the crown of her bright blond hair and smiled at Noel. And then, she turned her attention to Ike. "Who's this cowboy? Your protégé?"

"I'm his brother, Ike." He grinned. "Do you follow Noel around on the regular?"

"I do. I'm Anya." She walked toward them. "Did Noel tell you my dad and I want him to coach our bull rider expansion team next year?"

"He didn't. That's sweet." Ike grinned. "Noel is my idol. Nice meeting you, Anya." He left them, walking over toward the arena.

Anya approached Noel with that determined smile on her face.

He thrust out his hand. "If you want to greet me, the appropriate way is a handshake."

There will be no kisses today!

At least, not Anya's kisses.

Anya studied Noel for a moment before shaking his hand. "I'm learning a lot about personal boundaries in Clementine, thanks, in part, to Sophie Jean."

Noel frowned. "Sophie Jean?"

"We're friends, you see," Anya continued, gathering a lock of blond hair and pulling it over one shoulder. "She listened to my business pitch for you. The whole pitch, not just the job title and salary target. If you have time, I have all my research in my tote. Sophie Jean was impressed."

"No, thanks. I'm coaching kids in a few minutes." Noel's gaze drifted from Anya, to Sophie Jean's red truck, to the arena where she sat on a railing, and then back to Anya. The annoyance over being stalked was on the brink of turning into anger. "I think you'll find Sophie Jean respects my decisions about my career."

"She does. But she worries about you, too." Anya took a step closer, peering at Noel's face intently enough to make him uncomfortable. The woman was as unpredictable as a bucking bull. "I'm hard-pressed to find anyone on the circuit or around town who doesn't like you."

"What can I say? I'm a likable guy." Noel spread his arms briefly for emphasis. "But that doesn't mean I'd make a good coach. You should set your sights on someone with experience."

"You have experience coaching here." Anya gestured toward the arena where kids were gathered around Sophie Jean. "But more importantly to me, you're something of a living legend among the young bucks with ranking. Other coaching candidates... *Older* coaching candidates have been off the circuit so long that the up-and-comers don't know of their successes."

"That's flattering but—"

"You'll come around, Noel. This is a pivotal

year for you. Might make it through without injury. Might not." Anya's smile was casual, friendly almost. "You know what they say. A bull rider's age is closer to dog years given the abuse they put their body through. That means you're..." She paused, glancing up at the clear blue sky. "You're two hundred sixty-six years old. That's long in the tooth, isn't it?" Still smiling, she sashayed past him.

Two hundred sixty-six years old?

"I feel old, but not *that* old," Noel muttered, following Anya toward the arena at a slower pace. He was so preoccupied with her age comment that he didn't realize the woman was sticking around where she didn't belong until she climbed up on a rail next to Sophie Jean.

"ANYA, YOU SHOULDN'T be up here in your good clothes." Sophie Jean held out her hand, which was dirt streaked just from climbing up onto the top arena rail. "Your yellow jeans might never be the same again."

"My life might not be the same again if I don't get Noel to at least come to the bargaining table." Anya lowered her fancy white hat brim, leaving a small dirt smudge from her thumb. "My dad called this afternoon. He doesn't think we should waste any more time on Noel."

"He does seem rather adamant about staying in the game as a player, not a coach," Sophie Jean allowed in a sad tone of voice. She glanced over her shoulder, her gaze seeking Noel's.

He strode toward the barn, not looking her way.

Well, I did end it.

Her heart panged anyway.

The last of the big bulls were ushered out of the arena. A string of younger, smaller bulls had been loaded into a funnel toward the riding chutes.

"Well, this is sad." Ike rested his forearms on a railing nearby, staring at the bulls. "I'm looking at those bulls and I don't feel any desire to ride one."

Anya leaned backward to get a better look at the teen. "You're too tall to be a bull rider. What are you, six feet?"

Ike nodded. "Noel said as much. My dad had me convinced I was another Emerson bull rider."

"Your dad..." Sophie Jean felt for Ike. "You've got to follow your heart, Ike."

"Just might do that." Ike straightened, giving Sophie Jean a wry smile. "After the Fun Day tomorrow, that is."

Sophie Jean frowned. "Why's that?"

Ike rolled his eyes. "Because we need a bull rider on our team, obviously."

"Oh." In the chaos of wrangling five kids for the Fun Day, juggling work and interactions with Noel, Sophie Jean had forgotten how she'd negotiated with Griff about the competition. "Actually... You don't have to ride a bull."

"I don't?"

Sophie Jean shook her head. "We only need four competitors to ride something, and I think we should have the four younger kids mutton bust."

Ike squared his shoulders, expression turning fierce. "I'm not a slacker."

"I'm not saying that. Or that you wouldn't do well riding a bull for us," Sophie Jean was quick to clarify, trying to prevent Ike from an ego bruising. "You'll be in all the other competitions. I'm relying on you to rope."

"Sweet." Ike seemed mollified. "I'm going to grab some ropes for us to practice with." He headed toward the barn.

"Good kid," Anya noted. "You're a good coach, too."

Sophie Jean allowed herself a wry smile. "If you judge me solely on that one interaction, you should withhold your praise. And perhaps find a new way to evaluate Noel." Her Concierge of Fun.

"Where's my mutton busting team?" Noel called out. "Get your boots over here pronto."

Anya smiled. "He's got a different approach to coaching, doesn't he?"

"He's one of a kind." Sophie Jean's one of a kind.

"WHY ARE WE here at the swing set?" Sam stared up at Noel with a disgusted look on his face. "You're supposed to be teaching us how to mutton bust."

"Patience, good buddy." Noel tested the stability of the swing set. The cross bar was nine feet tall. Frank had once told Noel it was indestructible. Considering it had outlasted fifty or so teenage boys, Frank was right.

"What's a mutton?" Ford asked, mimicking Sam in expression and body language. At five, Ford worshipped the slightly older Sam the way Noel used to worship his older foster brother Chandler. "I wanna ride bulls with Ike."

There was a chorus of agreement among the members of Noel and Sophie Jean's team. All but Ike, that is. He was practicing roping around the corner, having told Noel that he didn't have to ride bulls in the Fun Day competition. Apparently, there were things Sophie Jean hadn't told Noel about the event.

He planned to get with her later and clarify things. Lots of things. For now, Noel had four young mutton busters to initiate.

"All the best bull riders start off riding mutton, also known as sheep." Noel grabbed hold of the swing's hanging bar and lifted his cowboy boots off the ground by bending his knees. "And all the best bull riders work on their grip strength. This is where I started. My personal record is hanging here for five minutes with my feet off the ground."

Sam scoffed. "Piece of cake."

"If you say so." Noel plopped his cowboy hat on top of Sam's, using the boy's head like a hat rack. Then, while holding the bar, he swung his feet up to his head and pushed his boots between the chains holding the hanging bar. It was easy from there to follow his boots with the rest of his body, until he completed the circuit by planting his feet on the ground. The world spun a little but Noel hung on to the bar until the dizzy spell passed and he managed to say, "A good bull or bronc rider has overall body strength."

There were gasps and cries of, "*Wow*," and, "*Let me try!*"

"I've seen tumblers do that on TV." That was Shay, the little girl with the glasses. "Can you do flips and cartwheels, too?"

"Only when a bull gets the better of me," Noel admitted, reaching back to touch the noticeably smaller lump on the back of his noggin. "Form a line." Noel reclaimed his cowboy hat. "Youngest to oldest."

The four kids scrambled to line up with Ford in the front and Sam in the back.

Noel had to lift Ford to the hanging bar because the boy was too short to reach it.

The tyke managed to hold on for a handful of seconds before dropping to the ground. Immediately, he shouted, "*Ow!*" and rolled onto his backside, sending his cowboy hat tumbling to land a few feet away.

"Are you hurt?" Noel leaned over Ford, seeing nothing amiss.

Instead of answering, Ford held his arms toward Noel, fighting tears.

"He wants you to pick him up," Sam said, coming to stand next to Noel. "You know, like moms and dads do."

Noel had no experience comforting little kids. He picked up Ford anyway, fitting the boy to his hip and patting him awkwardly on the back.

"My feet sting," Ford whimpered, tucking his head beneath Noel's chin. His straw cowboy hat remained on the ground a few feet away.

"Huh." Noel knew something about hard landings. "Sophie Jean's feet stung yesterday when she jumped off Shirley."

The kids whinnied, even young Ford.

"This swing thing isn't fun," Sam pointed out, always ready to see the glass half empty where Noel was concerned. The kid rivaled Noel's father for the title of Noel's Biggest Critic. Sam picked up Ford's cowboy hat and dusted it off. "I think this is a bad idea."

"That's only because you haven't tried it," Noel countered.

Sam harrumphed and gave Noel a look that seemed to say, "*You know nothing, Noel Emerson.*"

"It hurts when you fall," Ford told Sam.

"That's because it was a long way for you to drop, Ford." Something about having a child settle trustingly into Noel's arms was…nice. "You took one for the team, kiddo. Now we know that the shorter you are, the farther you fall. And the farther you fall, the more likely it is that your feet will sting."

Ford pushed away from Noel until they looked each other in the eye. "Can you catch me next time?"

"I sure can." Noel set Ford down.

Sam returned the boy's cowboy hat to his head. "You don't need to catch me, Noel."

"Fine." Noel held Sam by the arm when the kid would have returned to the back of the line. "Come over here and show our team how this is done."

"Can do." Sam strutted over to the bar like he had a string of bull riding wins under his belt. But he still had to jump to reach the hanging bar. And then he bicycled his feet wildly.

"You're making it hard on yourself." Noel grabbed Sam by the waist and held him still. "Let your feet hang."

"I was trying to flip upside down the way you did." Sam kept on pedaling his feet, nearly kicking Noel in the process. "Let me go. I can do it."

"You've got to walk before you can run." Noel let the kid go. Sophie Jean may consider the best way to learn was to incorporate fun but Noel was in the learn-by-failing camp. "Remember why we're doing this. We're trying to strengthen our grip so we can hold on to a sheep. Gripping is more important than flipping today."

"But…I…want…to…" Sam dropped to the

ground, panting. "Do it. I want to do the flip. Can I go again?"

"No. It's Shay's turn." Noel gestured for the girl to step forward in her pink boots and matching cowboy hat. He lifted her up until she grabbed hold of the bar, then he relaxed his hands though he kept them on her waist. "When you've got a good hold, say *go* and we'll start counting. The mutton buster with the longest time today wins an ice cream from me."

Shay grunted, adjusted her grip and then said, "Go!"

Noel counted out loud, "One, two, three…"

Shay's grip slipped. She shrieked.

"I've got you." Noel eased her to the ground.

"Did I win an ice cream?" Shay asked. "I was hanging up there a long, long time."

"Three is the number to beat." Noel smiled and patted the girl on the back.

"My turn," Mae said, pressing forward, eager to try.

Noel spent the next half hour lifting children so they could latch onto the bar and hang. No one made it to ten. He should have been discouraged.

But deep down, he was having a good time.

CHAPTER SIXTEEN

"You have solid technique," Sophie Jean praised Ike, having come over to watch him practice while Anya tried to charm Noel's foster parents.

Ike had thrown his lariat around the metal steer target easily and repeatedly.

Ike beamed. "Noel and I roped on horseback this morning with my dad. I don't want to jinx myself for tomorrow, but I was okay."

"You have solid mechanics, like Sophie Jean said." Frank joined them, carrying a lariat of his own. "Roping is the same as pitching in baseball. Both rely on proper form and technique." He made a loop and began twirling it at his side. "The same can be said of relationships."

"What?" Ike and Sophie Jean said at the same time.

Frank laughed. "Relationships rely on good habits to thrive and succeed." He brought the rope spinning above his head. "I love you in the morning. I love you at lunchtime. I love you before you go to sleep at night." He threw the rope. It landed around the neck of the metal target steer. As soon as it did, Frank yanked the rope to draw it tight. "Don't forget to finish, Ike."

"Right." Ike hadn't been.

"How about you come over once a week or so and we practice roping?" Frank offered.

"I'd like that." Ike nodded enthusiastically. And just like that, Frank had another roping student on his hands.

Sophie Jean had no doubt that Ike would be a competitive roper soon.

While Ike continued to practice, Frank gathered his rope. "What's your opinion of Anya and this coaching opportunity she's so eager to go on about?"

"She means well and the job seems legit," Sophie said carefully. The fact remained that the job offer was a prize Noel wasn't interested in. "But ultimately, it's Noel's choice."

Frank hefted the looped lariat in his hand and nodded. "Noel needs our support. And that insistent lady needs to learn how to accept a person's right of refusal."

"Here, here," Sophie agreed.

A truck pulling a large stock trailer arrived in the ranch yard, bringing with it the sound of sheep—*baaa*.

The muttons had arrived for the younger kids to practice riding.

Sophie Jean went in search of Noel and the rest of her team. She found them on the far side of the barn at an old swing set. Ford and Mae were swinging on the hanging bar on either side of Noel, who stood in the middle of them. Shay stood in front of him while Sam pushed Mae like a swing. The girl was giggling.

"How are we doing over here?" Sophie Jean asked.

"The Concierge of Fun is winning." Noel spared Sophie Jean a smile before lifting Shay up.

The little cowgirl's pink cowboy hat fell off when she grabbed the bar. She laughed. "Don't let go, Uncle Noel."

"I'd never drop you, dumpling." True to his word, Noel kept his hands on Shay's waist. "But you've got to hold on to the bar."

Shay hadn't been gripping the bar tightly. She adjusted her hold. "I got it."

The other kids started counting down. "Eight, seven, six, five, four, three, two, one." They cheered.

Noel lowered Shay to the ground. "Great job. You win an ice cream. Now that you've strengthened your grip, we're ready for the mutton wagon."

"There's a mutton wagon?" Sophie Jean didn't even know what that was. Moreover, she barely recognized Noel. Since when had he become so good with kids? "Do we need it? The sheep are here."

"Sheep!" Sam cried, eyes wide and mouth smiling.

"No one's riding a sheep without first mastering the mutton wagon. Come along." Noel led the group to the large, six-car-wide garage. "It's in here. We've just got to find it."

The kids scattered like scavengers, claiming to help, although they were exclaiming over each find—a toy lawn mower, a basketball, a discarded pair of soccer cleats.

"Why isn't Ike riding on the bulls?" Noel poked around on the lower shelves, lifting canvas sheets and plastic tarps as he moved along the storage wall.

"I told him he didn't have to ride," Sophie Jean admitted. "When I suggested selecting a young team, I gave Griff and Bess some caveats."

"Such as..."

"Only four of our five scores count on the timed events, while all six of their times count in calculating the overall average time." She wasn't a math whiz, like Anya, but Sophie Jean hoped the revised rules gave them a leg up. "Plus, we subtract ten seconds from our overall average."

Noel looked taken aback. "You're evil. That's something I would have gotten by Griff back in the day."

"I was trying to make it fair, not tip the scales in our favor," Sophie corrected, although Noel's praise pleased her. "Given that only four of our scores count in the bull or sheep riding event, I told Ike he didn't have to ride."

"But doesn't that mean we need everyone else

to ride a mutton for eight seconds?" Noel frowned. "What if someone balks or falls off?"

Sophie Jean bit her lip. She hadn't thought of that. "Maybe…but… How hard can it be to hang on to a sheep? The few times I've seen the event, they don't buck. They just run for the hills."

"Those bigger kids might be able to do that." Noel ran his hand around to the back of his head. "They got good at holding on. And the mutton busting wagon will help, too." His gaze returned to the search. "I hear you made a friend in Anya."

"I'd say we're friendly." It was too soon to call what they had a friendship. "She's…not what I expected."

"The world isn't ready for Anya Krantz," Noel said, heavy on the sarcasm. "Particularly me."

"You should listen to her pitch instead of her flattery," Sophie Jean said. "Not for my sake but just so you can make an educated decision."

"Two hundred sixty-six dog years." Noel shook his head. "That's how old she said I was. Not exactly what I'd call flattering."

"You look pretty darn good to me, old man." Sophie Jean should have resisted the tease.

Noel pinned her with a hot gaze. "Someday, Soph, we're going to figure this thing out between us and you're gonna marry me."

Sophie Jean's breath caught. Held. Until he looked away.

"In the meantime…" Noel bent and dragged a

large canvas off a mound of items. "Here it is." He pulled a red wagon forward, then straightened and swayed.

Sophie Jean grabbed hold of his arms, steadying him. "I got you."

"Thanks." Noel shut his eyes. "Give me a second."

"Is this it?" Sam came over to admire the wagon, throwing himself on top of it.

"That's a mutton wagon," Noel said, eyes still closed. "Made by Grandpa Frank."

"Are you okay?" Sophie Jean asked.

"I'm fine now." Noel opened his eyes. "Thanks to you."

"Look at me!" Sam called to the rest of the crew.

Sophie Jean tore her gaze from Noel.

The little red wagon had been given larger wheels on the front right and the rear left. The wagon itself had what looked like pillows stacked in the bed and was covered with sheep fleece. It was held in place by some bungee cords but it all looked rather…ramshackle, like it could fall apart if anyone played rough on it.

"Is that safe?" Sophie Jean asked.

"Who cares?" Sam shimmied onto his back and promptly slid off.

Noel caught him. "It's safer than riding a live mutton."

"That's not saying much." Sophie Jean noticed a trio of football helmets and child-sized crash vests nearby. She gathered them up. "Let's get out to the arena for practice."

The kids dragged the unsteady wagon outside, skipping and laughing in anticipation.

Noel paused in the garage doorway, catching Sophie Jean's eye. "Have I told you that I—"

"Nope." Sophie Jean swept past him and out the door before he could complete that sentence.

THE MUTTON WAGON was a big hit. Definitely fun. Definitely a challenge to the youngsters on Noel and Sophie Jean's team.

And although the kids trying it out on both Fun Day teams gave Noel a good laugh, including a stork-like attempt by his brother, Ike, Noel used the time to study Sophie Jean and work up the courage to say, "Meet me at the Buckboard tonight." Clementine's local honky-tonk.

Sophie Jean gave him a tart look, brows raised. "Are you asking me out?"

"Only if you're inclined to say yes." Noel felt his smile stretch into his cheeks. "I know it's only been twenty-four hours since we talked about my… uh…need to win. But I've thought about what you said and I'd like to talk through it. If I've well and truly been friend-zoned, then I'm asking you to meet me as a friend." He tried to look genuine as he delivered that friend tripe.

"You're incorrigible." She was onto him. Sophie Jean shook her head, smiling a little.

"But you like incorrigible." Noel remembered her saying as much years ago when they'd first started dating.

"The muttons are ready to be ridden," Chandler called from across the arena.

The younger kids abandoned the mutton wagon and ran over to Chandler, leaving the teenagers with their prize.

"We should help Chandler," Sophie Jean pointed out, heading after them.

Noel fell into step with her. "Why do you always look out for others before yourself?"

"That's an odd question." And Sophie Jean gave him an odd look. "I don't do that… Do I?"

"But you do. With Mary. With these kids. And when we used to date…with me." That was something of a revelation. "Back then, it made me feel loved."

"Maybe because I did love you," Sophie Jean's voice was pitched low and intimate.

But can you love me again?

"When you left…" Sophie continued, still in that intimate pitch, "I was devastated. My mom had just gotten married the year before and left town. I was at loose ends. But then I made a batch of your favorite cookies and came out here." Sophie Jean surveyed the ranch as if fondly remembering that day. "Frank met me in the ranch yard. He dropped off the cookies in the bunkhouse and took me for a ride. I don't know how many times you'd tried to teach me horsemanship. But your foster father… Frank knew just what to say to draw the best out of me."

"That's his superpower," Noel said softly, staring at their joined hands, unable to remember who'd reached for whom or when.

"Teaching the Western way is Frank's superpower?" she asked.

Noel shook his head. "Seeing someone is hurting and knowing what to do or say."

"That's how he turned all those teenage foster boys into angels," Sophie Jean surmised.

Noel chuckled. "We were never angels."

"Maybe not." Sophie Jean grinned. "But you all had good hearts. Mary always says so."

Laughter drifted to them from the kids near Chandler.

Sophie Jean tried to walk away.

Noel held on. "My heart was only ever good at loving you, Soph. I want to marry you. I want to put you first."

"WE SHOULDN'T DO this now. Here." Sophie Jean tugged her hand free while trying to hang on to her dignity. "Not with an audience."

"Then meet me at the Buckboard tonight at seven." Noel lowered his head and stared at her over the rim of his sunglasses.

"That's not a good idea." But her heart was pounding in her chest as if it was.

"I think it's an excellent idea." Noel moved closer, lowered his voice and stared at her as if she was always the only one for him. "My life is empty without you. And I want to make up for all the hurt I caused you."

Sophie Jean's mouth dropped open.

"Can we talk about the future?"

"You're quitting bull riding? Taking the job with Anya?" Sophie Jean glanced around, unable to see the flashy woman or her shiny silver truck.

"We'll talk," Noel said in a much-too-careful voice, one that set off alarms in her head. "Come to the Buckboard tonight."

Nothing has changed. Sophie Jean found the strength to finally tug her hand free of his. "We have nothing more to talk about. Besides, I need to find an Easter Bunny." She walked away.

But Noel couldn't help himself, he gave it one last shot. "Well, if you change your mind, I'll be waiting at the Buckboard tonight."

Sophie Jean was determined that he'd wait alone.

CHAPTER SEVENTEEN

THE BUCKBOARD HADN'T CHANGED.

The long bar still ran from the front door to the dance floor. Booths still lined the wall. Wooden tables between the two filled up the empty spaces. Small stage. Bad lighting. Good music. Line dancers on the dance floor.

There was one open booth. Noel settled in. Ordered an iced tea for himself and a pina colada for Sophie Jean, and then waited for her to show.

She'll show.

"And look what the cat dragged in." Anya slid into the booth across from Noel. She'd changed since he'd seen her last and was now wearing a green dress with ruffled sleeves. And, of course, she lugged around that bulky yellow leather tote. "I've been here every night since I got into town waiting for you to make an appearance."

"That spot's taken," Noel told her, hoping she'd move on.

The waitress chose that moment to deliver the drinks Noel had ordered. "Can I get you another beer, Anya?"

"No, thank you," Anya told the waitress politely. She pushed the pina colada to the center of the table as the server moved on. "I'm assuming this icy concoction is for Sophie Jean. After my business is done with Noel, I'll be leaving." She clasped her hands on the table. The waitress moved on.

Anya stayed put. "I made you a strong offer, Noel. And yet, you keep turning me down. Why? You can't ride bulls forever. Why not go out a winner?"

What she said made sense…more's the pity.

Noel slowly shook his head. "What you aren't factoring in is my heart, Anya. I have the heart of a bull rider. We don't quit until we're forced to."

"That's exactly what the Tulsa Travelers need." Anya put her hand in her large yellow tote, as if ready to bring something out for him to see. But she seemed to second-guess herself, and instead, settled her clasped hands on the table. "I could show you statistics on the probabilities of you being injured the older you get but I think you know that already, given the number of injuries you've reportedly sustained in the past year."

But he hadn't reported his latest injury.

"Every bull rider thinks he can ride forever," Noel countered, feeling the pressure to get rid of Anya before Sophie Jean arrived. "The truth is that I've never coached before." His foray into coaching youngsters with Sophie Jean didn't count. That was…fun. The acknowledgment gave him pause but only for a moment. "What if I did quit tomorrow and went to work for you? I'd have emotional baggage to work through. Is that what you want as a leader?"

Anya sat back in her seat, considering him. "You bring up a good point. And if your doctor told you tomorrow that one more blow to the head and you'd suffer permanent brain damage, would that change your mind? Would you have the same emotional baggage as if you'd made the choice to retire yourself?"

Noel rubbed his temples. "Those are hard questions." Ones he'd hoped to talk through with Sophie Jean.

"But those are the very same questions every bull rider knows he might face—control your own destiny or let fate and the bulls decide."

Anya continued to make good points, ones Noel had gone to great efforts not to think about. He was as bad as Ike when it came to imagining his future.

But the point now was to move her along. "That's thought-provoking but it doesn't change the fact—"

Anya tossed out an obscene number. "That's our best and final offer."

It was Noel's turn to sink back against the booth. That was some figure. Less than he'd make as a champion or top ten rider and more than he'd made as a competitor outside the top ten or away from the professional circuit. He struggled to swallow, struggled to form a rejection. His mind was a blank. And it shouldn't have been. If he accepted, he'd never have to worry about money again. Plus, he stood a better chance of winning Sophie Jean back. But…

"Noel, I know you think we're not making this easy for you to refuse. But you should know by now that bull riding isn't easy, start to finish." Anya's smile was surprisingly understanding. "Dad said that number would give you pause. Whether I hit you with all my charts, spreadsheets and probabilities or not."

"Two hundred and sixty-six in dog years might stick with me just as much." Noel tipped his hat to Anya. But he couldn't quite turn her down.

"You know how to get in touch. We'll give you until Monday." Anya got out of the booth and stared down at Noel the way one does when a deal seems like a sure thing or would be in another few seconds. She sighed when he didn't say a word. "I like you, Noel. You stand by your principles. But just so you know, Sophie Jean won't be meeting you tonight." Anya headed toward the door.

"Wait! Where is she?" Noel tossed several bills on the table to cover the drinks, then slid out of the booth.

"She's on a quest to find the Easter Bunny." Anya turned away, laughing. "I saw her over at Brown's Brewery earlier. If you hurry, you might catch her."

"WHY IS IT so hard to recruit an Easter Bunny?" Sophie Jean wondered aloud to the bartender at Brown's Brewery, half assuming he wouldn't answer given the noise in the place.

Brown's Brewery was packed with folks watching basketball and baseball games on the various big screens in the bar.

"I got you." The bartender turned around, reaching for various bottles of liquor.

"No. I didn't order another drink." Sophie Jean raised her voice, trying to be heard above the noisy crowd. And when it was obvious the guy couldn't hear her, she muttered, "Oh, never mind."

She sipped the last of her pina colada and pretended interest in the various games, using it as an excuse to scan the patrons of the pub. She was looking for someone who didn't have kids and wasn't going out of town on the weekend to compete or work in a rodeo. She'd been at it for over an hour. She'd asked at least ten different men but found no takers.

Well, no takers to play the Easter Bunny. She'd had several offers for a date.

A masculine body edged between Sophie Jean and the guy on the next barstool over. "Hey, Soph. I think we crossed our wires."

"Noel." Sophie Jean was glad to see him. She was smiling before she remembered she'd purposely bypassed the Buckboard. Right now, that seemed the least of her worries.

He wobbled his head as if it didn't matter. He was smiling at her the way she liked, plus he smelled nice, freshly showered, freshly shaved, with just a hint of woodsy cologne. "I hear you're looking for the Easter Bunny."

"The Easter Bunny is an elusive fellow," Sophie Jean replied.

The bartender placed a small plate in front of her on which sat a six-inch chocolate bunny, minus its ears. A straw and a small lavender flower protruded from the top of the bunny's head. "All done with your pina colada?"

"Yes but…" The bartender whisked her tall glass away. "What's this?"

"Just what you ordered. A Boozy Bunny." The bartender grinned. "Seasonal special. Served in a hollow chocolate bunny, not a glass. Once we run out of bunnies, we won't serve it anymore."

Boozy Bunny. Easter Bunny. I can understand the confusion.

"What's in this rabbit?" Noel asked, looking just as curious as Sophie Jean.

"The Boozy Bunny has cold brew, white chocolate liqueur and coffee liqueur." The bartender left them to serve someone farther down the bar.

Sophie Jean pointed at the chocolate bunny. "This is not the bunny I was looking for."

Noel leaned over and took a sip. Quarters were so tight, the brim of his black cowboy hat brushed across the top of her hair. "That's good."

He straightened, smiling at her. "It has a caffeinated punch, so expect to be awake all night."

She took a sip. "Oh, that's lovely. I bet if you move the straw around you can get some chocolate flakes in there." She stirred the drink with her straw, trying to scrape the inside edges of the bunny. She took another sip. "Oh, nice. Gold star to whoever created this beauty."

Noel laughed. "Now that you've found your Easter Bunny, how about we find a table."

"Oh, no. This isn't my Easter Bunny." She took another sip of her drink.

Noel stared deeply into her eyes.

She stared right back at him, waiting—*hoping*—for a kiss. A wish she knew she shouldn't put out into the universe.

Noel fussed with her hair, smoothing it behind her ear.

She was enjoying herself. His presence only added to her contentment. "I'll let you do that because I'm assuming your hat damaged my hairstyle."

"Right you are." He was smiling. "Tell me about your search for the Easter Bunny."

Sophie Jean told him about someone backing out of wearing the costume and how she'd promised Leigh she'd find a volunteer for Sunday morning's community Easter egg hunt. And she told him about her selection criteria—childless, available adults who had a bit of height on them. "But I'm running out of candidates."

"You could have asked me." He was stroking the shell of her ear with his fingers, making her sigh.

"Noel," Sophie Jean said in her best librarian voice. "The Fun Day is tomorrow. Mary's birthday is Saturday. For all I know, you might be gone by Sunday."

"But you still could have asked me," he said gently, softly, his words a caress.

Sophie Jean took another sip of her sweet bunny drink, sat up tall on her barstool and said, "Noel Emerson, will you be Clementine's Easter Bunny?"

"First, answer me this." He rested his elbow on the bar and eased closer until his lips were near her ear. "Is this a date or a friendly get-together we're having?"

Can't you just go with the flow, cowboy?

She leaned back to look at him. Sophie Jean traced the line of his jaw with one finger, a finger that seemed to have a mind of its own. "You should have qualified your question."

"Qualified it?" Noel laughed. "How?"

She brought that willful finger back to her lap. "If I would have shown up at the Buckboard tonight, would it have been a date or a friendly get-together?"

"Okay." Noel laughed again, then repeated the question using her caveat.

"If I could be sure…really sure that you'd never break my heart again…it might have been a date."

"If I could be sure," Noel began without a smile,

"really sure what the future has in store for me, I agree. It might have been a date. But first, I'd rather have spent time with you as my very special close personal friend, the one I discuss all my career and life options with before making a decision."

Sophie Jean was speechless. But her mind… Her mind wasn't at a loss for words.

Is he serious?

If he's serious, I blew it.

He can't be serious. Noel only sees one path forward—bull riding.

Noel smiled as if he knew something she didn't. "What's going on in that head of yours?"

Sophie Jean bit her lip before admitting, "I've just realized that the fates are against us."

"If I believed in fate, that'd be a real shame." He was still smiling at Sophie Jean the way she liked, looking happy and confident and just like the man she'd decided four years ago that she wanted to marry. "A real shame."

"It is," she said. And then she kissed him.

She kissed Noel as if she had four years' worth of time to make up for.

And the truly wonderful thing was…

He kissed her the exact same way.

NOEL WALKED SOPHIE JEAN HOME, holding her hand.

It wasn't far to her apartment. She lived a few blocks behind Brown's Brewery.

The sun had set and the breeze had died down. It

was a clear night with a full moon and a blanket of stars. Perfect for a romantic walk with the woman he loved. Or it had the potential to be perfect.

"I'm going to regret that kiss in the morning," Sophie Jean told him.

"Or not," Noel murmured, smiling.

"Or rather Sunday evening." She made a huffing noise.

"What's that supposed to mean?"

"You'll be gone by Sunday night. I can already tell. You're twitchy."

"I'm not twitchy." He didn't even know what that meant. "We'll talk through all the hard things, I promise." He imagined they'd need days, patience and plenty of reassuring kisses to find their way.

They reached her small apartment complex and crossed the parking lot, passing Sophie Jean's red truck.

"I don't mean you get the shakes, Noel. I mean you get twitchy emotionally right before you leave. You would always check to make sure everything was right between us before you left."

He didn't believe that was true. "I'll still be here on Sunday. I've made a commitment to volunteer at the Easter egg hunt. I'll be the guest of honor. Mr. Easter Bunny."

Sophie Jean scoffed, releasing his hand to hold on to the banister and climb the steps to her apartment.

He followed her. "I'll be here on Sunday night."

She shrugged as she reached the landing, digging in her purse for her keys.

"How about this?" Noel eased closer, drawing her into his embrace. "If I promise to be your Easter Bunny on Sunday, you'll promise to talk to me, the goal being to give us another try. Deal?"

"I think I'm going to need a retainer," Sophie Jean said, gazing up at him.

That took Noel aback. "A…a what?"

"A retainer. You know, a down payment on this promise." She wound her arms around his neck. "A kiss will do."

He was more than happy to oblige.

CHAPTER EIGHTEEN

"SOPHIE JEAN?" SOMEONE knocked on Sophie Jean's door Friday morning. "Sophie Jean? Are you up yet?"

"No." Sophie Jean rolled over in bed and curled her pillow over her ear. She was having a lovely dream about a date with Noel. They laughed. A lot. He walked her home under the moonlight and kissed her good-night next to her bright red geraniums flanking her apartment door.

"Sophie Jean?" Her bedroom door opened. Mom poked her head in. "Are you feeling all right?"

"Yes, Mom. I'm just tired." And wanting to cling to that dream, the one where she and Noel didn't argue, where he kissed her…

Sophie Jean sat upright in bed so fast that Kiki leaped off the mattress and raced out of the room. "Oh, no."

"I knew it. You're not feeling well." Mom sat on the edge of the bed and placed a palm on Sophie Jean's forehead. "You're clammy."

"I'm a fool," Sophie Jean countered, taking hold

of her mother's hand. "I think… I *know* I kissed Noel last night." More than once.

"I knew it. I knew you two would get back together." Mom stood and kissed the top of Sophie Jean's head. "When's the wedding?"

"There's not going to be a wedding. He's going to be gone by Sunday." After Mary's birthday celebrations. His head seemed clearer and he… "He promised to be the bunny for the Easter egg hunt."

"Well, if he promised—"

"He won't keep that promise. He's going to make this weekend great for Mary and be gone before we've made one deviled egg."

"Hmm." Mom smiled. "I have a feeling you might be wrong. Remember me? I'm a believer in rainbows, fairy tales and happy-ever-afters."

"Mom, I know you're trying to be supportive. But maybe…maybe if you patched things up with Byron I'd be more likely to believe there's a happy ending for both of us at the end of the rainbow."

"IKE, LET'S GET a move on or Griff will start the Fun Day without us." Noel had been doing chores around the ranch this morning, walking around whistling with a goofy smile on his face because his formerly messy life was falling into place really well.

"I'm not leaving without Dad," Ike said, stubbornly, standing in the middle of the living room.

Their father was resting in a corner of the couch

watching a live rodeo event on a tablet. Dad waved them away. "I don't belong at the Done Roamin' Ranch. You go have your fun."

"Everybody belongs there, Dad. Even you." Ike took the tablet from him and helped him to his feet. "Don't you want to see me in the roping competition?"

"Are you bringing Ace? Did you hitch the horse trailer?"

"No. There's such a disparity in the age of the kids competing that we're having them all rope from the ground." That had been decided by Griff and Sophie Jean but Noel didn't mind. It would bolster Ike's confidence.

"You can't take shortcuts in your training, Ike," Dad said in a grumpy, albeit softer-than-usual tone. "All rodeo ropers—calf roping, team roping, breakaway—are done on horseback. Makes no sense you'd rope from the ground."

"Other than to make sure your mechanics are good," Ike said defensively, sticking up for himself for once. "Get your hat and boots on, Dad. You're going." And then, Ike stomped out the door.

Without microwaving a burrito or making a sandwich to take along. It was a miracle.

But not as big a miracle as Dad doing what he was told.

And that's why Noel smiled, all the way to the Done Roamin' Ranch.

Not even the sight of Anya's truck could take a shine off his mood.

He brought his father over to greet Frank and Mary, who sat in Shirley's fancy surrey with two bench seats and a canopy to provide shade. It made a perfect viewing platform.

Frank and Dad started talking rodeo as if they were the best of friends. Noel went off in search of Sophie Jean.

"Hey," Noel said as he eased next to Sophie Jean and kissed her cheek.

She turned bright red. "Hey." In no way did she look happy to see him. "We need to schedule that talk."

"Right." Noel fought the sting of rejection but tried to smile.

"We can't do that now. Obviously." Sophie Jean wouldn't look at him. "And until we talk, you shouldn't kiss me."

"Right," Noel said again. "I'll have to be satisfied with that retainer kiss from last night."

Sophie Jean bit her lip and nodded.

Someone called to her and she hurried off.

Ike stepped next to Noel, taking her place. "The offer still stands."

"What offer?" Noel frowned.

"To talk to Sophie Jean for you. It's obvious you've done something to upset her."

It wasn't obvious. At least, not to Noel.

AFTER MARY WELCOMED everyone and explained the rules of the Fun Day games, Sophie Jean called her team together. "Today, we're going to have fun, just like we have all week together."

"Except on the day when Noel's dad almost died." Sam patted Noel's arm. "Did you feel sad, too?"

Sophie Jean's gaze accidentally found Noel's. She'd panicked when he greeted her this morning. They should treat each other like friends until she heard him out.

But as expected, the moment her eyes met his, the excitement of being with Noel from last night returned—the tender way he'd touched her ear and held her hand, the heat of his kiss that felt like a long-overdue homecoming, and his promise to be the Easter Bunny. Sophie Jean wanted things to work out with Noel even if she looked at their chances like a half-empty glass.

Something Leigh said to her about perseverance, overcoming prejudices and seeking compromise returned. Sophie Jean had embarked on this Fun Day experience with fun a top priority while Noel had wanted to win. Why couldn't they compromise and have both?

"Listen up, everyone! We're going to have fun, that's for sure," Sophie Jean told her team. "But we're fully capable of winning this thing *while* having fun." Out of the corner of her eye, she saw Noel's mouth drop open. "I know you've got it in you." She gathered their team in a circle and had them each put their hands in the center. "On the count of three, we're going to raise our hands and shout *win*! Ready?" She waited for them to nod. "One, two, three, *win*!"

The kids ran over to their assigned bench in a corner of the arena. They were excited, smiling and chattering happily. Even Ike.

Sophie Jean went to the barn to collect Shirley. Her team was going to ride the dapple-gray draft horse in the Bareback Ride-a-Buck event.

Noel joined her. "Are you okay?"

"Never been finer." Sophie Jean led Shirley toward the main arena gate.

"Well, you… And then…" Noel caught Sophie Jean's arm, bringing her to a stop. "Why are you suddenly focused on winning?"

Sophie Jean met Noel's curious stare. "Are you saying you don't want to win? That you only want to have fun?"

"No. I…" He removed his hat and turned it around, as if it was in need of a closer inspection, although Sophie Jean suspected he was really inspecting her, weighing her words, evaluating if this was some kind of trap. "I love winning. You know that. It's just…" He settled his hat back on that thatch of dark hair. "What exactly does winning mean for me, the Concierge of Fun?"

"You've got double duty, I guess." Sophie Jean took pity on him and smiled. "Your job, should you agree to it, is to make this day fun for the kids, so if we lose, it won't sting so bad."

"Oh…" he breathed more than said.

Sophie Jean smiled at Noel, reaching up to cup his cheek with her palm. "If you really want to win, you'll need to figure out how to do it. Remember, you can deduct ten seconds off the team's score for the first two events. Maybe there's a way to shave off some time in other ways. Fun ways."

Noel's bright blue eyes flashed. And then he gave her his trademark, mischievous grin. "I have an idea." He spun away, heading toward the barn.

Sophie Jean continued in the opposite direction, muttering to herself, "I really hope this doesn't backfire."

Her heart was on the line.

"I THOUGHT I was riding S-H-I-R-L-E-Y." Ike patted Chandler's bay gelding. His turn to trot around the arena with dollars beneath his knees was coming up next. "I don't even know this horse. You're making me nervous."

"A good rider can succeed on any horse." Noel clapped a hand on Ike's shoulder, needing to instill confidence in his kid brother. "And you're a good rider."

"Thanks. I…" Ike rolled his shoulders back and pressed his cowboy hat more firmly on his head. "What time do I need to beat?"

"You just need to cue a trot and keep those dollar bills under your knees. Let the horse do the rest." Noel was banking on the gelding's quick, smooth movement and removing ten seconds to give them an advantage when each team's averages were calculated. Since Chandler's kids were on their team, he'd been open to the use of his horse.

Ike nodded, looking far too serious. "I can tell you…" Ike cast covert glances around the arena. "I didn't have butterflies in my stomach until just now. Don't tell anyone else." His gaze landed in the direction of Piper and Ginny.

Noel thought some brotherly humor was in order. "Hey, it's not like Cindy Hidalgo is here."

"No," Ike said slowly, as one of the teenage boys on Bess and Griff's team successfully completed a circuit without losing any dollar bills. "Give me a hand up, will you?"

Standing at the bay's shoulder, Noel clasped his hands for his brother's foot. In no time, Ike sat on top of the horse, looking all business. He rode the horse to the starting position. Griff gave him a couple of dollar bills to tuck beneath his knees. And then at the drop of Griff's hat, Ike cued the gelding into a fast trot.

"Why didn't he ride Shirley?" Sophie Jean whispered when Noel came to stand next to her.

Noel whinnied softly. "You said we were going for the win. Good ol' Shirl has a smooth but slow gait. We need to take advantage of the ten-second deduction they're giving us."

"That's a winning strategy," Sophie Jean said softly, smiling.

"Maybe you're coming around to my way of thinking," Noel noted, giving her a tender smile.

"Only if your way of thinking is focused on a fun time." She arched her brows. "Is it?"

"Always." At least, for the rest of the day.

"OKAY, KIDS." SOPHIE JEAN had the team in a circle once more. "We won the Bareback Ride-a-Buck." Thanks to Noel's decision to have Ike ride a faster horse. "Now, it's on to Stepping Stones. Remember you need to ride at a controlled speed to the first bucket..."

Which Griff was setting up in the middle of the arena.

"...and dismount just fast enough that you don't fall off a bucket or tip one over." Which they then had to pick up. "You are all great at walking across the upside-down buckets and it's important to get back on your mount smoothly. No falling off because you let loose the reins on the last bucket and your mount makes a run for it without you."

"*Ford*," Sam said, pointing at his younger teammate.

"*Sam*," Ford said, pointing at the boy he worshipped.

They'd both lost their horses on the last bucket during practice. More than once.

"Okay, *win* on three." Sophie Jean thrust her hand in the middle of the circle. It was immediately covered by several smaller ones.

"I have an idea," Noel interrupted. "If getting on and off a horse is an issue, let's increase our chances of doing it cleanly by riding Baby Bear."

"No." Sam stuck his chin in the air. "Baby Bear is a pony. And we've all graduated from having ponies. Even Ford."

"Hear me out." Noel gathered the team closer, making a show of peering over their heads toward Griff. "Baby Bear is short—"

"And slow." Sam scowled.

"—and easier to get on and off of. What you lose in run time to and from the buckets, you'll gain in mount and dismount time."

"Could be a wash," Sophie Jean murmured.

"My feet might drag on the ground on a pony," Ike pointed out.

"Just don't let them drag." Noel looked at each team member in turn. "What do you say? Shall we try it? It could be fun."

The kids agreed. They got in their huddle and shouted, "One, two, three, *win*!"

CHAPTER NINETEEN

AFTER WINNING TWO EVENTS, Noel and Sophie Jean's team was sitting pretty.

Noel couldn't stop smiling.

While the horses were being put away, Noel went over to the surrey where Mary sat, along with Frank, Noel's biological dad and Anya, to his surprise.

"How's the Queen of Fun Day?" Noel asked, leaning on a wagon wheel. "Having a good time?"

"I'm having a great time because the kids are enjoying themselves." Mary smiled, adjusting the tiara on her head. She wore a white sash with her title—*Fun Day Queen*—spelled out in glitter. Some of the sparkly bits were sprinkled across the legs of her blue jeans.

Frank sat next to his wife, holding her hand and looking pleased. "Are you having fun, Noel?"

"Of course he is," Noel's biological father said from the back seat of the surrey. "He's won two events so far. I predict a sweep."

"I wouldn't go that far, Dad." Roping was next. Each team would line up in front of three sets of targets. An orange cone five feet away from the throwing line, a hay bale sheep ten feet away and a metal steer fifteen feet away. Contestants had four minutes to try and rope all targets. After that, it was the bull and mutton riding. "The next few events don't play to our strengths." His young team had gumption but inexperience usually showed when riding a living, breathing beastie.

"I like how you're using strategy instead of simply fielding a team," Anya piped up, wearing a Cheshire cat grin. "Didn't expect that from you given how you said you don't do teams."

That took some of the shine off Noel's satisfaction over early wins. "There are more ways to work the system to your advantage on a Fun Day than there are on a professional team."

"From the outside, you'd think that," Anya replied, as if she knew something he didn't.

"Noel has always been a winner." His biological father took up Noel's defense. "If he couldn't outwork a competitor, he'd figure out how to get in their head."

Sounds more like you.

"Gotta go. My team's lining up to throw first." Noel went to stand next to Sophie Jean, who was reminding the team of the mechanics of roping.

Each kid stood about ten feet apart and had their own set of three roping targets. The two girls looked frightened. Ford waved to his parents, unfazed. Sam held his rope with a determined expression on his face, tongue out. Ike looked tense enough to choke.

"Are you ready?" Chandler held up the stopwatch.

"Hold up." Noel instructed his team to set their ropes down and come in for a team huddle. "Why is it that only Ford looks like he's having a good time?"

"We're winning." Sam seemed to say what most of the team was thinking because all but Ford nodded. "Nobody thought we would. Now, we have to bring our best game."

Sophie Jean was surprisingly silent, a wrinkle in her brow.

"Can we all agree that roping is fun?" Noel waited for them to nod. "And can we all agree that waiting around for a roping turn isn't fun?" They nodded with more enthusiasm now. "Then we should just go out there for four minutes of fun, no waiting for a turn."

"Come on, Noel." Across the arena, Griff tossed his arms impatiently. "This is supposed to be a low-key Fun Day. Let's get a move on."

"Keep your pants on," Noel called back. "Fun takes a bit more preparation for some of us, obviously."

"I'm confused. Are we playing for fun?" Sam snuck a sly glance Sophie Jean's way. "Or are we out to win?"

Good question.

"How about this? For the next four minutes, let's imagine we're playing a roping game with each other," Noel said, smiling for all he was worth to reduce the pressure these kids were feeling. "And when anyone hits a target, you all cheer, okay? We'll play Cone, Sheep, Steer. Three throws. Three targets. Doesn't matter if you hit one and not the others. Keep throwing in that order. Cone, sheep, steer. Cone, sheep, steer. That way, you won't get hung up and frustrated trying to hit one target you keep missing. Okay?" He stuck his hand in the middle of the circle. "One, two, three, *win*!"

Sophie Jean helped the younger kids with their loops and then came to stand next to Noel. "Interesting idea."

"You wanted fun." Noel shrugged.

"Is this how you were when you had Fun Days here as a kid?" At his quirking brow, Sophie Jean added, "Encouraging your team to play for and with each other?"

"Naw." Noel scoffed. "I told you. We didn't have teams back then."

"Maybe you should have. You're a natural leader."

"More than just the Concierge of Fun?" He playfully bumped his shoulder with hers.

She grinned back.

THEIR TEAM LOST the roping competition to Bess and Griff's older, more experienced team of ropers. But only just.

Sophie Jean praised their team for their good work, having roped twelve of fifteen possible targets. Noel high-fived them all, smiling. His serious game face was nowhere to be found.

There was a break while the livestock was loaded into the holding pens with narrow paths that led to the bucking chutes. The young bulls for Bess and Griff's team were loaded first. Only four of his six team members were riding those bulls.

Sophie Jean went over to touch base with Mary.

"That was thrilling." Mary gave Sophie Jean a round of applause. "You only lost by three."

"The kids are doing so well." Sophie Jean climbed into the back seat of the surrey. "And they're having a lot of fun. Makes me think the Done Roamin' Ranch needs to organize and sponsor a junior rodeo team."

"I'd be interested in sponsoring a team like that." Anya wore a calf-length red suede skirt and matching vest. The white blouse underneath had long flowing sleeves. "You know… If Noel would ever come to his senses."

"Some folks take longer than others to make a career change," Frank said in that neutral voice of his. "Both of you might regret that Monday deadline, Anya."

"Maybe you could sponsor the local high school rodeo team, Anya," Sophie Jean suggested, adjusting Mary's tiara and smoothing her short, white flyaway hair from behind her. "They're about to start with the bulls. Is it wrong to worry about Piper and Ginny riding bulls when my stress level is much lower for Max and Dean?"

"Those teenage girls will be fine," Mary assured Sophie Jean. "They've ridden a mechanical bull practically all their lives. Plus, I worked with them this week. Showed them the ropes, you might say."

Sophie Jean leaned over the front seat to get a good look at Mary's face. "You rode bulls with them?"

"Not live bulls. The three of us rode the mechanical bull in the garage." Mary's voice rang with pride. "Seventy is the new thirty, you know."

Frank crossed his arms over his chest as if he didn't approve.

"Atta girl." Anya reached over to pat Mary's shoulder. "No fear."

"Oh, I have a healthy fear," Mary was quick to contradict the younger woman. "I was careful. And I was fine, Frank." She leaned over and kissed her husband's cheek.

Frank's expression softened. His body language relaxed. "I'm so lucky to have you, Mary," he said in an emotion-roughened voice. "But no one told me that love's give and take would require me to know when to bite my tongue and when to hold my breath and pray."

"Isn't that my line?" Mary chuckled.

For the first time, Sophie Jean realized the Harrisons must have been through rough patches. It was easy to imagine they'd always gotten along since they always seemed to now. If they can disagree and still love each other…

Well, it gave Sophie Jean hope that love just might last.

Mary glanced at Anya and Sophie Jean. "If Frank had his way, I'd be wrapped in cotton wool from head to toe and my big excitement would be a turn in one of the porch rockers."

Anya high-fived her. "You're my new idol."

"I WISH IKE was riding one of those bulls," Dad told Noel as they sat on the arena rails and watched Ginny stay on a mild young bucker for eight seconds.

Chandler rode in to sweep her off the bull when the buzzer sounded. The extended Done Roamin' Ranch family cheered. There was food on the barbecues now, buffet tables filled with dishes, and all they needed to do to eat was get through the last part of the Fun Day—mutton busting.

"Ike doesn't want to ride bulls, Dad." Noel faced his father. "Making him stick with it… It'd make sense if he was my height and build. But he's too tall. You know this. I know you do or you wouldn't have bought him Ace."

"It's tough to give up on a dream," Dad admitted, staring over toward the retreating bulls. "I wanted my boys to do better than me. And then my grandsons…"

Noel chuckled. "Putting the cart way ahead of the horse, Dad."

"Maybe not." Dad flashed a rare smile. "You've done better than I ever imagined. And there's hope for you and Sophie Jean yet."

Noel chose not to comment. Sophie Jean always tread so carefully where her heart was concerned. They still needed to find a way forward.

"Time for mutton busting," Chandler called out.

"You've got your work cut out for you this round," Dad told Noel as he climbed down the rail to gather his team. "All of Bess and Griff's team rode for eight seconds. Your little mutton busters all need to ride for eight to tie this event. That'd leave the score overall at two for you, one for Griff and one event tied."

"Right." Noel strode toward his small team, shoulders tensing. Sophie Jean was leaving this event to Noel to manage since she could offer nothing but moral support.

She and Ike were helping the kids don their protective wear—helmets, vests, gloves. Their mutton riders were so small that the gear looked out of proportion for their size. It took some time, but they got all four strapped in securely.

"Gather round," Noel said when they were suited up. He bent, hands on his knees, to be on their level. "You guys have been rock stars today. And that other team… They're worried they might lose to you." Whether that was true or not made no difference to Noel's message. "And they *will* lose to you if you hang on the way we did when we practiced."

They'd all been great at hanging on except when they got on live sheep. Then Mae had fallen off and couldn't be persuaded to get back on.

Noel checked in with her now. "All good, Mae?"

She nodded, eyes wide and face pale. She was far from good.

"I'm having so much fun!" Sam pounded his thin chest with his fists and released a yell that would make any world champion proud. "We're gonna win!"

"One step at a time, Sam." Noel tugged down the boy's crash vest. "One second at a time. Let's review the basics. You hold on with your fingers." He made claws with his own digits and gave a mild roar at Mae, hoping to inspire her. She looked less than impressed. "You cling with your knees." Noel moved his knees closer together. "And you keep your head down, face in the fleece. Got it?"

"Got it!" the team echoed.

"All right. Here's our order. Sam first." He was the bravest and best of the mutton busters. "Then Ford and Shay." Those two little ones had no fear. "Then Mae."

"You can do it, Mae." Sophie Jean gave the girl a hug. "And then you can tell all your friends you're a mutton buster. Won't that be fun?"

Mae nodded but her eyes hadn't gotten the message. She was frightened.

A win was within Noel's grasp and he felt that drive to win build in his chest. "You've got this, Mae." And he hoped she did. He hoped Mae surprised them all.

The mutton busting began. The rams were big and Noel had their team ride them nose to tail.

Sam lasted eight seconds.

Ford lasted eight seconds.

Shay lasted eight seconds.

"What happens if Mae can't hang on for eight seconds?" Ike asked, stroking those whiskers of his. "That would mean we won two and Griff's team won two."

"Yes. We didn't plan for a tie," Sophie Jean said, studying Noel's expression with a serious expression. "But I suppose that way everyone wins."

On some level, Noel knew the day had been a success. Everyone was smiling and laughing. Everyone but Mae. And she could do this. He knew she could. She'd been great hanging from the swing set bar and great hanging onto the mutton wagon. "If Mae can hang on, we win. And she can do it."

"But if she doesn't, that's okay, too." Sophie Jean's tone was as tentative as the emotion in her eyes when she looked at Noel. "The Concierge of Fun delivered."

The little girl looked over at her teammates.

"I can try. I want to try. We've all practiced and practiced."

Mae was eight and had been a townie up until her mama fell in love with Chandler. Now she lived on the Done Roamin' Ranch in the foreman's house but she wasn't as rough-and-tumble as the ranch kids and might never be.

The ram she was to ride was brought forward by Wade. That sheep was the largest of the day, nearly the size of a robust Saint Bernard.

Mae stumbled back, clearly spooked.

"You okay, Mae?" Chandler hopped off his horse, that fine bay that had helped Ike seal a win earlier. He hurried to his stepdaughter's side. "You don't have to do it if you're scared."

Noel crouched down and spoke to Mae. "You can do this, Mae. You did it yesterday, remember?"

"I fell. Twice." Her eyes were big and her bravado slipping.

"Mae, you got right back up after falling the way brave cowgirls do," Noel told her. "All you have to do now is hold on the way you did with the wagon and we'll celebrate. And tomorrow, I can take you downtown for doughnuts." Noel glanced up at his foster brother.

Chandler frowned. "We don't bribe our kids, Noel."

"Waffles are better," Mae said in a firm voice.

"With strawberries," Shay added, moving closer.

"And whipped cream." Ike rubbed his stomach, always thinking too much about food.

Sam squirmed his way to his stepsister's side. "You can do this, Mae. And if you do it, we'll all go for waffles. The whole team, including our Consurge of Fun."

"Concierge of Fun," Noel murmured.

"Okay." Mae nodded, although she didn't look any less scared.

But she was a trooper. She turned to face her fleecy nemesis.

The ram took one look at her and bleated, making her giggle.

"Hold on tight, Mae," Sam said.

"Grip him with your knees, Mae," Ford said.

"Nose to tail, Mae," Shay said.

"And have fun," Ike reminded her.

Noel lifted her onto the ram's back, placing her on the animal's shoulders so she was facing the ram's behind. "Grab hold tight."

Mae nodded. She thrust out her lip determinedly and lowered her torso to the sheep's back, digging her fingers into its thick fleece.

We're going to win!

But he celebrated too soon. The ram skittered sideways, sending Mae to the ground before they'd even begun.

She started to cry. "I can't do it."

Noel reached for her.

"That's okay, honey." Chandler got to her first, picked her up and carried her off.

Griff strutted over. "Tie game, then."

Concern for his young player receded behind a surge of competitiveness.

Noel hated ties. They were the same as losing in his book. And losing wasn't fun.

"We gave it our best shot, bro," Ike said, turning to walk toward the barbecues. "And it was a pretty good shot, too."

"Hang on." Noel caught Ike's shoulder and dragged him back. "We have one more competitor ready to go, Griff."

Ike stared at Noel in disgust. "Bro, I'm as big as this sheep."

"Yes, you are. But you can ride him. Then we can win." Noel patted Ike on the back. "Take one for the team."

Griff frowned. "He should ride a bull."

"He could," Noel allowed with a sly grin. "Except you and Sophie Jean agreed that our team would only ride sheep." He drew Ike closer to the ram. "You can do this."

"Noel…" That was Sophie Jean. She'd been in the background until now.

A teeny-tiny voice in Noel's head said a tie was good enough to win back Sophie Jean.

Griff laughed.

But a tie wasn't what Noel was looking for now. Now that they were on the cusp of beating Griff.

Sophie Jean reached Noel's side. "I don't know, Noel. This is a big sheep but…"

"I've seen bigger kids than Ike ride this size sheep." Noel directed his comment toward Griff. "And so have you."

Griff hesitated, then nodded. "All right."

"I have a bad feeling in my belly," Ike admitted.

"A tie for the day is fine, Noel," Sophie Jean said in a cool voice. "We had fun. That's what Mary wanted."

"You can do this," Noel told Ike in a low voice, ignoring the love of his life. All he could see was a victorious finish. "Hold on with both hands. You don't even need safety gear. Eight seconds and you're done." Earning Noel a win over Griff.

"Okay." Ike straddled the ram and tentatively took hold of the fleece at the animal's shoulders. "Is someone going to time me? Chandler left the arena with Mae."

"I'll do it." Griff drew his phone out of his pocket. "Ready when you are, Ike." He glared at Noel.

Loser, Noel mouthed.

Griff's expression turned thunderous.

Ike lowered himself to the sheep's back, his gangly legs set to drag behind him. And then he said, "Go."

CHAPTER TWENTY

"A TIE." NOEL still couldn't believe it. He stood with the other coaches in the middle of the arena. "We tied on Fun Day."

The sheep had bucked, protesting Ike's weight. His brother had fallen off after only two seconds and landed on his shoulder. Hard. Noel had apologized, then sent him inside the main house for an ice pack. The kids had exited the arena and were currently eating and laughing in the front yard with their parents.

"I can live with a tie," Sophie Jean said, not for the first time. "How about you, Bess?"

"Fine by me." Griff's wife nodded. "Griff? Noel?"

The two men stared at each other. Neither one of them wanted a tie.

"Buck off?" Griff tossed down the gauntlet. An oldie but a goodie.

"Buck off." Noel nodded his agreement. "Just you and me."

Together, he and Griff walked out of the arena, heading for the full-size bull-holding pens.

"What are you doing?" Sophie Jean tagged along after them.

"The winner will be decided by lasting eight seconds on a bull," Noel told her.

"Griff, don't get cocky." That was Bess, following closely at her husband's heels. "Noel is a seasoned professional."

"I've ridden more than my share of bucking bulls," Griff said hotly. "This competition isn't as lopsided as you think, Bessie."

Sophie Jean dug in her boot heels and pulled Noel to a stop. "What are you doing?" she whispered. "You have a concussion."

Oh, yeah. That.

Noel shook his head. "I have to do this, Sophie Jean. My honor is on the line."

"Your pride, you mean." She scoffed, staring into his eyes, searching for something. Hesitation? Fear? Noel had none. "It's no use arguing with you, is it? If I say this isn't fun for anyone anymore, you won't live with a tie?"

"I have to do this. And I'll be fine," Noel promised her, leaning in to kiss her briefly on the lips. "I'm not riding for points. I'm just going to stay on for eight seconds." Longer if Griff managed to last for the same. He stomped off after Griff and a second chance at victory.

Half an hour later, Griff lowered himself on a fine-looking young bull. The chute opened and darned if Griff didn't ride for a full eight seconds.

"You can still back out, Noel." Sophie Jean wasn't giving up. She stood a safe distance away from the chute.

The assembled had gathered to watch and there were two pick-up riders in the arena for safety. Chandler and Wade.

"Be smart," Sophie Jean continued.

"No can do, Soph. Sometimes a man's gotta do what a man's gotta do." A few minutes later, Noel was standing on the chute rails above a bull and having second thoughts. He still had a lump on the back of his head, small as it was. And he'd heard tales of bull riders ending their careers over a so-called simple practice ride. But he'd warmed up a little, strapped on a helmet, gloves and protective vest. There was no backing out now without looking like a chicken.

That wouldn't be fun.

"This is Rowdy Randy," one of the ranch hands was saying. "He's a spinner."

"Great." Normally, Noel loved drawing a spinner for a ride. That and good technique brought winning scores. But he wasn't certain his head was ready to be put on the spin cycle. He tightened the straps on his borrowed gloves and lowered himself down. "Hey, Chandler, be ready for me to land on the back of that horse of yours when time's up."

Just like he had over twenty years ago.

Rowdy Randy shifted his weight and started huffing like a freight train engine gearing up for a big hill. He knew what was coming. And he was ready.

Noel wrapped his right hand in the rigging, then raised his left arm in the air. "Ready."

The chute opened. The bull lunged out. Noel leaned back, squeezed the bull's flanks with his heels. And then the spinning began. Leaving nausea in its wake.

Noel had to close his eyes and focus on the feel of the beast beneath him or he would have lost his lunch and the competition. Habit took hold. If only that small voice in his head wouldn't stop talking.

You're blowing it with Sophie Jean.

Riding this bull isn't going to make you happy.

You need to grow up.

That last might have been shouted by Sophie Jean. But it didn't mean his voice didn't take up that mantra too.

"YOU ARE THE most foolish man." Sophie Jean hadn't realized she'd run to Noel's rescue when he hit the dirt in a sprawl of limbs after more than eight seconds on Rowdy Randy. "Are you breathing?" Her hands roamed his extremities, looking for injury.

"My hand got stuck in the rigging." Noel swallowed thickly, eyes still closed. "Is the world still spinning?"

Sophie Jean didn't know whether to be relieved or angry with his response.

"Leave it to Noel to try his famous flying dismount," Chandler said from his seat atop his bay. "Some things are best left to the glory days of our youth, brother."

"It's your fault, Chandler. You didn't have your horse in position for me to ride piggy-back properly." Noel still hadn't opened his eyes, which was making Sophie Jean worried. "I almost stuck that landing." Instead, he'd overshot the mark and flown over Chandler's horse and into the dirt.

"My bad." Chandler rode off. "I'm calling this Fun Day a tie."

"Lovely," Noel murmured. He hadn't opened his eyes.

Worry filled Sophie Jean, from her gut to her throat. Everything was clenched. Stressed. Anxious. "You stay where you are a bit longer. I hope you didn't make your head worse."

Noel blew out a breath and opened his eyes. "I'm fine. I just like you fussing over me. Could get used to that on the circuit." And then he drew her down and kissed her before she could process his words.

KISSING SOPHIE JEAN was the best decision Noel had made all day.

He gathered her close, heedless of the dirt and such beneath him.

I missed this.

I missed her.

Several cowboys let out catcalls.

Sophie Jean drew back, her cheeks flaming, her eyes a watery brown. "*On the circuit?* I thought you were going to talk with me about life *off* the circuit." She popped to her feet and hurried off, calling over her shoulder, "You can keep that retainer."

Chandler rode back over, staring down at Noel, still sprawled in the dirt. "You might want to run after her."

Slowly, Noel sat up, feeling a bit of vertigo, a bit of nausea, a bit of fuzz around the edges of his vision. "You think?"

"Yep." Chandler made a sound of disgust. "You kissed her and she bolted. Get after her, cowboy."

Noel got to his feet and looked around.

But the object of his affection was nowhere to be seen.

RUNNING WAS Sophie Jean's best defense. She always ran from the bad stuff. Always. And what had happened in the arena, in front of everyone, was bad.

Why did I believe Noel was quitting bull riding? I should have known better.

But she was her mother's daughter, a hopeless romantic who believed in rainbows, fairy tales and happy-ever-afters. And look where all that had gotten her.

She was walking out in the back acreage of the Done Roamin' Ranch with no clear destination in mind other than to get away from everyone who'd witnessed that kiss, including Noel.

Especially Noel.

She was so mad she couldn't trust herself around him.

Sophie Jean kept walking, lengthening her stride.

She walked far enough that she could no longer hear the shouts or laughter at the ranch proper. She walked far enough that birdsong and crickets provided a backdrop to her pace. She walked far enough that…she hadn't realized she was walking in the pasture with the new roping steers, the ones that weren't domesticated enough for safe handling. There were about twenty nearby and they were all staring at Sophie Jean as if debating whether or not to charge.

A vulture wheeled above her.

Sophie Jean froze. "Hello, all you tame cows." Wishful thinking, that.

The herd began walking her way at a speed that indicated purpose.

To trample me?

Fear spread through Sophie Jean. She broke out in a sweat.

The herd seemed to walk faster.

Hooves pounded behind her.

Sophie Jean whirled, heart racing, wanting to see what was going to stomp her into the ground.

It was Noel atop Shirley. He rode bareback. They galloped toward her.

And she'd never been so happy to see Noel in all her life!

Noel drew Shirley to a stop, positioning the large draft horse between grounded human and feral steers, and looked down at Sophie Jean. "Hi. Is now a good time to talk?"

"No." Sophie Jean stomped her boot heel. "I can't believe you'd do something as stupid as riding a bull when you have a concussion. You could have killed yourself. And for what? To show off in front of—"

"I kissed you and all you want to do is argue about me riding a bull?" Noel scoffed. "Send mixed messages much?"

"Yes! All the time! And I receive mixed messages from you." She pointed at him. "I thought you could be trusted. Forget about my heart. I thought you could be trusted with those kids." Her arm fell to her side. "A tie is something to be proud of, not belittled."

Noel looked remorseful. "Agreed. I got caught up in the moment and I'd like to talk more about my flaws, the decisions I need to make about my career and our future. It was a thoughtless comment I made about the circuit."

Sophie Jean resisted the impulse to give in. It was too soon. Her hurt and anger were too raw. She flailed her arms in the air. "What's the point? I don't trust you. You'll be back on the circuit before I can say *lickety-split*. What happened in the past twenty-four hours should be forgotten. Wipe it from your wounded brain. Delete it from your addled memory banks."

Noel guided Shirley closer to her. "Soph, you're being too loud. The bulls are getting restless."

They were, in fact, closing in on them. The steers in the back were trotting to catch up with the leaders of the pack.

"Time to giddy-up." Noel extended a hand toward her, booted foot held away from Shirley's flank to be used as a step. "You can berate me all the way home."

Sophie Jean grabbed hold of his hand, lifted her right foot until her boot sole slid over the top of his foot, and gave a little hop, the way she used to when they'd dated and he'd drawn her up behind him. But they'd never done this on a horse as tall as Shirley. Sophie Jean had no leverage.

"Change of plan." Noel hopped off Shirley and handed Sophie Jean the reins. He cupped his hands together. "Come on. I'll boost you up."

The roping steers continued to approach at a faster pace.

"What about you?" Sophie Jean was too scared to hop onto Shirley's back.

"I'll be fine." He held his cupped hands closer to her. "Let's go."

"You won't be fine." Her heart was pounding so hard in her chest, it hurt. "We need a plan B."

"I'll be fine," Noel repeated. "I'll get up behind you. But first, I have to get you up."

Sophie Jean relented, placing one hand on his shoulder and one foot in his cupped hands.

Noel lifted her onto Shirley's back as if she weighed nothing.

Shirley shifted her rear haunches away from Noel. Sophie Jean steadied her with her feet and the reins.

"Easy now." Noel tried to grab hold of Shirley's mane and keep her steady. But the mare was agitated now, eyeing the coming herd.

"They're getting closer." And Sophie Jean could do nothing to help Noel up. Her hands trembled on the reins. "Noel—"

Shirley bolted. It was all Sophie Jean could do to stay on her back.

But the draft horse didn't gallop toward the barn and home. Oh, no. She charged the bulls with a shrill whinny.

The steers turned tail and ran off.

Only then was Sophie Jean able to regain control of Shirley. She got her turned around and headed back toward Noel. "Good girl. You showed them, didn't you?"

"Over here." Noel stood on a large, fallen log. "This is high enough to work as a mounting block." He was grinning.

Grinning.

"You shouldn't be smiling. That's twice today

you've been lucky." Sophie Jean maneuvered Shirley sideways next to the log. "First, with a soft landing after that bull ride. Second, with Shirley and her bravery."

The mare whinnied on cue. Sophie Jean gave her another pat on the neck.

Noel grabbed a handful of mane and leaped behind Sophie Jean. He placed his arms around her waist. "I'd consider myself very lucky if you said yes. Why don't we head on over to the courthouse in Friar's Creek on Monday and get hitched?"

Sophie Jean's heart melted a little.

"Why don't you come on the road with me, Soph?"

Sophie Jean stiffened. "Because… I have a job and a life here?" She stopped herself from adding that this was where her dream was. She had to face facts. That might never happen.

"Take a sabbatical. We'll come back after I retire in a few years." Noel gave her a gentle squeeze. "I love you, Sophie Jean. I don't want to spend any more time apart."

Something inside her went cold. Something that felt very much like her heart. "This isn't what I expected your talk to be like. And…" She had to admit it. "Even though I want to be with you, I can't go on the road with you. And I can't ask you to retire, either. This isn't going to happen."

Noel was silent. "There was a reason we broke up before." And, Sophie Jean realized, a reason she hadn't taken the leap of opening her own salon. She'd always held out hope that Noel would return, retired and ready to start a new life, one they would build together here in Clementine. Because that was easier. But she drew the line at marrying him to tag along. "You charge ahead without thinking things through," Sophie Jean continued as gently as she could, knowing if her heart was breaking his must be, too. "Just like those bulls you ride, never with a worry or a plan for five days down the road, much less five years. While I… I save for a pipe dream and rainy days. I don't know what's coming beyond the next four weeks in my client booking calendar but I do have a life with family and friends nearby. That's important for someone like me. Don't you see? We're opposites. And opposites don't really attract."

She felt him sigh behind her. That rather hopeless sigh tugged at her heartstrings. But she had to finish this.

"I can't marry you, Noel. And someday—" someday when she wasn't around "…you'll understand why."

CHAPTER TWENTY-ONE

SOPHIE JEAN DIDN'T want to talk. And after trying for several minutes on the ride back to the ranch proper, Noel stopped trying to argue his case.

They returned to the barn and she left, making her excuses to Mary by telling her that Charlene needed her back in town.

Noel hit the buffet table even though he wasn't hungry. He sat at a picnic table even though he wasn't feeling social. And he smiled at all Griff's jokes even though he couldn't work up the energy to laugh.

How can we love each other and still get it wrong all the time?

Noel knew the answer. He'd made a mistake. He hadn't thought things through. He had little concept of the future, just as Sophie Jean had said. But that was no consolation.

"We should do this every year," Griff said happily. "It was fun, wasn't it?"

Noel nodded. He had fun working with the kids. They were each unique with a different way of approaching the competition. Someday, when he was over his heartache, he might even be able to joke about this day.

But not today.

At some point, Anya came to sit down next to him. "Do you know that half of all marriages fail?"

"Not now, Anya," Noel growled.

"Noel..." Anya broke apart a chocolate chip cookie with nuts and gave him half. "I'm here to cheer you up. Did you know that those who date more than five years before marriage have a better chance of staying married?"

"What's your point?" Reluctantly, Noel took a bite of the cookie. It was Sophie Jean's recipe. He could tell. She used vanilla pudding in her dough.

Sophie Jean...

He struggled to swallow.

"My point is that the folks who stay together instead of rushing into something have a better chance of staying with the one they love." She gave him a sad smile. "Charlene told me you dated Sophie Jean for ten years or something. You should look at this like a bump in the road."

Bump? The bridge between them had collapsed!

"You're single, too, aren't you, Anya? How come you're handing out love advice?" Against his better judgment, he popped the rest of the cookie into his mouth, hoping this time when he swallowed, the lump in his throat would go away.

No such luck. His luck had run out an hour ago.

"What I'm doing is spouting statistics, which I

love." Anya slipped on a pair of very thick classes, dug a pile of papers out of a large yellow leather tote and placed one sheet in front of Noel. "I feel partly to blame for Sophie Jean refusing whatever you offered. I showed her this the other day."

Noel picked up the sheet of paper and stared at the numbers. "What am I looking at?"

"Statistics that prove you're riding bulls on borrowed time." She ran her finger down a column. "That set of numbers indicates the probability of injury. You'll note the chances of catastrophic injury increases with age."

Well, duh. Any rodeo fan knew this. "Why aren't there any numbers after age forty?"

"Because there's no data." Anya gave him a pitying look. "There aren't enough riders who last past thirty nine to calculate a probability of injury or death."

Griff took the sheet of paper from Noel, glanced at it, then handed it to Bess, who was a high school math teacher. "What do you think, Bessie?"

Bess bent over the sheet. "I think…Noel is lucky. So lucky that he should go buy himself a lottery ticket because he's defying the odds of death."

"I knew that already," Noel said gruffly. "According to Anya, I'm over two hundred years old in bull rider years."

"I didn't show you my data to convince you to come work for me." Anya reclaimed her facts and figures. "It occurred to me that you make decisions slowly, like with Sophie Jean. And since I respect you as a bull rider and a person, Noel, I thought you should know the facts, one of which is my observation. You're a good coach."

Noel wasn't certain he agreed. He'd lost badly today.

He stood. "The facts are that I've always blazed my own trails at high speed with little thought to the future. That's not exactly the characteristics of a good leader. Now, if you'll excuse me, I need to spend some time with my mother."

But even Mary couldn't lift his spirits.

"MOM, I'M BACK." Sophie Jean entered her apartment with her head down and her hopes for a future with Noel crushed beneath her own boots. She dropped her purse and keys on the entry table and turned. "Oh."

"Hey, Sophie Jean." Byron sat on the couch with his arm around her mother and Kiki in his lap. "Thanks for the call the other day."

"My daughter the meddler," Mom said, although happily. "You were right, though, so I can't complain."

"I'm so glad that things worked out for you two." Sophie Jean headed to the kitchen with Kiki at her heels. "I'm going to feed the cat and then spend the night binge-watching all my shows in bed."

"Why don't you come to dinner with us?" Byron asked, beaming. "I'm taking your mother to the

Buckboard. Or we could go to that Mexican restaurant you like."

"That's kind of you to offer but I wouldn't be much company." As it was, she needed a good cry. "I started work early and have been out in the sun all day."

Kiki rubbed her head against Sophie Jean's legs, purring loudly.

"Does this mean you two are heading back to Oklahoma City?" Sophie Jean was just getting used to having her mom around again.

"We're thinking of moving here." Byron sounded blissful. He really was one of the good ones. "Charlene enjoys her job at the Cozy Clip and I can run my business from anywhere."

"And I'll have my daughter in town to keep me company." Mom also sounded over the moon.

"There is that," Sophie Jean murmured, thinking she'd celebrate having family close tomorrow.

"I rented us a room at a bed-and-breakfast in Friar's Creek." Byron kept up the conversation while Sophie Jean fed the cat. "We'll be out of your hair as soon as we leave for dinner."

Which meant it would just be Sophie Jean and Kiki tonight.

She swallowed a sob, trying to cover it with a cough.

Based on her mother and stepfather's concerned expressions, she hadn't fooled either of them.

"I'm fine. I promise. But before you leave town,

can you pick up a pint of ice cream for me?" Sophie Jean was going to wallow. And the best way to do that was with junk food. She moved into the kitchen. "Oh, and a bag of Hawaiian chips, any flavor."

Mom followed, slipping her arm around Sophie Jean's waist without a word. "I'm sorry things didn't work out the way you wanted them to with Noel."

Sophie Jean didn't ask her mother how she knew the day had been disappointing. It was just more proof that her mother knew Sophie Jean like the back of her hand.

"I'M STUFFED," IKE announced from the rear seat of Noel's truck. "I had a great time, too. Will I be too old to compete in the Fun Day next year?"

"You'll be competing in junior rodeos," Dad said, rubbing a hand over his chest.

"You all right?" Noel asked. Not that he was in any great shape himself. His heart was doing a slow break. Nothing clean about it.

"I'll be fine. I shouldn't have eaten the chili is all," Dad admitted, slowly, as if still assessing his body's reaction. "I'll need to take something when we get home."

They drove along Main Street. It was Friday night and places like the Buckboard and Brown's Brewery had full parking lots.

"Frank offered to give me roping lessons." Ike

wasn't just stuffed with food. He was overflowing with words. "And Griff invited me to practice with the high school rodeo team over at his ranch. I didn't realize a lot of the kids practice together year-round."

"Emersons don't do teams," Dad grumbled.

Noel flinched. "I recall you saying that when I was younger." Too many times. He slowed for a stop sign. "I hadn't attributed the no-teams thing in my head to you…until now." Another mental block tied to his past. He accelerated through the intersection. "Was that part of your enemy mantra?"

"The other guy's gonna get you if he can," Ike quipped.

"That's right." Dad smiled, not realizing how he'd brainwashed Noel and ultimately lost him Sophie Jean with that kind of thinking.

Oh, no. You did that all by yourself.

"Bull riding is an individual sport," Dad was saying, confirming all the old beliefs that Noel would need to shed to be happy. "No one is on your side but you. And if you're winning, you ride that streak as long as you can."

This. This is what's holding me back. The things Dad told me. Over and over.

Noel drove the rest of the way home in a fog. Not a brain fog, not exactly anyway. He was lost in thought, shoving hurt to the back of his mind and letting the facts about the day try to fit themselves together in a way that made sense for both himself and Sophie Jean.

I liked coaching those kids. It was fun.

My strategies and Sophie Jean's helped us stay ahead.

Those figures Anya showed me struck a nerve.

There might be a way to make everybody happy.

When they got home, Noel grabbed a cold beer and sat on the back porch to continue thinking.

CHAPTER TWENTY-TWO

SOPHIE JEAN SKIPPED Mary's happy-hour party at Brown's Brewery.

Instead, she took some of Twila's early afternoon appointments so Twila could get home to her family. When the last client left, Sophie Jean closed the Cozy Clip and went to the library to pick up the Easter Bunny costume from Leigh.

I wonder if Noel will show up to wear it.

I wonder what I'll say if he does.

"You're a lifesaver." Leigh passed a very large cardboard box to Sophie Jean. "Have you had a chance to read *The Old Man and the Sea*? Hanging in there, remember?"

"Not yet. But I have started *Pride and Prejudice* again. Though it's hard, there's a lot to be said for staying true to oneself."

"Good point, Sophie Jean." Leigh scurried ahead to hold the door for her. "So long as pride doesn't get in the way of your happiness."

Sophie Jean returned home to a house empty of all visitors except her cat, who had the zoomies.

The fluffy calico raced around the apartment as if chasing the devil.

Someone knocked on the door.

Sophie Jean steeled herself to it being Noel.

It wasn't. That was deeply disappointing.

Anya barged right in. "I didn't see you at Mary's party." She wore plain blue jeans and a yellow T-shirt with her company logo on it. Her hair was in a simple ponytail and her glasses were on. "And since I could use some cheering up, I thought I'd crash your break-up-with-Noel pity party." She set a grocery bag on the kitchen counter.

Kiki ran around the corner and slid into Anya's feet before gathering herself, arching her back and then scampering back to the bedroom.

"I'm starting to think that cat doesn't like me." Anya unpacked chips, dip, diet soda and pint-sized cartons of ice cream.

"Kiki is in awe of you." Sophie Jean was, too, when it came down to it. Anya knew how to hang in there. How to pivot and persevere. "Given your style selection today, I'm wondering if you're back to being a plain old ranch hand."

"I don't know." Anya shrugged. "I kind of like the bravado a fancy appearance gives me. But I like the regular me, too."

Sophie Jean thought about that and other things the younger woman had said to her while she put the ice cream in the freezer for later, next to a box of frozen lasagna her mother had left.

That frozen package made her smile, which reminded her, "Why do you need cheering up?"

"My dad doesn't want to give Noel until Monday to decide. He's got his eye on one of his favorite bull riders ever for our coach." She dropped a name Sophie Jean had never heard of. "That man is old-school. Not only does he not treat other riders right. He's been known to use a cattle prod on the bulls he uses to train other riders with."

Anya took a bag of chips and a can of dip and went to sit in the living room on Granny Oswald's high-backed gold chair. "I had such high hopes for our team. For Noel. Even for you."

"Me?" Sophie Jean brought the other bag of chips and dip can. She folded herself into the couch corner. "You had hopes for me?"

"You have what it takes." She ate a chip loaded with dip.

"To do what?"

"Succeed."

Sophie Jean scoffed. "Not hardly."

"All you need is one little tweak to believe in yourself." Anya stared at the ceiling as if thinking. "Come work for me and we'll find what you need. Together."

"Work for you? What position could I possibly be qualified for?" Sophie Jean smiled weakly.

"Isn't it obvious? My assistant manager." Anya paused to eat another loaded chip. The bees Mom had painted on her nails looked cheerful. "I'm bad with people and better with numbers. I need someone who won't back down when these bull riders try to ignore me."

"You need an enforcer? Like in the movies?" Sophie Jean took an extra-big scoop of dip, chuckling. "That's not me. I'm more of a conflict avoider."

Anya scoffed. "Don't sell yourself short. You're subtle but you can organize the troops."

Her belief in Sophie Jean was bolstering. "You mean I can wrangle a passel of kids for Fun Day."

Anya grinned. "Them, too."

NOEL WOKE UP early on Sunday morning determined to fulfill his promise to play the Easter Bunny for Sophie Jean. He had more to say to her and hoped she'd listen.

But when he went to the bathroom, he heard a soft cry for help. And he went running. "Dad?"

"WE NEED THE Easter Bunny out on the main park lawn," Leigh told Sophie Jean just minutes before the Easter egg hunt was supposed to start. They stood in a cramped park storage room. "Now."

"I was waiting for…" *Noel.* "…my volunteer." She couldn't believe he hadn't shown up. "But I can put the suit on." And Sophie Jean quickly did that because Leigh was in panic mode. The legs of the costume bagged around her ankles. The bunny shoes were oversize, more like clown shoes than bunny feet. "I never should have expected him to come. We had an argument on Friday and…"

"That story can wait until later." Leigh continued to sound unusually out of sorts. "Carla's started the Easter march music. She's early. As usual. You'll have to rush, Sophie Jean."

Not only that, she'd have to persevere. In holding herself together.

RUSH. RUSH. WAIT. WAIT.

Noel sat in the same emergency room cubby at the hospital on Sunday morning. Dad had another "heart event" and they were running tests to determine why it had happened when they'd put in a trio of artery-opening stents earlier in the week.

"I'm hungry," Ike said, stomach growling to prove it.

"I'm fine," Dad said, having picked up his mantras from days before. "Right as rain and ready to head back home."

"We're staying. Even if we miss Easter supper at the Done Roamin' Ranch." Noel glanced overhead at the clock on the wall. Eight thirty. He pushed himself out of the chair. "I was supposed to be the Easter Bunny today." Sophie Jean had told him to be there by seven thirty. "It's too late." He sank back in his chair. Anya was right. He took too long to figure things out, and now he'd blown his chance at winning Sophie Jean back.

"Son…" Dad rested a hand on Noel's shoulder.

"I'm in the best place I can be right now. I've called Iona and she's on her way. If you need to be somewhere, you can go."

"No." Noel shook his head. "My place is here. With you and Ike. Plus, our teenage lad is starving."

"I can fast," Ike said cryptically. "I mean, I don't have to eat right now. I can wait until Iona gets here to grab something from the vending machine. We'll be fine"

"Yes. Fine." Dad crossed his arms over his bare chest. "Go on."

And after a moment, Noel sprinted out of there.

THERE WAS A line to greet the Easter Bunny.

Sophie Jean acted her way through the morning, giving out hugs, exclaiming with her hands over the number of eggs in each child's basket and generally keeping her mouth shut.

It's not such a bad gig.

Everyone was happy... Well, almost everyone. She'd made a few of the younger kids cry and run screaming in the opposite direction.

Wait until you meet Santa Claus, kiddo.

She was definitely in a jaded mood this morning. Losing at love would do that to even the most persevering of Hemmingway's book characters. No sense reading *The Old Man and the Sea* now.

Near the end of the Easter egg hunt, Anya walked over the dewy green grass to greet Sophie

Jean on the park lawn. She was dressed once more as an everyday ranch hand. No bling in sight. Even her cowboy hat was plain old straw. "I thought I'd find you here. It is you in there, isn't it, Sophie Jean?"

Sophie Jean bobbed her oversize bunny head.

"The librarian told me and I…I'm leaving town. Noel won't return my calls." For once, Anya looked like she might cry. "Wanted to say goodbye properly."

Sophie Jean hugged her, regretting the big round bunny head that bumped Anya's cowboy hat to the turf.

"Sophie Jean!" Noel ran across the lawn to join them. "Leigh told me you filled in for me."

I have nothing to say to you, buster.

"I'm so sorry," Noel continued, looking frazzled. "Dad had another heart attack this morning and by the time I remembered I was supposed to be here, the hunt had long since started."

Sophie Jean held a bunny rabbit hand over her heart. Poor Steve.

You are forgiven.

"Hey, Anya. I wanted to talk to you, too." Noel looked around at the quickly emptying park. "But first, can we go somewhere and get Sophie Jean out of that suit?"

Sophie Jean led them back to the storage shed. It didn't take long to remove the costume.

"I've been thinking about Anya's proposition,"

Noel began when Sophie Jean sat next to Anya on a park bench with a broken armrest waiting to be repaired.

I can't get my hopes up.

But Sophie Jean did anyway.

Noel paced the long, narrow storage shed, avoiding various boxes of holiday decorations and sports equipment. He stopped and faced them. "Based on the offer as is, Anya, I've got to turn it down."

Anya and Sophie Jean both slouched on the bench.

"This is why you rushed over here?" All Sophie Jean's hopes…

"Well, no. I…I want to make Anya a counteroffer." Noel rolled his shoulders back. "Apologies if I'm babbling. After Dad… Well, I need to work out the details for you, Anya, but I want to coach the Tulsa Travelers."

"Tell me more," Anya said, smiling a little. She bumped Sophie Jean's shoulder with her own, as if to say, *"Things are looking up."*

Sophie Jean didn't dare put too much stock in Anya's current outlook.

Noel drew a deep breath. "Yesterday, when you offered to sponsor a junior rodeo team, it got me to thinking. You can't spread yourself that thin, Anya, at least at first. I understand you have a working cattle ranch but you've told me you don't have accommodations for bull riders or a state-of-the-art training facility. You'll need money and time for construction."

Suddenly, it occurred to Sophie Jean that if Noel took the job with the Tulsa Travelers, he'd be living and working in Tulsa. Not Clementine. She sank lower on the broken bench.

"But there are a lot of resources available for you through the Done Roamin' Ranch," Noel was speaking to Anya. "We already have a professional arena. Competition-quality bulls. A workout facility. A nearby town with local services."

Anya was uncharacteristically silent.

"Noel, what are you saying?" Sophie Jean asked, feeling confused.

He turned toward Sophie Jean. "That Anya and her father should take the Done Roamin' Ranch on as a silent partner. Or maybe not so silent, since I'd like the Done Roamin' Ranch to be listed on the team gear as a sponsor." Noel drew another deep breath, as if he needed to slow down his racing thoughts. "What I'm saying is that I have roots in this town. My family, my found family and, if I play my cards right, my fiancée." He spared Sophie Jean a tender glance. "I can be the Tulsa Traveler's coach if we base the practice facility here. In Clementine. Professional sports teams aren't always located in the city they call home. And all it would take to make this work is for Anya and her father to finance another bunkhouse at Frank and Mary's ranch."

He's thinking beyond the next rodeo.

His outlook on life is changing.

And he probably didn't read any of the books Leigh had recommended.

Anya sat back, looking as stunned as Sophie Jean felt. "What a…a novel idea. I'd have to crunch the numbers to see if it makes financial sense. But—"

"Great. Go forth and crunch numbers, Anya," Noel cut her off. Shooed her off. Then he turned to Sophie Jean once more. After a moment, he sat next to Sophie Jean on the broken-armed park bench. "I spent the past two days thinking about everything you've told me since I've been back. Not just you. You and Frank and Mary and everyone else, including Anya, my dad and Sam."

"Sam? You're taking advice from Sam?" Although when Sophie Jean thought about it, the energetic kid dropped bits of wisdom like breadcrumbs.

"I didn't want to retire and be a nobody, Sophie Jean. So, I didn't think or live as if retirement was an option. But things have changed. I've changed. Here." He tapped a spot over his heart. "For the better, I hope. Winning is great but it's not winning that defines me. It's who I make a positive impact on, the relationships I have with my family and friends, and who I love."

"Like Frank and Mary," Sophie Jean said quietly.

"Exactly." Noel got down on one knee in front

of her, taking hold of Sophie Jean's hands. "Soph, I love you. I want to make a life with you. Without you, my life is incomplete."

Tears welled in Sophie Jean's eyes. Tears clogged her throat, making it impossible to speak. She'd lost hope in him and in herself.

"You reminded me that winning isn't everything. And those kids we coached... Those kids showed me how to have fun *and* compete. I just didn't want to see it. Not when we tied. Not even after Griff and I rode those bulls and tied again."

Sophie Jean leaned closer. "What made you see it?"

"My dad, of all people." He chuckled and gave her hands a squeeze. "He reminded me that he's the one who put the idea in my head that everyone who can't help you win is the enemy. I spent twenty years trying to prove to him that I was my own man but deep down inside, I was still the man he'd made me. Until now."

He inched closer, resting his wrists on her knees. And his eyes, those bright blue eyes, were shining with the promise of a future. "We have what it takes to go the distance together. We... *I*...just needed time to realize there's a lot more to life and not everything is a competition meant to be won. Will you marry me, Soph? Right away, I mean. We've waited so long to get this future of ours off the ground. And we need to be on the same page as we move forward."

It was everything she'd wanted to hear him say and more. "Of course I'll marry you. I love you. I'll marry you as soon as I can find a fancy dress and shoes to match." Sophie Jean laughed self-consciously. "I'd marry you tomorrow at the county courthouse but I know myself well enough to admit *I'll* have regrets if I don't dress up for the biggest day of my life. Of *our* lives."

"That's just it, isn't it?" Noel got to his feet and drew her up along with him. "You have to know yourself inside to truly give yourself to love without regrets. To make room for all love has to offer."

Sophie Jean twined her arms around his neck. "That's a proper piece of good advice." She grinned. "Don't tell me that came from Sam."

"It came from me, Soph. Now, I owe you a Boozy Bunny for taking my place this morning." Noel grinned. "But since Brown's Brewery isn't open yet, will you settle for breakfast at the hospital? And then maybe later, I can meet you at the ranch for Mary's Easter supper."

"I'd like that." She snuggled closer. "But since we just got engaged, can't we kiss on it and make it official? Like a… Like a retainer?"

"Oh, honey." Noel grinned. "It was official the moment I got back to town and you roped me."

Sophie Jean sighed. "Stop talking, Noel. Stop talking and kiss me."

EPILOGUE

A YEAR HAD come and gone since Noel retired. And plenty had changed.

There had been two Emerson weddings in Clementine. Soon after he was fit with a pacemaker, Noel's father had rushed to the altar to marry Iona and move to Friar's Creek to live with her and her boys. A month later, Noel and Sophie Jean tied the knot at the local church.

She'd moved into the Emerson Ranch with Noel and Ike, who was old enough to decide that he'd like to stay in school with his friends in Clementine. Ike and Ginny were doing all right as a roping team and as a budding couple. There was no more talk about bull riding or Cindy Hidalgo.

The Krantzes had cut a deal with Frank and Mary with a contract that named the Done Roamin' Ranch their official training site. Noel was attending the ribbon-cutting ceremony at thc fancy bunkhouse the Krantzes had built behind the barn. It came complete with a sauna, hot tub and cold-plunge pool.

Sunday morning after church, Noel brought a

mug of tea out to Sophie Jean, who was sitting on the back porch. She was reviewing a lease-to-own agreement with Helga, who'd decided she wanted to semi-retire. Sophie Jean was going to achieve her dream of running the Cozy Clip, and someday in the future, she'd own the salon her grandmother started.

Life was mighty fine.

"I should have Anya look at this for me." Sophie Jean set the thick sheaf of papers on the patio table. "Vickie knows her real estate but Anya can project future numbers like nobody's business."

Even the rodeo circuit cowboys and executives had been impressed with the young woman's skills…once she found a happy compromise in her appearance and professional demeanor. She had Sophie Jean do her hair now. And Noel to keep her father from unrealistic investments in and around the team.

"I have another opportunity to discuss with you, Soph." Noel sat in a chair next to her. "Babies."

"Have you been talking to my mother again?" Sophie Jean chuckled. She'd changed out of the dress she'd worn to church and into a pair of black leggings and white T-shirt. "Mom can't wait for us to have kids."

Noel took Sophie Jean's hand and pressed a tender kiss on her knuckles. "I can't wait for us to have kids, either." It had been a year and he was always ever hopeful. "I've grown awfully fond of Sam and Mae."

"You can't wait for kids?" Sophie Jean smiled at him, curled in her chair the way Kiki curled in her lap sometimes, with her legs tucked under her, looking content. Her long brown hair spilled over her shoulders. "Says the man who's about to go on the road again for a weekend team competition."

"Yes. That's me. I'm only on the road four days a week, twenty weeks a year." That might sound like a lot, but it was significantly better than his fifty-week schedule had been while he was riding bulls.

"As it so happens, Noel Emerson..." Sophie Jean's smile grew and she leaned forward to whisper, although no one else was at home, except Kiki sitting just inside the sliding glass door. "I think we're having a baby."

"What?" Noel leaped from his chair and drew her to her feet. "When did you find out? When are we due?"

"I saw Doc Nabidian yesterday," Sophie Jean said softly, blushing a little. "You fell asleep so early last night that I hadn't figured out how to tell you."

Noel gave her a loving squeeze. "Next time, wake me up."

She chuckled, wriggling free. "The doctor said the baby's coming sometime in January. We'll learn more when we go in for a sonogram."

"Soph." Noel swept her into his arms again and

held on tight. "I love you. I love you so much." He eased his embrace and cradled her dear, sweet face in both hands. "I hope it's a girl. I hope we have a houseful of girls."

Sophie Jean scoffed, placing her warm palm over his cheek. "Whatever we end up with. One kid, a houseful, boys or girls, we're going to love them for who they are and respect who they want to be."

"And we're going to stand by them, no matter what." Noel kissed her, happy and grateful. He'd very nearly let his life progress on its empty, messy path. It was only the faith and good heart of this woman, as well as Anya, plus a pack of ranch kids, that had been able to teach him that he could have more.

That he deserved more.

And that he could still keep it fun.

* * * * *

For more romances with the
foster sons of The Cowboy Academy,
visit www.Harlequin.com today!